The Case of the Poisoned Pumpkin

Witch Haven Cozy Mystery - book 11

K.E. O'Connor

K.E. O'Connor Books

While every precaution has been taken in the preparation of this book, the publisher assumes no responsibility for errors or omissions, or for damages resulting from the use of the information contained herein.

THE CASE OF THE POISONED PUMPKIN

ISBN: 978-1-915378-38-5

Written by: K.E. O'Connor

Preface

The Witch Haven series has been created so you spend time with four amazing witches:

Books 1-3 tell Indigo's story: Spells and Spooks, Hexes and Haunts, Curses and Corpses

Books 4-6 tell Luna's story: Muffins and Moonlight, Cupcakes and Cauldrons, Pancakes and Potions

Books 7-9 tell Odessa's story: Hauntings and High Jinx, Hauntings and Havoc, Hauntings and Hoaxes

Books 10-12 tell Storm's story: The Case of the Screaming Skull, The Case of the Poisoned Pumpkin, The Case of the Cursed Candy

And there are two bonus origin stories to enjoy:
Fire Fang and **Silvaria**

Chapter 1

"Did you have to give your scarecrows the entire day off?" I groaned like a two thousand-year-old witch as I stood and stretched my back. My fingernails were stained orange, my muscles ached, and my dark hair stuck to my face like a geek squad helmet.

Odessa Grimsbane looked up from where she was sorting her own pile of pumpkins. As usual, she had a sunny expression on her face, despite being as grime splattered as me. "They deserved it. Besides, it's good to get your hands dirty. And Fire Fang mentioned you needed more exercise."

I grimaced. There were times when I regretted having a hellhound who could talk.

"Don't be like that. The fresh air is good for you. Breathe it in good and deep." Odessa gulped in the crisp afternoon air. "Better than medicine or magic. It helps me recharge."

I wasn't buying it. "We should use magic to sort these pumpkins."

Odessa stood and rested her hands on her hips. "Storm Winter, don't tell me you're afraid of hard work. You're happiest when you're grubbing around

1

in some out of the way place full of demon goo and monster droppings."

"Monster droppings?"

She waved a hand at me. "You know what I mean. You enjoy gross places like Bog Valley and Night Shade Hollow. Yuck. Just the names make me grumpy."

"I wouldn't say I enjoy those visits, but that's where the work takes me." My private investigation agency was the most successful firm around for five hundred miles. Maybe even the best in the world. I wasn't bragging. It was a fact. I had the dubious contacts, didn't mind facing off with whatever scumbag caused my clients trouble, and I had a deep sense of making sure justice was done. The little guy got downtrodden too often, and that's where I stepped in and ensured the bullies lost. There was nothing better than uncovering pond scum and flushing it out.

Well, the bullies and the pond scum lost most of the time. There was one case I'd worked on for years that continued to defeat me. A case buried deep in my heart.

"Think of pumpkin sorting as a strength training day," Odessa said. "You need muscles to defeat the demons."

"I have magic. So do you." I twirled my fingers, and a pumpkin hopped off the dirt.

Odessa grabbed it. "Careful! This one could be the winner."

"Hey, ladies. I figured you could do with these." Sol Vossen stepped off the porch of Odessa's farmhouse and presented us with a tray of drinks and cookies.

"I was just thinking about refreshments." Odessa planted a kiss on her new husband's cheek. "What would I do without you?"

"Get an enchanted scarecrow to see to your every need," I muttered under my breath.

I turned away as Odessa and Sol cooed over each other. They were a new couple and had gone through a few near-death experiences and a whirlwind romance, which had resulted in Odessa asking Sol to marry her. After a close encounter with a fake ghost, who turned out to be a shape shifting demon, they were now a blissfully happy couple.

I focused on the pumpkins. I was happy for Odessa. She deserved someone as decent as Sol, but I was never comfortable with public displays of affection, and these two were always all over each other.

"Storm, come get a drink," Odessa said.

I glanced up to make sure they weren't canoodling, then headed over and grabbed a large glass of fizzy water, which I downed in one. I eyed the cookies. "Is there pumpkin in those?"

Sol chuckled. "You get used to it. It sneaks into every meal we have."

Odessa gave him a gentle swat with the back of her pumpkin-stained hand. "You don't like my cooking?"

"I adore your cooking. And these dark cherry and pumpkin cookies are the best." He planted an affectionate kiss on her forehead.

Even though there was pumpkin in the cookies, I was starving, so I grabbed three and stuffed them down. And they were good, if you ignored the pumpkin aftertaste. Where there was Odessa, there were pumpkins. And since she'd dragged me over to help her manually sort her latest crop to find a pumpkin to display at the Witch Haven County fair, I had to accept a pumpkin-filled life for the next few hours.

I took another drink, turning as the ground shook beneath my feet. Fire Fang, my temporary furry lodger, bounded past. He was chasing Tuffin, Odessa's cat familiar. Although he was growling, which was his default noise, his tail wagged, showing it was just a game.

They raced around the pumpkin patch a couple of times, Tuffin shooting insults over one shoulder, while Fire Fang huffed out small fireballs. They only just skimmed Tuffin, so I knew he wasn't that intent on destruction.

"Odessa, have you noticed anything weird about Fire Fang?" I said.

"Weird how?"

I'd been mulling over the results of Fire Fang's blood tests since I'd gotten them three weeks ago. According to the vet, Fire Fang wasn't a hellhound. He was a mortal. Which was impossible, unless he was wearing an amazing fancy dress costume that had fooled us all.

"You know, anything odd that makes you wonder what he is."

Her gaze was full of questions. "I don't spend much time with him, but he seems like your average hellhound to me. You've mentioned he levitates, and the color changing thing is odd. I can't think of anything else."

"It's just I got some strange test results back from the vet."

"Fire Fang's sick?"

"No. Does he look sick to you?"

"He looks the same as always." Odessa gasped as Fire Fang's teeth snapped too close to Tuffin. "He has too much energy. That could be a problem."

"They're only playing." Fire Fang was always on hyper alert when we were out of the office. He felt like he had to protect me. It was kind of sweet but also annoying. I had weather witch powers, so I could take care of myself. "There's something going on with his magic. Maybe I should get more tests done. Or take him to a vet who specializes in hellhounds."

"Do whatever you have to if you're worried about him," Odessa said.

"He looks healthy to me," Sol said. "Fire Fang never runs out of energy."

Fire Fang and Tuffin had reversed roles, and Tuffin was chasing Fire Fang through the bare pumpkin patch, tiny sparkles of magic shooting out and catching the end of his tail.

"I want a second opinion," I said. "To be on the safe side. Maybe Luna knows someone local who won't mind taking a look at him. She must have contacts now the animal sanctuary is operational."

"And growing daily. She had a delivery of five orphaned fanged gray bats. They're cute, but they nip." Odessa showed me two small puncture wounds on her thumb.

The sound of wood splintering had us turning. Three scarecrows were slamming through a barn door.

"Should they be doing that?" I said.

"No! That's my newborn scarecrow barn. Those guys aren't ready for the outside world. They have no social skills. They also nip."

"And tear and destroy." Sol's expression had turned grim.

I ducked as half the door flew toward us. "They missed the memo about no fun day trips outside." They looked ready to explore, taking out anyone who tried to stop them.

Odessa and Sol were racing toward the barn before I'd finished speaking. Orange magic blazed around Odessa, while Sol sparked his magic ring to life and flared out a white ball of magic toward the escaping scarecrows.

I grabbed another cookie from the abandoned tray. Scarecrows weren't my area of expertise, and Odessa knew how to handle them better than anyone else. She was Queen of the Scarecrows, after all, and I didn't want to cramp her style.

As I watched the rampaging scarecrow show, Fire Fang loped over.

"Good game of chase?" I tossed him a piece of cookie.

"Tuffin cheated. That cat's a monster. Grubby little fuzz bucket."

"You were having fun."

"My tail got goblin nobble singed." He flopped down on his side and exposed his belly.

I ignored his pinky-gray gut. Ever since I'd learned Fire Fang was mortal, I wasn't comfortable with our living arrangements. It had been different when I thought he was a hellhound. We'd shared a bed, food, and I didn't mind leaving the bathroom door open when he was around. But this was too weird. Fire Fang wasn't who he said he was, and I didn't know if that was because he couldn't remember his life as a mortal, or he was deliberately hiding things. It made for an uncomfortable situation. One I'd been doing my best to avoid. And that meant no belly rubs.

Fire Fang wasn't getting the message. He lifted a leg, exposing more of his warm, furry belly.

I tossed him another cookie. Rubs were off the table until I figured out what Fire Fang was. If I'd been rubbing a mortal's belly all this time... I shuddered and pushed the awful possibility to one side. This mystery needed solving, and fast.

Fire Fang grumbled his unhappiness but ate the cookie.

"I've been thinking about your visit to the vet," I said.

He lifted his head and growled. "Something's burning."

I looked around, and sure enough, there was fire licking the back of the newborn scarecrow barn. I stuffed the last of the cookie in my mouth, waved my arm in a large circle, and conjured a downpour, directing it over the barn and extinguishing the fire.

"Odessa needs to watch those newborn pumpkin-headed nightmares," Fire Fang said. "Fire and straw are a terrible combination."

"Apparently, customers are requesting fire abilities with their scarecrows. It's the latest upgrade."

"Those chicken armpits are already too strong. They don't need fire as well."

I grinned at Fire Fang's persistent inability to cuss. "What can you do? Customer demand. And you know Odessa loves to keep her customers happy. Most of the time, her scarecrows are well-behaved. It's only if Odessa has an off day that things go awry."

"This isn't an off day?"

I tilted my head from side to side. "This is a typical day."

Odessa jogged over, looking slightly sweaty but happy. She shot me a thumbs-up. "Thanks for the save on the barn. Those boys are naughty. They think they're ready for the outside world, but they still haven't gotten through basic training."

"Did you cull them?"

"No! They're tied down. Sol is dealing with the rest and getting everyone calm." She knelt and scratched Fire Fang's head. "How are you, beautiful boy?"

"I'd be happier if you fixed this speech spell, you crazy buttoned witch. I still can't cuss."

"Which makes you even more perfect." She kissed the top of his head. "Let's go inside and clean up. And we deserve a treat after dealing with those rambunctious scarecrows."

I looked at the empty plate of cookies. I'd missed breakfast, so needed more fuel. "Sure, I could go for a treat."

Odessa washed up in the sink, while I lounged in a seat by the kitchen table. Her farmhouse was a huge, rambling affair, with creaky floorboards and wood everywhere. The kitchen always smelled of pumpkin spice, and she was never happier than when she was baking treats with her magical pumpkins and looking after people.

She served a tray of pumpkin scones and tea and sat opposite me. "I was just saying to Sol how quiet it's been around here the last few weeks."

"You call a burning barn and escaping scarecrows quiet?"

Odessa chuckled as she poured the tea. "That's everyday life here. And I can tell you're not that busy, either."

"I'm busy. I have cases."

"Nothing to get you thinking hard. You have that look on your face."

"What look?"

"Your grumpy, bored witch face." Odessa scowled at me and wrinkled her forehead.

"I don't look like that."

"You don't when you're busy. You just look average grumpy, then. No new, interesting cases coming your way?"

I shrugged. "It has been quiet. I don't know what's going on with all the criminals. Vacation time, maybe?"

"Indigo was saying even the Magic Council is quiet, and Olympus has been hanging around the house much more. She can't decide if that's a good thing." Odessa munched on her scone. "I take that as a positive sign. Witch Haven is at peace. No one wants to bother us, and we can get on with our lives and be happy."

"Or the evil is resting up, preparing for a big bang."

"Trust you to look at the gloomy side of things."

"It's the realist side. Take off those pumpkin colored glasses, and you'll see what I mean."

Odessa played with her scone for a few seconds. "No new sightings of Eden?"

That question did make me scowl. "Nothing since the last fake report."

I'd been sent a picture of my missing sister a few weeks ago that had me convinced I'd finally found her. But when I got to the location and asked around, I realized it wasn't Eden. The young woman I found looked like her, but it was a big waste of time. Just like every other sighting I'd ever followed up.

Odessa squeezed my hand. "She's out there somewhere."

"I know. And since work is quiet, I can focus on Eden." Although I didn't know what I would focus on. I'd followed hundreds of leads on my sister, and they'd all come to dead ends. Wherever Eden was, she didn't want to be found. Or maybe whoever had her didn't want her to be found. Well, tough. I'd made it my life's work to find that person and destroy them, while getting my baby sister back where she belonged.

"Here's something positive to think about. We're overdue a girls' weekend away," Odessa said. "Now's a good time. I could speak to Indigo and Luna and see if they're free."

"Luna's probably still fixing up the wedding of the century. She'll be too busy for a weekend away."

"She can make the time. It's probably just what she needs. Her demanding werewolf almost in-laws and her Type A parents are tricky to control."

"Suggest it. But something quiet. Maybe a cabin in the woods with no internet or TV."

"So we can get murdered in our sleep? No, thanks. I was thinking a luxury spa hotel."

I groaned. I was never comfortable having strangers rub oil in my skin and exfoliate my pores. "I'm probably going to be busy."

"Don't make excuses."

"I'm not. I'm just—" My phone rang. "Look at that. Saved by the bell." I pulled out my phone and answered it.

"Storm. It's Laris Brack. I need your help. Gaian Grimm is dead."

Chapter 2

I sat up straight in my seat. "Who's Gaian Grimm?"

"An old friend of mine. I'm so..." The words choked out of Laris, and he took a few seconds to compose himself. "Sorry. It's all been such a shock. I only found out a few hours ago."

"I'm sorry to hear that. What do you need from me?" I'd known Laris for years, so I didn't think he'd called for tea and sympathetic words.

"Something's wrong. The investigating officer thinks Gaian's death was an accident."

"You don't?"

"He was an advanced magic user. You don't blow yourself up with a misfiring spell when you've had his years of experience."

"A misfiring spell killed him?"

Odessa cleared away the plates, knowing not to interrupt when I talked business. I appreciated the privacy she gave me.

"Storm, I don't like to ask, but it's time to call in that favor. Gaian's death was no accident. I believe he was murdered. And I want you to look into it."

I gritted my teeth. I knew this day would come. And I was obligated to help Laris after he'd gotten me out of a trial involving werewolves and a battle to the death. And he was a decent guy. The only magic wielding lawyer I trusted.

"I can help."

A relieved exhale came down the line. "Thank you. Let's meet to talk about this. Are you free for dinner?"

"Always. Where do you want to meet?"

"I'll make a reservation at Silver Pine Lodge. It's not that far from Witch Haven."

"What time?"

"I'll see you there in two hours. I can't believe Gaian is dead. I have to know what happened."

"No promises, but I'll see what I can do."

We said our goodbyes, and I checked the time. Silver Pine Lodge was only a thirty-minute drive from Witch Haven. It was an exclusive community of wealthy magic users. The sort of place I never visited. But Laris, being an influential partner in Waggle, Tang, and Brack, was used to that kind of luxury. And so long as he paid, I was happy to tag along for the luxurious ride.

Odessa returned to the kitchen. "Everything okay?"

"My days just got busy again. That was Laris Brack. He wants me to look into the death of a friend."

Her eyes widened. "Poor Laris. This friend was killed?"

So much for her not listening in. "That's what Laris thinks. We're meeting for dinner to talk it through. I owe him a favor, so I said I'd help."

"The werewolf favor?"

"Yep. The wolves that demanded I go hand-to-hand with an alpha over one tiny comment."

"You said his biological bits and bobs were invisible to the naked eye. Werewolves are sensitive about that kind of thing. No, scrap that. All men are sensitive to those comments."

"It was all his fur. That werewolf had super shaggy fur. I'd never seen such a fluffy wolf before."

"You said it in front of his entire pack and the female werewolf he planned to make his mate."

"I was doing her a favor. The guy was a jerk."

"Who almost killed you."

"It was under control."

"Thanks to Laris pleading your case." Odessa pursed her lips. "You're going out to eat?" Her gaze turned concerned as it traveled over me.

"Sure am. Laris is treating me to dinner at Silver Pine Lodge."

She squeaked. "You need to change. And use the shower upstairs. Make sure you scrub under your fingernails."

I looked at my usual uniform of black boots, black jeans, plain sweatshirt, and leather jacket. "I'm good like this. I'm not getting changed to go to dinner. But I will wash up."

"Borrow some of my clothes. Look through the closet. Leave your things here, and I'll launder them. Or burn them. How old is that sweater?"

"Hey! Not old enough to burn." I gripped the front of my sweatshirt. "Keep away from my clothes."

"Fine. But change. Please. Silver Pine Lodge is respectable."

"And I'm not?"

"Not dressed like a bit part actress in a biker movie."

"Orange isn't my color."

"Not all my clothes are orange." Odessa looked at her black dress with a huge orange pumpkin face on the front. "Storm, Silver Pine Lodge is exclusive. They'll have a dress code."

"Laris has clout. I'm sure they'll let me in once they know I'm with him. I could show up nude and I'd get in by giving Laris's name. He's always a generous tipper."

"You're impossible. You need to take better care of yourself."

"Why bother, when I have amazing friends like you to cluck over me."

"Maybe one day, you won't have me to cluck over you, then what will you do?"

"Find new friends who realize I'm a grown woman who can wear what she likes."

Odessa threw a dishcloth at me. "Go scrub those disgusting nails and run a comb through your hair. The scarecrow look only looks good on actual scarecrows."

I chuckled as I headed to the bathroom to freshen up. I washed the dirt off my face and ran my hands through my hair to unstick it. I even gave my nails a going over. But if people had a problem with my appearance, it was their problem, not mine. I had more important things to worry about. Maybe I forgot to change my sweater for a few days and eat a decent meal, but my friends looked out for me, so I knew I'd be okay.

I headed back into the kitchen and twirled in front of Odessa.

She tutted. "You've made no effort."

"Ta-da." I lifted my hands to show my clean fingernails. "I have the nails of a hand model."

"A hand model showing the before pictures of a fungal nail cream product."

"They're not that gross." I glanced at Fire Fang, who was waiting by the door. "You stay here, if you like."

"Nope. Where you go, I go. Especially when there's fancy food involved."

"It'll be boring. The restaurant won't let you in."

"I'm still coming with you."

"Suit yourself." I'd been leaving Fire Fang behind a lot. I just wasn't comfortable in his company. And I still hadn't figured out a way to tell him: *hey, you know you think you're this awesome hellhound with amazing abilities? Well, somehow, you're a mortal trapped inside a magical shell. Good luck with that.*

Was I avoiding a difficult situation? You bet your goblin nobble I was. I might keep avoiding it until I figured out a solution. If there even was a solution.

After a quick goodbye to Odessa and Sol, we left the farmhouse and headed to the beaten up car a client who'd come up short on their final bill had given me. It was rusty, but the engine was reliable, and it meant I didn't have to keep renting cars.

The engine turned over smoothly, and we headed onto the road.

"Don't think I haven't noticed," Fire Fang said.

I kept my attention on the road. "Noticed what?"

"I've been counting the days."

"You've lost me."

"Twenty days without a belly rub."

"And that's significant?"

"I used to get daily belly rubs. Why are you being weird?"

"I'm not."

"And you keep kicking me off the bed."

"You take up too much space. It's a small double."

"It never bothered you before."

"It does now."

"And you've started shutting the bathroom door. What's going on?"

"Nothing's going on. I'm setting boundaries."

"Why do we need boundaries? Everything was great until you got weird about your personal space."

"Everything is still great." I glanced at him. He was sprawled on his side on the back seat, his anatomy on display. "Have you ever thought about dog pants? It's getting cold."

"Dog pants are a thing? What would I do with my tail?"

"I guess there's a hole in the back. You don't want your bits exposed for everyone to see, do you?"

"You've never complained about seeing my bits before."

And I hadn't. But that was before I knew what Fire Fang was. I snuck on my mental to-do list the need to get more tests done on him. If somehow he was a mortal trapped inside a hellhound's body, I needed to pull the two apart. It couldn't be healthy for either of them to be stuck like that long term.

After complaining about trying to force clothing on him a few times, Fire Fang went to sleep, and the rest of the journey was me and my thoughts, which was never a good thing. I focused on counting the number of red cars I passed. Distraction was always better than dealing with an unfixable issue.

I cruised through the open black gates of the Silver Pine Lodge, stopped the car, got out, and passed my keys to the waiting valet. "You need to pump the gas a few times if she plays you up."

He did an excellent job of hiding his horror about the rust bucket I'd presented to him.

I headed inside with Fire Fang and stopped by the head waiter's desk. "Storm Winter. Laris Brack has a reservation for us."

He nodded as he checked his records. "Very good, madam. Unfortunately, your companion animal must stay outside. No familiars in the restaurant."

"Told you," I muttered to Fire Fang. "Can you send him out something on a plate?"

"I like steak," Fire Fang said. "Lots of it. Medium rare. And a side order of fries and garlic bread. Heavy on the garlic."

The head waiter nodded. "Of course. There are shelters around the side if you wish to join the other familiars. Your food will be brought out."

Fire Fang grumbled again, but headed off.

I followed the head waiter, who led me to a table at the back of the restaurant where Laris was already seated.

He greeted me like an old friend, with a hug and a back pat. Even though our relationship had started out as purely business, it was hard not to like Laris. He was a huge bear of a man, with large mutton-chop whiskers turning gray and warm brown sparkling eyes.

They weren't sparkling this evening as he pulled back from our embrace. He looked tired, and his eyes were bloodshot, suggesting he'd shed more than a few tears over the last few hours.

"I'm glad you could come. I'm still in shock by all this. And as soon as I started poking around, I had to get in touch with you. I knew you wouldn't dismiss my concerns." Laris had a firm grip on my arms as he rushed out his words.

"Take a breath. Sit down. Tell me everything. Start at the beginning."

We took a moment to order, then Laris settled into his seat, his hands clasped together. "I've been friends with Gaian my whole life. Our mothers gave birth to us on the same day, and we were always brought together for play dates. We genuinely liked each other."

"Maybe not go back that far," I said.

"Sorry. My mind is a mess. I can't believe this has happened. Why kill Gaian?"

"Tell me about him. I don't know the name."

"Gaian is... Sorry, Gaian was a decent man. We went to the same college. I studied law, while he got into diplomatic relations. He served a number of high up families, travelling the world to ensure successful alliances continued. He spoke multiple languages and loved the finer things in life. Although he was perhaps a little too fond of gambling. That was his only flaw. He was an excellent person."

"It sounds like he had high up connections in the magic community." I sipped the ginger beer Laris had ordered for me. He knew I wasn't a big drinker and always got me something I'd enjoy.

"Yes. Most recently, he served the royal line of the Grimlows."

"He moved in high places. How did he find working with them?" Grimlows were powerful water loving magic users. They not only could control water but spent a lot of time in it. They had palaces on several continents, all close to the sea, and were a powerful influence over many magic groups.

"Gaian had his struggles, but he enjoyed the complicated jobs. As you can imagine, working with the Grimlows wasn't without its complexities. He enjoyed telling me about them, but he was always discreet."

"He'd need to be. Especially since they love using intimidation and kidnap to force loyalty and maintain power. I can't see how any amount of diplomatic negotiation would fix those actions."

"Gaian made it work. He defused several potential battles the Grimlows tried to start. He was a charming guy. A people person. He could always find a compromise to any difficult situation. He'd been working with them for several years."

"Is it possible he fell out with a member of Grimlow royalty? They're quick to react, and their methods are harsh."

"No! Well, I don't think so. Why kill such an asset? Without Gaian, they'll be fighting with the other royal families within weeks. And according to the initial investigation, it was his own misfiring magic that killed him. Grimlows would most likely drown their victims."

"Not if they used someone to do their dirty work."

"Oh! Yes, of course. You see, I'm not thinking straight. I should have considered that." Laris sipped on the heavily scented glass of red wine he'd lifted from the table.

"Why do you disbelieve the possibility it was a spell gone wrong? None of us are perfect when we use magic."

"Because Gaian worked hard to master his power. And he was a sensible warlock. He never overstepped his ability. Some magic users think they can control any spell, but not Gaian. And his main ability was to defuse other magic users' power. When he touched someone, it nullified their magic."

"It completely took it away?" That was something some spell casters would consider a threat.

"Not completely. It balanced it out and made any magic coursing through an individual stable and calm. It helped defuse many reactionary situations. That was why he was so popular with the Grimlows. He softened their sharp edges during negotiations. He was well regarded in all circles because of his ability to keep a situation calm. But he never overstretched." Laris gave a rueful chuckle. "When you get to our advanced years, you know not to tinker with magic that is beyond you."

"If his ability wasn't the problem, what about his gambling?"

We paused as the food was served, and I enjoyed carving into a huge plate of roasted butter salmon and vegetables.

"Gaian was in a little debt when he died, but he always settled any outstanding bills after he got paid."

"How can you be sure about that?"

"He was an honorable man. He wouldn't take without giving back."

"We should start there. After dinner, how about we go play the slots? Do you know where Gaian liked to gamble?"

Laris looked dubious at this suggestion. "I do. I even went with him a few times. More to keep him company than anything else."

"Perfect. We'll eat, I'll grab a doggy bag of leftovers for Fire Fang, and then we'll spend your money and see what we can find out about Gaian and his liking for taking a gamble."

I was hoping he hadn't taken a punt on something that cost him his life.

Chapter 3

"You're welcome inside, sir, but the lady's dress is inappropriate. This is a high-class establishment." The security guy barring our way into the Golden Elephant Casino had an apologetic but firm expression on his face.

"That's discrimination," I said. "Women can wear pants these days. This isn't the eighteen hundreds."

His gaze flicked my way. "Of course. But we don't allow jeans and boots on anyone in here, regardless of their gender. No gentleman or lady is allowed in unless properly attired."

"We won't be long. And we'll be discreet," Laris said.

"And as I said, sir, you're welcome inside. But your friend and her hound must stay out here."

"What if you looked the other way while we snuck in?" Laris pulled out his wallet and extracted a wad of money. "We're not here to cause trouble."

The security guy shifted from foot to foot and glanced over his shoulder.

Laris kept counting out the money. "Can I persuade you?"

"She has to change. I'll lose my job if I let in anyone dressed like that." The security guy grabbed the cash.

"These pieces are classic. This leather jacket is vintage." I kicked a piece of dried mud off one boot. "The clothing stays on."

The security guard shook his head. "You must wear a dress."

"How's that going to work? I don't carry an evening gown for such an occasion. Stop being a jerk and let us in."

He thought for a second. "We have clothing for staff out back. They're plain black dresses. I'm not sure I can do anything about the boots, though."

"The boots stay on. I'm not going barefoot." I looked at Laris and lifted my hands. "I could wait out here and question people when they leave."

"No hassling the customers," the security guy said. "Fine, the boots stay. But you have to—"

"Yeah, I get it. Change into a dress so as not to let the side down." I looked over my shoulder. Maybe it wasn't too late to back out of this.

Laris touched my arm. "I don't want to go in on my own. I know this is an inconvenience, but would you mind changing?"

I would. I very much would. I opened my mouth to protest, but I owed Laris big time, and I hated to be in debt. Plus, he looked like he might collapse with exhaustion. If putting on a dress would get me a step nearer to helping a friend and getting out from under his obligation, I'd do it.

"Nothing low-cut," I said to the security guy.

"The uniforms are discreet. Come inside. I'll find a room for you to change in."

"And Fire Fang is coming in, too."

Fire Fang growled. "But I'm not wearing a donkey helmet dress."

"Err... sure. But he can't bother the customers. Put him on a leash." The security guy tucked away the money. He opened a door and ushered us into the coat room. "Wait in here."

"Sorry about this," Laris said once the door was closed. "I forgot about the dress code. I think you look fine. Lovely. It's a quirky style. All the black, and... well, more black."

I waved away his awkward attempt at improving my mood. "Let's get in there and find out what we can about Gaian."

The security guy reappeared and handed me a dress. "It's clean. The uniforms get laundered every night."

The dress looked fine, although it would be too long for me. I wasn't short, but the owner of this outfit must be almost seven feet tall.

"I'll wait outside while you change," Laris said.

"I'm still not sure about the hound. Can't you leave him outside?" the security guy said.

"That's not up for debate. He's my... familiar. I need him by my side. My magic gets unstable without him. You don't want me accidentally blowing up this wonderful casino, do you?"

His lips pursed. "Just make sure he behaves."

"I know how to go out in a public place, you chicken armpit." Fire Fang growled at the security guy, and he backed out of the room.

Laris followed him. "I'll be outside whenever you're ready."

I swiftly changed my clothes. The dress hung down to my ankles. "This is for the greater good," I muttered to myself.

"I'm your familiar, am I?" Fire Fang huffed out smoke. "First I've heard about it."

"I had to get that jerk off my back. Would you rather be stuck outside?"

He did a doggy shrug.

"What's up with you?"

"Nothing."

"Hungry?"

"Nope."

"Tired?"

"Nope."

"Just being a goblin nobble?"

He didn't reply.

I glanced at Fire Fang. "How do I look?"

"Like you borrowed your granny's dress before she went on a diet."

I shoved him to the door. "Just the style I was going for."

We met Laris outside the coat room and headed into the main casino area. The lighting was muted, there was calming music playing in the background, and laughter filtered through the air. Everything looked expensive and new, and the clientele was from a class I didn't associate with. There were lots of dinner jackets and bow ties. Even Laris looked a little shabby in comparison, and he was always well turned out.

"You wander around and chat to a few people. I'll go to the bar. The servers often have the inside scoop on their customers," I said.

Laris nodded and headed to a nearby blackjack table.

I stopped at the bar and waved the server over.

"Good evening, madam." His gaze flickered over me. "Or are you new here?"

"Yes to the new, but I don't work for the casino. I need information about one of your regular customers."

"Happy to help. I can recommend the nineteen sixty-four claret. It's full-bodied."

"I don't want a drink."

"Then I don't have information for you." He turned away.

People never talked out of the kindness of their heart. "How much is the wine?"

"Five hundred a bottle."

I grimaced. "Find a bottle for a hundred."

"I work on commission. It's not worth my while."

Fire Fang dropped his head on the bar and growled. "It will be, unless you want to be missing a thumb. You can't pour drinks accurately with a missing digit, goblin nobble."

The server backed up. "We have a size limit on familiars. He's too big to be in here."

"I agree. He's huge. And grumpy. He could snap that whole hand off if you don't answer my questions. How would you shake a fancy martini, then?" I passed him some money across the bar to soften the threat. "This is yours. You don't need to sell me a drink. I just want a few questions answered."

The server cast a cautious look at Fire Fang, his hand sliding out from behind him. He grabbed the money and tucked it under the counter. "What do you need to know?"

"Gaian Grimm used to come here. Do you know him?"

"Sure. He's a great guy. He comes in a few times a week."

"He gambled regularly?"

"Yes, but he wasn't out of control, like some of our regulars. He had a limit and usually stuck to it."

"Usually? Did something change?"

"Gaian started spending at the high roller tables." The server lifted his chin in the direction of games at the back of the casino. "They have a big buy-in. The people around those tables take no prisoners. They gamble for a living."

"And Gaian wanted in on that?"

"I got the impression he was looking for a thrill rather than wanting serious money. After all, the guy isn't short on cash."

"He didn't owe anyone money around here?"

"It's hard to know for sure but not that I'm aware of. He spends generously at the bar and enjoys himself. And he never seems down on his luck. I guess that's what you get when you run with the royal circuit."

"Anyone here he used to spend a lot of time with?"

"Gaian is a sociable guy. Most of the people in here would consider him a friend."

"No one he had a problem with?"

The server considered the question as he polished a glass. "No one I can think of. Gaian is one of the good ones. Why the questions?"

"He's dead. We think he was murdered."

His jaw fell open. "I had no idea. What happened to him?"

"That's what I'm trying to find out."

"You're looking in the wrong place for whoever did this. No one here would kill Gaian. This is a classy establishment."

"Gaian could have gotten on the wrong side of someone. Point out the people he hung out with the most," I said.

The server's gaze swung around the room. "The two blond guys over by the poker table. They often spent time with Gaian."

I looked over to where he gestured. Two guys of around thirty with shaggy blond hair, wearing similar dark suits and white shirts, were laughing and joking with several people. "They're brothers?"

"No, but everyone thinks that. That's Micky Cox and Chance Starlight. They often played cards with Gaian or just sat around shooting the breeze."

"Gaian was older than them by about thirty years. I'm surprised he picked such young friends."

"They picked him. And I should warn you, Micky and Chance aren't to be trusted. They spend decent money here, but they don't get it through the regular channels like us hardworking types."

"Explain."

"Watch and you'll see. Luckily for them, they never run up debt behind the bar, and no one's made a complaint yet, but it's only a matter of time. I've asked around other local casinos. They're known on the circuit."

"For doing what?"

"You'll see. I should get going. Other customers to take care of." The server paused. "I'm sorry about Gaian. I hope you catch whoever did it."

I nodded, but my attention was on Micky and Chance. They were classically good-looking and could easily pass as siblings. They had artfully messy dark blond hair and big smiles that lit up their faces. Kind of cute, if you went for the surfer look.

"They're too smiley to be murderers," Fire Fang said.

"There could be dark hearts hiding behind those warm smiles. Let's see what their game is." I looked around to check Laris was doing okay. He was talking to someone at a card table and seemed comfortable, so my attention returned to the two guys.

They stood from their seats, still chatting and laughing with the other players. One of them crouched for a second. His hand slid into a jacket on the back of a chair, and he took out a wallet. He lifted some money, then placed the wallet back. He clapped a hand on the other guy's shoulder. That must be a sign the mission was accomplished, because they left the table a few seconds later.

They were smooth as they worked their way around the room. Some places they came away with nothing, but most of the time, they lifted money, the occasional watch, and even some playing chips off a table.

"You think Gaian caught them stealing from him?" Fire Fang said. "He confronted them, so they silenced him?"

"It's a possibility. They're clearly professionals and wouldn't want their shady business revealed. They'd be banned from every casino in the area."

One of the guys, I wasn't sure whether it was Chance or Micky, looked at me. He smiled, whispered something to his friend, then strode over.

"We've been made," Fire Fang grumbled.

"It doesn't matter. We needed to talk to them, anyway." I watched as the guy approached.

"Hey, I've not seen you here before. First time at the casino?" He was even cuter close up. He had dimples and brilliant white teeth that looked like they'd been bleached.

"No, it's not my sort of thing. I don't like playing games."

"You sure? I'm a regular. Micky Cox. And you are..."

"Storm Winter."

"A beautiful name for a stunning angel. I can show you around. Fix you up with a game. I love a flutter."

"So I've noticed. You're good at what you do."

"You've been watching us, haven't you?" His easy smile didn't falter, but the warmth faded from his eyes. "You wouldn't happen to work for the Magic Council, would you?"

"Nothing so grand. I don't enjoy bureaucracy."

"I thought maybe you might be working here, given what you're wearing."

"You don't like my dress?"

"It's great. The boots give it a unique twist."

"That's what I thought." My gaze traveled over him. Micky was all charm and smiles, but it was a front.

He shifted under my scrutiny. "I like your dog."

"I don't like you, turkey goblet," Fire Fang grumbled out. "No one likes a cheat."

Micky's eyebrows flashed up. "Who did I cheat? You sure you're not Magic Council?"

The time for small talk was over. I flashed him my PI credentials. "You have light fingers."

His smile had gone, and he glanced over his shoulder. "I don't know what you're talking about."

"I'm not interested in how you make your money, but I am interested in what you know about Gaian Grimm."

"Oh! I figured..." He gestured behind him.

"You figured wrong. I want to know about your friendship with Gaian."

The smile returned. "He's not in trouble, is he?"

"You will be if you don't answer my questions."

Raised voices on the other side of the casino had me glancing over. Two guys were arguing at a table. A drink got knocked over, and a woman joined in the yelling.

"Go check that out," I said to Fire Fang. "It could be about Gaian."

"You sure? I don't like the look of this goblin nobble."

"We're good." My attention turned back to Micky. "I'm waiting to learn what you know about Gaian."

"There's not much to tell. He's an all-round good guy. Generous, fun to hang out with. I like him."

"Did you two ever argue?"

"No, he's not that kind of guy. He gets on with everybody. He works for some royal family in diplomatic relations, so knows how to smooth over tense situations. Not that he gets in them. I was wondering where he was. What's he been up to?"

"Dying."

Micky blinked rapidly, and one hand pressed against his chest. "Gaian is dead! How? When? I only saw him a few days ago. That can't be right."

"It's very right."

"Um... jeez. That's terrible." He grabbed a stool and leaned on it. "Gaian is really dead?"

"Yes. Most likely murdered."

"What! No way. Gaian is everyone's friend. I mean, he was. I don't understand what's going on."

"Tell me about the last time you saw Gaian. How was he behaving?"

Micky scraped a hand through his hair. "The same as always. We hung out for a while, but then had some... work to do. New customers had come into the casino, and we wanted to make them feel welcome."

"You work as a team with your friend, Chance?"

"We're double trouble." Micky shook his head. "I still can't believe it. How did Gaian die?"

"You tell me."

He jerked upright. "This is the first I've heard about it. I can't be any help to you."

"Did you and Chance work over Gaian? You thought you were on to a pot of gold because of his connections. You've admitted you knew about his influential job working for the royal family."

"Hold on. Don't throw around accusations like that. Everyone knew what Gaian did." Micky backed away, his hands raised. "I didn't kill him. I liked Gaian."

"Maybe you liked his money more. He discovered you were stealing from him and confronted you. Or he didn't like the fact you stole from other people and told you to stop. You must have hated that."

"No, no, no! You've no clue what you're talking about. When did Gaian die?"

"Less than twenty-four hours ago. Tell me your movements for that time."

"I'm not going down for this. Sure, I lift a few wallets, but that's it. I'm not a real criminal."

"I'm yet to be convinced of that. You and your friend need to come with me."

"There's not a chance of that happening. Once you get hold of me, you won't let me go. You'll fit me up for this crime."

"Stay calm. I just need you to answer some questions. We can do it here, but you won't want potential customers realizing you're being questioned about a murder. Or that you steal from them. It might all come out if you don't cooperate."

Micky kept backing away, so I followed him.

A searing pain slammed into my back, and I hit the floor. Footsteps raced away from me, and by the time I'd staggered to my feet, Micky and Chance were racing toward the exit.

I'd been played. While Micky distracted me, Chance must have snuck up and whacked me with a spell.

With a throbbing back and aching knees, I raced after them. The dumb dress tangled around my ankles, and I almost fell again. I hitched it to my thighs and kept running.

I barged past the security guy, ignoring his protests, and into the cool evening air. But I was too late. The only thing I heard was faint laughter in the air, and I had no idea which direction Chance and Micky had escaped.

But by running, they'd proven one thing. They were guilty of killing Gaian, and I was taking them down.

Chapter 4

"I'm sorry again about what happened this evening." Laris sat next to me in my car as I drove home after the failed mission at the casino. His private car tailed us, so he could get a ride when we were finished talking.

"Don't apologize. It was my fault. I got taken by surprise." I was angry at letting Micky and Chance get away, but there was no point in taking it out on Laris.

"I should never have left you on your own. I didn't think we'd find the actual people who killed Gaian tonight." Laris patted my knee.

"I'd have caught them, but the dress slowed me down. If that idiot security guard had let me wear my usual outfit, none of this would have happened." I was back in my usual jeans and sweater combination and already more comfortable.

"At least we have the prime suspects," Laris said.

I nodded as I stopped the car outside my apartment. "We'll catch up with them and get a confession. Gaian's murder is almost solved."

"I appreciate your help. It finally feels like we're making progress. I'll speak to the Magic Council first thing tomorrow and let them know what you discovered. They'll have to take me seriously when they learn Gaian was associating with criminals. They killed him to silence him." Laris took out a hankie and mopped his eyes.

"That's my thinking." I opened the door to let Fire Fang out, and after saying goodbye to Laris and seeing him to his waiting car, I headed inside and up the stairs to my apartment.

My knees were sore from where I'd landed heavily, and my back bruised from the spell I'd been whacked with, but it was mainly my ego that felt dented. I'd let down my guard and hadn't taken this case as seriously as I should. Lessons learned. Trust no one, always watch your back, and everyone is guilty until you prove them innocent.

I glanced at Fire Fang, who hadn't spoken the whole journey back. "What's up with you?"

"You."

I unlocked the apartment door. "I don't get it."

"You're only happy when I'm not around. You sent me off the second there was something else going on in the casino. If I'd been watching your back, that guy would never have snuck up on you."

I winced and took a moment to take off my jacket and boots, giving myself time to figure out what to say. "Maybe not. And I am happy you're around. It's just..."

"Just what? You've been moody and distant for weeks."

I headed to the kitchen and looked inside the fridge. It was almost empty, as usual.

Fire Fang padded after me. "Storm, I know something is wrong. And I also know you're terrible about sharing your problems, and you keep everything in until it bursts out in an ugly mess."

"You're being dramatic. I never burst. I'm sure there was some cheese in here." I closed the fridge door. "Maybe that stray cat snuck in and ate it."

"Is it something I've done? Is it because I stole food from the trash?"

"Since when did you steal food from the trash?"

"Forget I said anything. It's not that."

I leaned against the kitchen counter and considered revealing his test results. The vet must be wrong. How can a mutant hellhound be a mortal? "You never talk much about your past."

His ears flipped up. "That's because I don't have much to tell. You know I have memory loss. Is that what the problem is? You're worrying I'm some dangerous, out-of-control creature who'll eat you in your sleep?"

"I already know you're that."

He huffed out a smoky laugh. "My memories before I was a hellhound are blurry. It's mainly gaps, but I occasionally get unhelpful images."

"Of what?"

"A different place, other people. Sometimes I see a red brick house."

"You think it was your home?"

His muzzle wrinkled. "It could have been."

"Where is this house? If we find it, it could bring back your memories. It would remind you of what you really are."

"Does it matter? I like what I am now. I'm strong, powerful, and help you out of tricky situations."

"Which rarely happens."

Fire Fang growled. "Have you learned nothing from tonight, you crazy buttoned witch? You need me by your side. I know you don't like asking for help, but that's my job."

"What if it wasn't? What if your job was something different? Your life was different?"

"Then I'd change it, so it was more like this. Although with better food in the cupboard and my place back in your bed."

I hunted out some dog chews and threw him a couple. "You must want more than this."

"I could go for another dog chew."

"I mean, I'm happy with a basic life and focusing on work, but don't you have ambitions?"

"Even though you've refused to bond with me, I'm your familiar. My path is chosen. That's my ambition. Mission achieved."

"You're not bound to me. You're free. You should explore your past more."

More smoke plumed from his nose. "Why are you suddenly so keen to get rid of me?"

"I'm not. But things could change in a heartbeat. You could get your memories back. You could turn back into..." I just couldn't tell him his test results showed he was mortal. Shifting from magic user to mortal would be a tragedy. Mortals had no special powers and no knowledge of how incredible the world was. They just shuffled around in a gray acceptance that life was tedious. It was the worst threat to hold over a magic user to take their power.

I couldn't give Fire Fang that terrible news. I didn't know how he'd become a hellhound, but I wasn't going to smash his world apart.

A soft thump from my bedroom had me turning. A second later, the stray black cat who'd been haunting me for what felt like an eternity appeared, blinking her eyes and yawning.

"How did you get in there? Did you steal my cheese?" I strode over to scoop her up, but she scuttled under the coffee table, hissing at me.

"She's back!" Fire Fang raced over, his tail up.

"She can't stay." Although I had wondered where she'd been these last few weeks. I'd almost missed her howling under my window. Okay, that was a lie, but I had been concerned about her safety. She was a scrawny little thing, and a gust of wind would knock her over.

"The cat stays." Fire Fang stuck his nose under the table. "At least for the night. It's cold outside."

I groaned, too tired and sore to protest. "Just for one night."

"For good. You'll only waste energy chasing her away. We're keeping her. She's kind of cute." Fire Fang poked his nose under the table again, then shot back as claws raked down his nose.

"Yeah, she's a sweetheart. She's not sleeping on my bed, though."

"You need to give her something to sleep on," Fire Fang said. "I've got the couch, so that's not free."

"I've got an old box somewhere. Give me a minute." I headed down the stairs, grabbed a large shoebox, put an old blanket in it, and returned to the apartment. When I returned, I discovered a small pile of ginger fluff next to the table.

"Did you put that there?" I asked Fire Fang.

"The cat did. When you left, she spat it out."

"Gross. And it's not her color. Maybe she fought a local ginger tomcat." I set the box beside the coffee table. "That'll do. We'll figure out something else in the morning."

"Because she's moving in?" Fire Fang poked the box closer to the table, then sniffed the ginger fur.

"Because I'm too tired to have this debate."

I left the cat to do whatever she was going to do, had a wash, changed into my comfiest oversized T-shirt and shorts, then climbed into bed with my laptop.

Fire Fang wandered in and settled on the floor beside the bed.

I flicked through multiple webpages, looking for information about Micky and Chance. There was surprisingly little about them online, although I found a few photographs.

They must have killed Gaian, but I needed to make sure I wasn't missing anything. If those two were as tricky as I thought they were, they'd already be figuring out alibis to get away with his murder.

After another half an hour of searching, I found a social media page showing Micky was in a relationship with a woman called Ashley Ellis. She looked uptight, with a sharp face and pointed ears. A pair of intense, brilliant purple eyes glared at me from the page.

I scribbled down her information, stifling a yawn behind my hand.

"Did you find what you were looking for?" Fire Fang mumbled, sounding half asleep.

"I think so. First thing in the morning, we're going to question Micky Cox's girlfriend."

I couldn't feel my feet. I jerked upright in bed and discovered the stray cat was asleep across my ankles. Fire Fang was sprawled out on the other side of the bed.

Why did I bother setting rules? These two were in control around here.

After wriggling my toes out from under the cat, the whole time her feigning sleep, I snuck into the bathroom and showered.

My night had been full of weird dreams about Eden. There'd been no new leads on my sister for weeks, but my subconscious was still hard at work, and it wouldn't let go.

It was strange, but she felt close to me. And for weeks, I'd been looking over my shoulder and studying any woman who looked vaguely like her. I just needed to keep looking. Eden was out there.

I dressed, drank coffee, and checked the bedroom. Fire Fang and the cat were still asleep, so I let them have a lie-in. I could visit Micky's girlfriend on my own.

A quick scan of her social media page revealed the town she lived in. It was a half-hour drive from Witch Haven. I poked around some more before hacking into the electoral roll database and getting her address. Information obtained, I left the sleeping fluffies behind.

I grabbed a pastry from Fandango's bakery, said a quick hello to Albert, and was on my way.

It was a good drive, barely any traffic, and the crisp, warm, sweet pastry had set my mood to not gloomy.

I pulled up outside a small, single-story house with neat flowerbeds and hopped out. I walked to the door and knocked on it.

Ashley Ellis opened it. She wore almost the same sharp expression she had in the picture, although from her crumpled clothing and bleary eyes, it looked like she'd only just gotten out of bed.

Those bleary eyes narrowed. "Is there something I can do for you?"

"I hope so. I'm Storm Winter. I'm looking for your boyfriend, Micky Cox."

She snorted. "Good luck with that. I haven't seen him in days."

"You've had a fight?"

She crossed her arms over her chest. "What do you want him for?"

"I'm a private investigator. I've been hired to look into a suspicious death. Micky's name came up in conversations about the deceased."

That caught her attention. Her spine straightened, and her eyes widened. "You think Micky murdered someone?"

"He knew the victim. And they were seen together recently."

"Not Micky. He's a joke and takes advantage of people, but he's no killer."

"When was the last time you saw him?"

"Four days ago. Who's dead?"

"Gaian Grimm."

She shook her head. "I don't know him. He was friends with Micky?"

"They hung out together at the same casino."

Ashley rolled her eyes. "Of course. That's what we were always fighting about. I kept telling him to get a legitimate job, or he'd end up in trouble. He said all those rich people didn't notice when their wallets went missing. He said he was owed that money. He showed them a good time and made them happy. It was his payment."

"I doubt the people he stole from would agree with that. I'm not interested in how he gets his money, though. I'm interested in whether he murdered Gaian."

Concern crossed Ashley's face. "You're wasting your time hunting Micky. He's a lot of things, but he's never violent. We've had our fair share of rows, and he never even raised his voice to me. He's a charmer and a trickster. He even tricked me out of money."

"Does he have his own place?"

"No. He moves around a lot. His best friend, Chance, is always with him. They sneak into hotels and get away without paying the bill. And they're always on the lookout for empty vacation rentals. They once stayed in a mansion for six weeks before the owner realized something was wrong. Micky's whole life is one big gamble. He loves a challenge."

"Maybe he upgraded the challenge to see if he could get away with murder."

That earned me a vehement head shake. "No. He's a lover, not a fighter."

"So you've no idea where I can find him?"

"I wish I could help. If you ever catch up with him, tell him to pay me back what he owes me. The big, dumb idiot." Although the words were sharp, the tone wasn't. There was still affection here for Micky.

My phone buzzed in my back pocket, and I pulled it out to see the call was from Laris. "Thanks for your time."

She raised a hand. "When you find him, tell him... tell him to call me."

"Sure. But I think you can do better than a thief." I headed away from the house and answered the call. "Hey, I'm already working the case. I should have Micky and Chance by the end of the day."

"Storm, I'm sorry to say this is becoming a habit, but Micky Cox has been found dead."

Chapter 5

A brisk wind whipped off the water of Serpent Lake. I stood beside Laris, waiting for a small team from the Magic Council to finish their examination of Micky's body.

A tall skinny guy, wearing a Magic Council uniform—black clothing with a wide-brimmed hat—strode over and shook Laris's hand. "Lord Brack. I was told by my manager you wanted to be kept informed about this case. I'm Darnel Tharris. If you have questions, please let me know."

"Thank you. I appreciate that," Laris said.

I sometimes forgot how important Laris was, as Darnel simpered around him.

Darnel glanced at me before turning his attention to Laris. "Is there anything in particular you want to know about this individual?"

"Do you know how he died?" Laris said.

"We need to complete an examination, but early indications suggest drowning."

"Are there signs of injury on the body?" I said.

Darnel glanced at me. "And you are?"

"Storm Winter. I'm working with Laris. Lord Brack."

"Very good. Another lawyer?"

My eyebrows lifted. "Do I look like a lawyer?"

"No, you look like... a friend of Lord Brack." Darnel tugged at his collar. "We'll be moving the body soon. I'll be able to tell you more in a day or so."

"Have you got a time of death?"

Darnel hesitated. "Not an exact time. Most likely between two in the morning and six. He's not been in the water long."

"Excellent work. Thank you, Darnel," Laris said. "Anything else you need to know, Storm?"

"Not for now."

"I should get back and supervise," Darnel said.

"Of course. Don't let us stop you," Laris said.

I waited until Darnel walked away before turning to Laris. "What strings did you pull to get news about this drowning so quickly?"

"It pays to be connected. And lucky. I was speaking to a contact at the Magic Council this morning and giving her an update about the casino. It just so happened a call came in about a body discovered in the lake while we were talking. They found out the victim's identity from Micky's wallet. I called you right away when I heard what was going on."

"If only the Magic Council was this helpful when I worked cases."

His smile was indulgent. "You don't need their help. You do a fine job without them."

"You know flattery gets you nowhere with me."

His smile turned genuine, and he patted my shoulder. "It never hurts to attempt to crack that tough exterior of yours."

"It's there for a reason. You won't like what's on the inside. Any sign of Micky's friend, Chance? I was with Micky's ex-girlfriend, Ashley, when you called. She said those two were close. They did everything together."

Laris took a moment to look around the lake. "I haven't seen anyone who shouldn't be here. Surely, if Chance knew his friend was dead, he'd stay around and find out what happened."

"Perhaps they both drowned."

Laris grimaced. "They could have been fooling around in the lake and gotten out of their depth."

"Pun intended?"

"Oh, dear. That was tactless. No. I mean, perhaps they were bad swimmers. If they fell in after a heavy night of drinking... well, this would be the result."

"Or they were both killed," I said.

He startled and smoothed a hand down his neat red tie. "You don't think this drowning was an accident?"

My gaze traveled over the stony banks of Serpent Lake. "It's too soon to say. But it would be an odd coincidence for us to look for them in connection to Gaian's murder, and then for one of them to turn up dead the same night."

"Perhaps we're not the only people who wanted to speak to them. Someone they stole from could have discovered their theft and gone after them. We caused a stir at the casino, and it got them noticed."

"I caused the stir. You were charm personified, as usual."

We were silent as we watched the body being moved.

"How's your back?"

"I've forgotten about it." It ached, but there was no point in concerning Laris about my injury from last night's fight. "Maybe no one else is involved in this. Chance and Micky argued. Chance killed Micky and dumped the body. This is a tidal lake, so he hoped the corpse would be dragged out to sea before anyone found it."

Laris simply nodded, watching as the team bagged Micky's body and moved it into a vehicle.

"Any idea where Micky entered the water?" I said.

"No, and the Magic Council found nothing when they looked around the shoreline."

"No drag marks or signs of a struggle?"

"Nothing. And I checked myself. Magic Council employees are competent—"

"Occasionally."

A small smile flickered across his face. "Yes. But they can miss things. I walked around the edge while waiting for you. Nothing was out of place. And I've visited enough crime scenes to know what to look for."

"I'll head back to the ex-girlfriend's house. Ashley might have more useful information when she learns what happened to Micky."

"I'll go with the Magic Council and see if they discover anything useful when they conduct the autopsy." Laris sighed. "Perhaps this is over. Micky got the punishment he deserved after killing Gaian."

"What about Chance? He's still on the loose. We should speak to him. It could be Micky was panicking about what they did to Gaian and wanted to turn himself in. Chance wasn't willing to give up his freedom, so he killed his best friend to keep him quiet."

Laris's forehead crinkled, and he tugged at the gray whiskers on his cheek. "You're right. We find Chance. We see this through to the end."

"It's all guesswork at this stage. We need to get answers out of Chance."

Laris briefly clasped my hand. "Thank you, Storm. I'll let you know if I hear anything useful from the Magic Council."

"I'll do the same with the ex-girlfriend." I jumped in my car and drove back to Ashley's house. I was just climbing out when her front door opened.

She slowed as she saw me. "You again. I told you everything I can about Micky. And I still haven't seen him. I need to get a move on. I'm starting work in twenty minutes."

"I'll walk with you. I have news about Micky."

Ashley didn't look happy about my suggestion, but simply shrugged and slung her purse over one shoulder. "Whatever you like. And I don't care about Micky, so you're wasting your time."

I fell into step with her. "It's not good news."

"He's finally been caught? Serves him right."

"No. Well, in a way, he's been caught. Ashley, that call I took when I was here, was from a friend who has connections at the Magic Council. They discovered a body in Serpent Lake. It was Micky."

Ashley stopped walking and turned to stare at me. "He's dead?"

"He is. The Magic Council is looking into what happened."

Her eyes filled with tears, but she blinked them away. "Big, dumb idiot. I'm not surprised. It's horrible news, but Micky was always risking his life for fun. He probably had too much to drink, stole a boat with that loser, Chance, and they lost control of it."

"Was that the sort of thing he'd do?"

"Micky lived in the moment. It was one of the many things we argued about. He never thought ahead about the consequences of his actions. If he thought something would amuse him, he did it." She pulled a crumpled tissue from her pocket and blew her nose. "Such a dummy."

"How long were you two together?" I said.

Ashley continued on her journey once she'd stopped sniffing and wiping her nose. "On and off for three years. It was more off than on, if I'm honest. I fell for his charm initially, but after months of Micky never taking anything seriously and treating life like a game, it got boring. I wanted to settle down. I've been saving for my own home for years and wanted someone to share it with, have a family with, and build a life together."

"Micky wasn't on board with that?"

"He pretended to be. But Micky's charm and good looks only got him so far. I saw through the charade and ditched him. But he always found a way to get through my door again. He promised he'd change and wanted the same things as me. But it never lasted. Now we've come to this. I'm sad, but I was waiting for the day when someone told me Micky Cox had pushed his luck too far."

"Were you angry things didn't work out between you?"

"Sure. But I was also relieved. I got sick of my things going missing and having to buy them back from the pawnshop Micky took them to. He needed money to get in the casinos. He promised he'd double my money and buy me all the jewels I wanted, but that wasn't the point. He always had some silver tongued lie to trick me. It wrecked our relationship."

"Wrecked it enough for you to drown him?"

Ashley smirked, then glared at me. "I wouldn't waste my time killing Micky. I was done with him. I was moving on. Of course, occasionally, I thought about strangling him when I discovered another of his lies. But it wasn't me."

"What did you get up to last night? Between about two and six in the morning."

"You're seriously asking me for an alibi?"

"You were his girlfriend."

"Ex-girlfriend."

"You asked me to pass a message on to him to call you. You still cared about him."

"Which means I wouldn't kill him."

"Your relationship was troubled. Maybe he took something from you he shouldn't and you wanted revenge."

"I have nothing that valuable. Nothing worth killing for."

I shrugged. "Don't be surprised if the Magic Council comes by and asks you the same thing. I could keep them off your back if you give me a decent alibi."

She choked out a laugh. "I have one. I worked the late shift at the herbal wholesalers on the other side of town. I did an eight-hour shift and finished at midnight. I grabbed a late dinner with my colleagues, and then we walked home. We traveled as a pack because it was late. They'll all be there now if you want to check where I was."

"What time did you get home?"

"About one-thirty. I had a shower and crashed out. I had no desire to sneak out, find wherever Micky was lurking, and drown him. I wouldn't waste my time or risk losing my freedom to get rid of him." She tilted her head. "Do you even know for sure he was killed?"

"It's an open avenue of investigation. I'll come with you to the wholesalers, check your alibi, and then you won't be bothered anymore. Providing you're innocent."

I got another unhappy glare. "Sure. Just don't tell my friends I killed someone. I don't want to lose my job. Micky already cost me enough."

"I can be discreet." We continued walking. Ashley wasn't acting hyper nervous, just shocked over the news. She certainly wasn't acting like she was trying to get away with murder. "If someone drowned Micky, any idea who might have done it?"

She was quiet for a moment, her fingers playing with the strap on her purse. "He had serious debt built up with Thad Dedopulos. Do you know him?"

"I've not had the pleasure. What does Thad do?"

"Loans money with an extortionate rate of interest. Micky was in over his head. He loved to live the good life but couldn't afford it, so he borrowed. When the usual lines of credit dried up, he turned to loan sharks. Thad is the worst around. Micky started with a small loan, but then he got greedy, and so did Thad. The last I heard, Micky owed him over ten thousand, and Thad wanted it back with all the interest on top and late repayment fees."

"Was it just Micky in debt to Thad?"

She glanced at me. "You're thinking about Chance?"

"Maybe Chance needed money, too."

"Maybe he did. Have you spoken to Chance yet? He did everything with Micky. They were like twins. Handsome, annoying, idiot twins."

"The Magic Council is still searching the lake in case there's a second body."

"Oh! You think Chance could be dead, too?"

"He wasn't at the lake, and there haven't been any sightings of him nearby. Has he been in touch with you?"

"No! We weren't close. He didn't like Micky having a girlfriend." Ashley shook her head. "They could both be dead? That's horrible. I really hope it was an accident, but there are people out there who weren't fooled by Micky's charm. They both had enemies."

"Have you got Thad's details? I'd like to speak to him."

Ashley's nose wrinkled. "I don't. I kept away from that nastiness. Thad even had the cheek to show up at my place a time or two to see if he could get money out of me for Micky's debts. I sent him away with a warning not to come back, or I'd report him to the Magic Council."

"Did he listen?"

"I didn't see him again. Even though Micky was a jerk, I think he told Thad to stay away from me. Moronic fool." She dabbed at her eyes. "And poor Chance. I don't like the guy, but what if he saw what happened to Micky, and he's in hiding? He'll be devastated. They had a real bromance."

"He won't be so devastated if he killed Micky."

Her hand went to her mouth. "I didn't think about that. No! Not Chance. Those two never really argued, not about anything serious. I was jealous of their relationship. If anything bad happened to Micky, and Chance saw it going on, he defended him, even if Micky was in the wrong. They stood up for each other. It was one of those true friendships that are so hard to find."

"I plan on talking to Chance, providing he's alive. But I'll start with Thad."

"Thad hated them. He was waiting for an opportunity to crush them. You could try the Jade Bar on Sharpe's Row. It's near here. Thad used to meet Micky there."

"I'll do that. But first, I need to check your alibi."

Ashley grumbled under her breath but had no choice but to take me into work with her.

Forty-five minutes later, I was heading away from the herbal wholesalers in my car. Ashley had been exactly where she said she was last night. She'd work the late shift, had dinner with her colleagues, and then they'd walked home together.

Although it was impossible to check the last part of her alibi, since she'd been in bed alone, I didn't get any sense Ashley wanted Micky dead. She'd had a soft spot for him, no matter how much she protested. Ashley was at the bottom of my suspect list.

I parked, walked to the door of the Jade Bar, and pulled it open. The place was almost empty, given it was early, but there was a small group tucked away at a table at the back and a couple of guys sitting at the bar drinking alone.

I headed to the bar. The scent of macaroni and cheese made my stomach growl as I arrived.

A woman in her mid-forties strode over, a smile on her prematurely lined face. "Honey, I heard that stomach of yours from a mile away. You want something to eat?"

A short pit stop to refuel would do no harm. I checked the specials board and discovered mac and cheese was the only option. "I'll take a ginger beer and a large plate of your special."

"Coming right up." She walked away and grabbed my ginger beer before setting it down. "You new in the area or just passing through?"

"Passing through. I'm looking for someone. Thad Dedopulos?"

The woman's eyes narrowed. "What would you want with Thad?"

"A friendly chat." I set my PI credentials down for her to see. "He could have gotten himself in some trouble."

She spent a few seconds looking over my credentials. "That wouldn't surprise me. How serious are we talking?"

"The murder kind of trouble."

Her thin black eyebrows flashed up. A bell rang behind her. "Hold on a second, honey. That's your order." She dashed away and returned with a steaming mound of gooey mac and cheese that she set in front of me.

I grabbed a knife and fork from the container on the bar and tucked in, almost burning my mouth. It was good. Creamy, salty, and carb-loaded.

"My husband is the chef. It's great, isn't it?" The woman grinned as I stuffed down the food.

I gave her a thumbs-up, since my mouth was full.

She stepped closer. "My best advice is to eat and leave. Thad won't be any help. He never talks to the Magic Council or any kind of PI. You're wasting your time and possibly getting Thad's attention. And that's never a good thing."

"I wouldn't be so sure about that, Bonnie," a low gravelly voice said from behind me.

Bonnie backed away and raised a hand. "I was just saving this lady some trouble."

"Too late for that."

I glanced over to see a tubby guy with a bald head covered in tattoos take the seat next to me. I swallowed my mouthful of food. "Thad Dedopulos?"

"Depends who's asking."

I pushed him my credentials as I ate more mac and cheese. "What can you tell me about Micky Cox?"

He grunted. "What's that little gutter rat got himself into?"

"An early grave. He was pulled out of Serpent Lake today. What do you know about that?"

"Huh! He's dead. He owed me. What a waste of an investment."

"I'll pass on your condolences to his family. Did you kill him?"

Thad smirked. "I never kill people who owe me money. Well, I rough them up if they don't come up with the funds, but why would I bump off someone when they're giving me money?"

"It seems common knowledge you and Micky did business. The Magic Council will be here soon, wanting to know if that business turned bad."

"You see me shaking?"

"I can keep them off your back."

His narrowed eyes suggested he didn't believe me. "You have influence with the idiots in the black hats?"

"I have a friend who does. What do you say? You talk to me, and I make your life easier." I slurped up more food.

Thad tapped his fingers on the bar. "Since you brought me useful information, I'll bite. But no Magic Council. Those guys give me the chills."

"Got it. Where were you between two and six in the morning?"

More finger tapping happened. "Right here. The bar stays open till one, and then we had a lock in, just me and the boys." He pointed over his shoulder at the five men who were watching the conversation intently.

I looked at Bonnie, and she nodded. "They were here. They put cash behind the bar and drank until it ran out. I never turn down an offer like that. Business isn't exactly booming."

"What time did you leave?" I said to Thad.

"The sun was coming up. I can't give a closer time than that."

"It was after five," Bonnie said.

Thad tipped back, rocking his stool. "Although it's a shame one of my assets is dead, I'm not unhappy. I can't stand people who cheat others."

"Isn't that what you do? I heard your interest rates aren't friendly."

Bonnie hissed a warning at me and shook her head.

Thad waved her away. "They know what they're getting into. My terms and conditions are wide open if anyone bothers to read them. Which they don't. Micky and his friend, Chance, liked to play at being nice guys, but they're as twisted as me. They trick and deceive. They sneak around and steal. It was shady. I hate that behavior."

"You didn't hate it enough to not lend Micky money."

"Because it served my purpose."

"Did you ever have to rough him up to get a payment?"

Thad cracked his knuckles. "Yeah, and I enjoyed every second. He was a worthless trickster, and I needed to teach him a lesson."

"You're not painting a pretty picture for me. If you two came to blows in the past, it could make you a suspect if this turns out to be a murder investigation."

"I can't be a suspect. I was here. There are six people who can confirm it." Thad rolled his shoulders, although there was a glint of warning in his eyes. "I can relax now Micky is dead. Chasing after that idiot for my money was a hassle. He's a problem gone. Thanks for telling me."

"Always a pleasure to assist the criminal fraternity." I tipped back my bottle of ginger beer.

Thad eyeballed me for a second before sliding off the stool and heading back to his friends.

"Honey, have you got a death wish?" Bonnie kept her voice low.

"Not this week."

"It must be your lucky day, then. You got off easy. Thad usually throws people out the second they ask questions he doesn't like. You caught him in a good mood."

"And he caught me in a good mood, thanks to your excellent food." I pushed away my empty plate. "My compliments to the chef."

"Thanks, honey. I'll pass them on. You'd better go. I don't want there to be any fights. And the way Thad is looking at you, things could get nasty."

I'd gotten what I needed, so I finished my ginger beer, paid the bill, and left.

It had been easy to rule out the only other suspects in connection to Micky's death. That left me with Chance Starlight.

As I strolled back to my car with a full belly, I smiled. It was nice to work a simple case for once. All I had to do was find Chance, get a confession, and I'd get a double murderer off the streets.

Chapter 6

The next morning, I was in my office, feet on the desk, as I made my way through my contacts. I'd been making calls for hours, trying to find Chance. He was good at hiding, but I was better at finding. I was going to snag this trickster and get a confession.

Fire Fang stomped into the office and rested his head on the edge of the desk.

I slid him a glance. Uh-oh, he looked huffy again. "Everything okay with you?"

"You've still not said sorry."

"For what? There's food in your bowl, fresh water down, and I took you for a walk this morning. I'm the perfect hellhound owner. Gold star for me."

"For yesterday. You left me behind."

"You and Stray Cat were asleep on my bed. Which, by the way, neither of you were supposed to be doing. Anyway, I figured you could do with a lie-in."

"You went to a possible murder scene and then questioned two suspects without me. What if you'd needed my help?"

I pointed a finger at myself. "Powerful weather witch. I look after myself."

"You've got me to protect you. And Binky."

"Who's Binky?"

"I named the stray cat. We can't keep calling her Stray Cat."

"We're not calling her anything. This homestay is temporary."

"Yeah, you said that about me, but there's a food bowl on the floor with my name engraved on it."

"I had a moment of weakness when walking past the pet store. It won't happen again." I set aside my phone. "Besides, you'll get your memories back soon, and then you'll leave. There's no point in me getting attached to you."

He huffed out smoke. "Is that what this is about? You have abandonment issues?"

"I'll abandon you if you psychoanalyze me." Although I would get a few pangs of loneliness when Fire Fang finally went. As for Stray Cat, I was happy never to see her skinny behind again. I'd lost too many nights of sleep to that one.

Fire Fang snorted out more smoke. "I'm going nowhere, you crazy buttoned witch. Neither is Binky. She likes it here."

"She told you that, did she?"

"No, but we could try the speech spell on her to get her talking, too."

"One talking fuzz ball is enough, thanks. Besides, that spell may not work on her. It took enough trial and error to get this one working for you." I leaned back and checked my coffee mug. Empty. "Where is Stray Cat, anyway?"

"Binky."

I arched an eyebrow at him. "She will always be Stray Cat to me. Where's she hiding? She'd better not be under the covers on my bed."

"I don't know. I haven't seen her. She went out and didn't come back."

"That's good news. Maybe she's gotten the message, or she realized living with us is no walk in the park and moved on."

"Not now you've given her a shoebox. That cat is staying."

My phone pinged with an incoming message. It was from Tulip, one of the PIs I used when I had a busy workload.

I got a sighting of the guy you're looking for. A second later, an address came through with the name of a club. *Enjoy Lumbagos.*

"Lumbagos?" I muttered. "That can't be right."

"Something wrong with your back?" Fire Fang said.

"No, apparently, it's a club name. This has to be a joke, right?" I texted back Tulip to see if her auto correct had gone haywire.

LOL. I got the spelling right. It sounds like a treat. Mexican fusion with karaoke.

I checked the address. It was a couple of hours away from the casino Chance and Micky were last seen in. It would have been easy for Chance to make it that far without being picked up.

I grabbed my jacket from the back of the chair.

"Are you leaving me behind again?" Fire Fang said.

I hesitated. I was the one who had the issue with his test results. I didn't know how to tell him or even if I should tell him. Would I want to know I was a mortal, rather than a fab magic user who had control over the elements? Not likely. I'd be happy to live in glorious ignorance.

Fire Fang nudged me with his head when I didn't respond. "You need me. I'm coming with you."

"You are. But after this, we have to talk."

He backed up a step. "It sounds like you're breaking up with me."

"No, but you might want to break up with me. Or at least get professional help."

"I'm almost scared. Storm, what's going on?"

"Later. Let's focus on this case. Once we've found Chance and had him arrested for Gaian and Micky's murders, we can deal with the other stuff."

"Other stuff like what?"

I grabbed my keys and headed to the door. "Other stuff like you'll see. Now get a move on. We're going to Lumbagos."

Two hours later, I was staring at six enormous plastic palm trees outside a set of double doors painted a brilliant red. Loud Mexican music blasted out of outdoor speakers, and the smell of nachos and chili was thick in the air.

"It looks terrible, but smells amazing," Fire Fang said. "I suddenly need a huge bowl of chili."

It didn't sound like a terrible idea. I opened the door and walked into a riot of red and yellow splashed around a large open plan bar. There were small tables and a dancefloor at the back. A circular bar was decked out with its own mini palm trees. Even a few flamingos made it into the mix.

The place was busy with the lunchtime rush, everyone getting in some Mexican vibes. There were even a few sombreros floating around on people's heads. Tacky but tasty. That was a vibe I could handle.

I headed to the bar and had to wait a few minutes before I got the server's attention.

He dashed over in a bright red shirt with frills on the front that bobbed when he moved. "You look like a fancy cocktail kind of woman. What will it be? A Juicy Lucy, a Short Trip to Hell, or a Dancing Wench?"

"I'm not here for a cocktail."

"We'll have some chili, though," Fire Fang said. "Two huge bowls. The hotter the better."

"A pup after my own heart. Any drinks to go with that?"

"No. And we'll take the chili to go. We're looking for someone. Chance Starlight. He was spotted here earlier today," I said.

"Don't know him. You'll definitely need water to go with your chili. Still or sparkling?"

I pulled up a slightly grainy photograph of Chance and held it out for the bartender to see. "This is the guy. I know he was here."

He peered at the picture for a few seconds. "He could have been in and left. I'm not the only one serving here today. I might have missed him. Is he someone important?"

"Yes. Mind if I look around, ask a few customers if they've seen him?"

A pained expression crossed his face. "I don't know about that."

"He's in trouble."

"What kind of trouble?"

"Trouble you don't want connected to this place." He lifted his hands, palms up. "Be quiet about it."

I nodded and slid a big tip into the jar on the counter. I looked around Lumbagos. There was a group of older guys sitting around one table, sharing a plate of nachos. I headed over to them.

"Hey, are you regulars here?"

"Every week when they do the early lunch special," one guy said.

"I'm looking for someone." I held out the picture of Chance for them to see.

"Don't know him."

"He's not a regular."

"He looks too wet behind the ears to handle the chili they serve here."

They chuckled at that last comment.

"The Magic Council wants a word with him," I said.

"Sweetheart, you're not fooling anyone." The oldest guy in the group, a grizzled man with a huge white mustache, crunched on a nacho.

"I'm not?"

"He's your boyfriend. What's he done, cheated on you, and you want revenge?"

My top lip curled. "He's not my type."

"You don't work for the Magic Council, though. I've had dealings with those morons over the years, and you're not giving out the moron vibe."

"You're right, I'm not. But I'm still looking for Chance. He's wanted for questioning on a possible double murder."

That wiped the smug looks off their faces.

"Murder, you say. Well, that changes things. You're sure you're not after your sweetheart because he abandoned you at the altar?" White Mustache said.

"She looks like she'd eat him alive," one of the other guys said.

"I won't eat anyone alive, but let me introduce you to Fire Fang."

Fire Fang stepped up and grumbled a growl so deep, the table shook.

The guys cringed back. One of them grabbed the nachos. Food before friends.

"None of us have seen him. Stop bothering us or we'll complain to the management." White Mustache threw a bread roll at Fire Fang, which he caught and ate. "We'll have you tossed out of here. We're loyal customers, and the manager won't want to lose our business because of some angry witch and her grubby mutt."

"Wait, wait. Let's hear what the little lady has to say." A guy with a tattoo on his neck looked the least fearful of the group. "Who did this fella kill?"

"Does it matter? Two people are dead because of him." Most likely, but they didn't need all the details.

Tattoo Neck's gaze flicked to the back of the bar. "We want no trouble here. This is a family place. We like to keep things friendly. People come here for fun, not to wile away the hours with a killer."

"And they can still come here for fun. All I need to know is if you have seen this guy. Any of you?"

The sound of glass breaking caught my attention. I turned, looking for the source.

Tattoo Neck nodded at the corner of the room. "You might like to try the public restroom. They have real fancy soap in there."

I raced to the restrooms at the back of the bar and discovered Chance sliding out of a broken window. "Don't move! You're coming with me."

His gaze flashed my way. He slipped through and disappeared before I could grab him.

I poked my head out to see him racing along an alleyway.

"We'll head him off outside." I sped out of the restroom, Fire Fang speeding ahead of me, almost sending several servers flying as they dodged out of his way.

"Hey! What about your chili?" the guy behind the bar said.

"Another time." I was out the door, heading toward the alleyway. We should be able to cut Chance off before he made it to the end and merged into the crowds. He couldn't be that fast.

I was wrong. But I got a glimpse of him weaving through a crowd of people past a row of restaurants.

"There he is." I pointed him out to Fire Fang, and then we were moving again.

I waited until the crowd had disappeared before swiping my hands through the air, conjuring a powerful wind to knock Chance off his feet. I slammed the spell at him, but it was as if he could predict my thoughts. He dodged to the right just before the spell hit, and it zoomed past him.

"This needs some muscle. Go get him, Fire Fang."

Fire Fang growled and raced away, but Chance was either smart or lucky, because another crowd appeared, and he vanished from sight.

I wasn't worried. Fire Fang would sniff Chance out, and his huge teeth would make sure he didn't get away.

I ran past the crowd, making sure Chance hadn't hidden among them. He wasn't there. He must have dodged through and into a side street. I reached the end of the road, where it diverged in three directions. Chance was nowhere to be seen.

Fire Fang was sniffing the ground and growling, but he also seemed at a loss as to where Chance had gone.

"How does he keep slipping away so easily?" I said.

"His dad must have been an eel."

We spent ten minutes surveying the junction, hoping to glimpse Chance, but he was long gone.

"What do you reckon, Fire Fang? Which direction?"

"Back to Lumbagos. We have chili waiting."

I was tempted by that idea, but I hated letting anyone give me the slip. Chance had to answer for his crimes. "Let's head to the shopping district. That'll be the busiest place this time of day. It'll be easier for Chance to hide there."

"Then we're going back for chili, right?"

"Sure. If we have time, then we can eat chili."

We headed toward the shopping district. It was never my favorite place. I was a bargain basement shopper, and the designer frills and sparkles of a place like this set my teeth on edge.

We hunted around, checking the different levels and shopping areas, but there was no sign of our sneaky trickster anywhere.

"I've changed my mind. I want fried donuts." Fire Fang jerked his head toward a red and white painted food truck. The delicious smell of deep-fried sweet goodies drifted out of the open hatch. The queue of people waiting for their orders suggested the offerings were as amazing as they smelled.

"Ten more minutes. Then I'll reward you with donuts."

"Dipped in chili?"

"Don't be gross."

After another ten minutes of searching, I was about to admit defeat when someone yelled. It wasn't a cry of excitement. Terror was laced through the noise.

I headed in the direction of the sound, which took me away from the main stores and into a gray corridor that looked like it led to a delivery entrance.

"Please, don't do this. I've done nothing to you." The guy begging sounded petrified.

There was a low rumble of reply, which I didn't catch.

"You've got the wrong person. If this is about money, I can repay you. Whatever you want."

I rounded the corner with Fire Fang to see Chance on his knees, his hands shielding his face. A guy dressed head-to-toe in black had a fireball over his head and was about to slam it on top of Chance.

Chapter 7

I slashed my hands through the air, conjuring a lightning bolt, which I slammed by the attacker's feet. He was flung back against the wall, and his fireball disappeared.

I raced toward Chance but only made it a few steps before a punch of magic to the gut knocked me off my feet. My breath shot out of me, and I crashed to my knees, pain splintering through me.

Fire Fang kept running, but a second later, he was lifted off his paws and crashed into the floor.

I rolled over, casting a messy lightning bolt spell to whack our attacker. But I didn't finish casting before I was hit with another flare of strong magic, and a sharp pain blasted through my shoulder, making my vision fuzzy.

The black-clad attacker slung several fireballs at Chance, but he rolled away at the last second, and they skimmed over him. Another lucky move from this trickster.

I got a look at the attacker's face, or rather, the mask he wore. It was black and molded to fit the contours of his face, with holes for his eyes and mouth. From the build and height, I assumed it was a guy. He was tall, with broad shoulders, but every inch of his skin was covered.

My head throbbed and my shoulder ached, but I scrambled forward, casting a tornado spell by whipping my fingers in a half circle and thrusting them out.

It hit him, and he careened back, slamming into a pile of boxes. They smashed to the ground, whatever was in them breaking.

Chance was scrambling away on his hands and knees, a terrified look on his face as his gaze darted between me and the attacker.

"Are you good, Fire Fang?" I kept my attention on the attacker, watching for his next move.

"I definitely deserve donuts with chili after this," he grumbled as he staggered to his feet.

"You deal with Chance. I'll get the other guy."

"You sure you're up to it?"

I gritted my teeth. "Not really, but I need to know who's trying to kill Chance." I staggered forward, holding my arm so my shoulder throbbed less.

Three enormous fireballs headed my way. I threw myself to the floor, casting out a lightning bolt. But my aim was off, and it slammed to the right of my attacker.

His masked face turned to Chance and then back to me. I was too far away to be certain, but he had some kind of red badge emblem on the collar of his shirt. Before I could get a better look, he turned and raced along the corridor.

I staggered after him but went down on one knee. Doing so much weather magic in such a short space of time and with an injury was never a clever move.

Chance yelped as Fire Fang sat on him.

After waiting a moment to be certain the attacker wasn't coming back, I dragged myself over to join them. "Hey, Chance. You're not an easy person to find."

Recognition hit his face once the initial fear of being sat on by a hellhound faded. "Oh! It's you. The Goth waitress from the casino. I thought you were here to kill me, too."

"It's tempting. Did you get injured?"

"Just bruises. But that guy wanted me dead." Chance looked at Fire Fang. "You can get off me. I'm not going anywhere."

"You stay there for a moment. You're a little too quick to run the second you get an opportunity." I conjured a basic healing spell and applied it to my wounded shoulder. It took away the worst of the pain, but it still throbbed like an angry ogre with concrete boots had stomped on me.

"I only ran from Lumbagos because I was scared. Someone let me know you were asking about me. They said you looked mean. You don't look mean. You look... um, really pretty."

"Sure I do. Get him on his feet, Fire Fang. I need to treat my injuries. And yours."

Fire Fang snapped his teeth around Chance's arm and dragged him up.

Chance gave a mouse-like squeak. "You saved me. I won't run. I promise."

"I doubt your promises are worth much. Fire Fang will keep an eye on you. Where's the nearest magic apothecary?"

Chance pointed a trembling finger back toward the stores. "I saw one closed for renovation that should have what you need."

"Perfect. We can find a quiet place, then you're telling me everything you know about Gaian Grimm."

"Errr... why?"

"Let's move." I did my best to look like I hadn't been in a magical fight and punched every which way by super strong spells as we merged into the shoppers. Although we got a few odd looks, it was easy to find the apothecary, and with a simple unlock spell, we snuck inside and were welcomed with a quiet warmth, the air smelling of citrus and basil.

I hunted through the supplies, half an ear on the door in case anyone caught us. I mixed a potent healing potion, gave some to Fire Fang, and downed the rest. The second Fire Fang had swallowed his dose of the potion, he grabbed Chance again.

Chance tugged ineffectively to get his arm free from Fire Fang's mouth before turning an imploring look my way. "I appreciate the help, but I don't know anything about Gaian. And I can see you're a busy lady, so I'll just get on my way."

"No, you won't." I pulled up a seat and settled in it. "You knew Gaian. You and Micky Cox spent time with him in the casino."

"Oh! That Gaian. I thought you meant someone else."

I raised my eyebrows when he didn't continue.

"I... I heard what happened to him. He was a good guy. It's a shame. He was fun to hang with."

"Why did you kill him if he was so much fun?"

Chance's eyes flashed wide. "I've never killed anyone. I liked Gaian. He was always generous with getting the drinks in. I had no problem with him."

"Did he discover you stole from him, like you do all the easy targets at the casinos?"

"I took nothing from Gaian. I think he knew what Micky and I got up to, but we never targeted people unless they could afford it. We thought of ourselves as modern day Robin Hoods. We took from the rich and gave to ourselves." Chance shrugged. "It's not as if I'm rolling in cash. And we were never greedy. If anyone was down on their luck, we didn't touch them."

"That's hardly a noble cause, goblin nobble," Fire Fang mumbled around Chance's arm.

"We have to get our kicks, and our money, from somewhere," Chance said. "The rich have too much. There should be an equal distribution of wealth in this world. We simply try to change that."

"Sure you do." My shoulder was feeling better, and my head was clearing. "It seems you've annoyed a lot of people. Why did that guy want you dead?"

He lifted his shoulders. "No idea. I don't know who he was. That mask was creepy, though. I was hiding from you and your... adorable dog, when he came out of the shadows. He grabbed me and dragged me into the corridor. He didn't say a word, simply made me kneel, and was about to blast me with that fireball when you showed up."

"Was he someone you stole from?"

"I never took enough to warrant being killed. That's not how we operate."

"How do you operate?"

Chance tried one more time to free his arm, then gave up. "We pick wealthy individuals or couples and skim a little off the top. A few hundred here or there. We don't go after the same people more than twice. And only the rich get targeted. No one would kill over that."

"Maybe it was another loan shark."

"Loan shark? Nope, not me. Never go near them."

"What about Micky?"

"Oh! Well, maybe he used them now and again. You think it was someone sent by Thad Dedopulos?"

"Could be. Do you owe him money?"

"No, although he was hassling me to get repayments. But that is Micky's debt. I help him when I can, but neither of us has been flash with the cash recently. That's how casino life gets you. Some weeks you win—"

"But most weeks you lose."

"I mean, sometimes. It evens out in the long term."

"The guy who wanted you dead had serious power."

"Tell me about it. He wasn't messing around."

"You're sure you've never dealt with him before?"

"He was in disguise, so I can't be certain our paths haven't crossed."

"Did you see a symbol on his clothing?"

"I mainly kept my eyes shut. I didn't want to see my death flying toward me."

"This guy must have been following you. That wasn't a lucky grab. You were his target."

Chance chewed on his bottom lip. "It seems like it. Do you think he'll try again?"

"He might. It depends how badly he wants his money back."

Chance slumped against the wall and sank down until he was sitting on the floor. "Things have gotten out of hand recently. All I want to do is have fun with my best buddy. Now someone wants me dead, and I can't get hold of Micky. I know he'd get me out of this mess."

My eyebrows flashed up. "You know why you can't get hold of Micky, don't you?"

He looked up at me. "Sure. He met a girl, and they went on a date. I assumed he'd gotten lucky and wasn't answering his phone because he was busy doing something much more enjoyable."

I glanced at Fire Fang, and he gave me a doggy shrug. "Micky's definitely not doing anything enjoyable. He's dead."

"Yeah, good one."

"This isn't a joke. He was pulled out of Serpent Lake. He drowned."

The smile vanished from Chance's face. He blinked rapidly and opened his mouth, but only a gurgled noise came out.

"Did you kill him, too?"

He gulped, and tears filled his eyes. "Micky is dead? That can't be right. What happened?"

"I just told you. Did you fall out and things got out of hand, so you shoved him in the lake?"

Chance's head bowed, and he didn't speak for several minutes. "We did argue. I was jealous about him getting a date. He always gets obsessed with new relationships. I made some dumb joke about him not putting girlfriends before best friends, and he didn't like it. The last words I said to Micky were mean ones. Now he's... gone?"

"You argued with Micky, then he turns up dead?"

His head whipped up. There were tears on his cheeks. "Not because of me. Sure, we got into a fight. I'd had too many drinks and said stupid things, but I wouldn't kill him. No! This can't be right." Chance tried to stand, but since Fire Fang still had hold of his arm, he didn't get far before he dropped back to the floor.

"Who was the girl he was on a date with? Maybe they fought over something." Chance's shock was genuine. He also wasn't hiding that he'd argued with his best friend just before he died. Maybe he hadn't killed Micky, after all.

"Just a cute redhead he met in the casino. We were considering lifting her purse, but Micky took a shine to her. He bought her a drink, with my cash, and the next thing I knew, they were arranging a date."

"Which you weren't happy about."

"We work as a team. It's easier to distract people if there are two of you. Micky hooking up with some new girl meant there'd be less money for both of us. And I don't like going hungry." Chance swiped tears off his face. "You said he drowned?"

"In Serpent Lake. When was the last time you were there?"

"Not for ages. But that makes no sense. Even when he was drunk, Micky was a great swimmer. He bragged that his greatest achievement was the dozen swim badges he got at school."

"Serpent Lake is tidal. He could have gotten pulled under."

"It wouldn't happen. He loved swimming in the ocean but was always careful about riptides. He knew what to look for." Chance's eyes grew wide. "It was the guy who just tried to kill me. He wants us both dead. He succeeded with Micky, and now he's coming for me."

"Why would he do that?"

"I don't know! But there's no way Micky would drown. His great-grandfather was part merman. Micky adored the water. It was in his blood. There's something else going on." He reached forward to grab my hand, but a warning growl from Fire Fang set him back on his butt. "You need to help me. You saved me from that guy with the fireball, so I know you're powerful. I haven't killed anyone. I'm innocent. I could be the next target if you don't look after me."

"You want to hire me as your bodyguard?"

"Yes! That's an amazing idea. Of course, I can't pay you right away, but give me a few nights in the casino, and I'll cover your fee."

"I'm expensive."

"It doesn't matter. I need to be protected. I've got magic, but it's basic. It's mainly sleight-of-hand stuff and distraction magic. I can't protect myself. Not from someone as powerful as that masked guy."

"I'm no one's bodyguard. I'm here to bring you in for questioning over Gaian and Micky's murders."

"But... but I just told you I had nothing to do with those deaths. And why would I kill my best friend? I still can't believe he's gone."

"That's for the Magic Council to find out." I pulled out my phone and called Olympus Duke. "Hey, are you up to speed on the Gaian Grimm and Micky Cox murders?"

"I am. No thanks to you."

Olympus was so grumpy when I didn't keep him in the loop. "You'll thank me in a second. I've got your prime suspect."

"You found Chance Starlight?"

"Yep. We're in the magic apothecary in the Whispering Willows shopping center."

There was a pause. "I'm glad you found him. We need to talk to him."

"What's with the hesitation?"

"There's been a complication in this case. Micky didn't drown."

"How did he die?"

"He was poisoned by a pumpkin pie."

Chapter 8

After learning a few more details from Olympus about the actual cause of Micky Cox's death, I ended the call and glared at Chance. "What do you know about poison and pumpkin pie?"

"Err... not much. It's usually delicious, although not if you add poison. Why do you need to know my views on pumpkin pie? And what's with the poison angle?"

I huffed out a breath and continued to glare at him. Something didn't feel right. There were too many loose threads floating around. Gaian was dead, apparently by a misfiring spell, but Laris thought he'd been killed. Micky Cox shows up drowned, but he was poisoned. And a mysterious mask wearing man, who wielded magic like a master, almost killed Chance.

"In all the chaos, I didn't ask for your name," Chance said.

"Micky didn't tell you?"

"He couldn't remember. He said it was something like Suzanne."

"It's not important. But it's not Suzanne."

"You saved my life. I owe you a debt. I'd like to know the name of the person who saved me."

I held in a sigh. "Storm Winter. I'm a private investigator."

"It's great to meet you, Storm. How did you get involved in this mess?"

I gently probed my tender shoulder. "My friend, Laris Brack, asked me to look into Gaian's murder. That led me to you and Micky."

"But now Micky's been murdered, so we can't be involved. And I could be next."

"I'm thinking about that." I couldn't let a few tears and a passable show of grief distract me. Chance must have done this. There were enough pieces that fit together to convince me he was far from innocent. This had to be about money. Gaian was going to reveal what Chance and Micky were doing, and that meant the end of their fun.

But I needed proof before I could go any further with this investigation. "What were you doing yesterday between two and six in the morning?"

"Was that when Micky died?"

I nodded.

He sucked in a shaky breath. "I usually get done at the casino by about one. It gets quiet after that. Fewer tourists dropping in."

"And where did you go after that?"

"Nowhere. I walked around, went to a late night café, and nursed a coffee for a couple of hours. I kept waiting to hear from Micky. When he didn't message me, I decided to lie low. After you came after us at the casino, I figured discretion was the best option. I messaged Micky, so he knew where I was going, then caught a bus, had a nap, and hung out at Lumbagos. The chili there is great."

Fire Fang spat out Chance's arm. "Thanks to you, we're never going to find out if that's true. I also didn't get my donkey helmet donuts, either."

I shot Fire Fang an apologetic look. Food would have to wait. "Can anyone vouch for your movements?"

"I was being discreet. I used distraction magic to ensure no one paid me attention." Chance tilted his head. "How did you find me?"

"You're not as good as you think you are. One of my contacts spotted you."

He pursed his lips. "It's because I'm tired. My magic gets shaky when I haven't had enough sleep. Or food. Speaking of which, I'm hungry. What about going someplace that has pumpkin pie? Since you mentioned it, I've got a craving for something sweet and orange."

"It doesn't take much to stop you from caring about your dead friend or the fact someone just tried to kill you."

"No! I just... I mean, I love pie. Doesn't everyone? It's comfort food, and I've just had several shocks one after the other."

Fire Fang grunted an agreement.

"The pie does add a layer of complication to this mystery. Did you and Micky eat any pie when you were together?"

"Pumpkin pie and poison. Hey, you're saying Micky didn't drown?"

"It doesn't look that way."

Chance was quiet for a few seconds. "I knew he'd never go out that way. And as for the pumpkin pie, I don't know. Micky could have eaten it when he was on his date. Maybe the girl he was with poisoned him."

"Why? Did he also steal from her?"

"Hey! That's mean. We don't steal from everyone we meet." Chance heaved out a sigh. "We loved pie but hadn't eaten any recently. I still can't believe it. What will I do without Micky?"

I left him to his miserable musings and mixed another healing potion, while Fire Fang kept an eye on Chance.

Chance had no alibi, and it was unlikely anyone could tell me what his movements were when Gaian or Micky were killed. Things looked bad for this trickster.

I downed the potion, still not happy about all the information rumbling in my head. I was missing something, but I wasn't sure what. All I knew for certain was that Chance had fought with his best friend. He knew Gaian, had no money, and was great at tricking people. He also had a poor alibi for the time of Micky's death. But the poison was odd. I couldn't get that to fit.

But it wasn't up to me to put the final puzzle pieces together. I'd take Chance to the Magic Council and leave him there. Chance was a criminal. They'd be able to hold him while I tidied up any loose ends with Laris.

"Are you going to let me go?" Chance said.

"The opposite. The Magic Council still wants to see you."

"Can't you look the other way while I disappear? I won't be any trouble. I'll hide."

"It's too late. You have crimes to answer for. Maybe even two murders."

"Only maybe? You don't think I did it, do you? Please, help me. I'm innocent."

"You haven't spent your career cheating people?"

"Not that! I'm not talking about stealing a few wallets. Something else is going on, and you know it. The guy who tried to kill me meant business."

"People who plan murder usually mean business."

"But he was powerful. He even got you, and you seem like a super strong witch, as well as an attractive one."

"Cut the smarm. You're not getting away with this. Maybe there are a few questions that need answering, but the Magic Council will figure it out. And my friend lost someone he cared about because of you."

"Not because of me. And I've lost someone, too. I cared for Micky. We've always looked out for each other. I'd never hurt him. I want to find out who killed him as much as you do."

"Maybe I'm looking at his killer."

"There you go again with the maybes. I can be useful. We could look into Micky's death together. I have connections."

"You don't. On your feet. We'll head to my car, and I'll take you to a local branch of the Magic Council."

Chance hesitated, but a growl from Fire Fang got him to his feet. "This is wrong. You should look for the guy who tried to kill me. That'll give you the answers you need. It'll also prove my innocence."

"There's nothing innocent about you. Let's move. And just to be clear, if you run, Fire Fang will take you down and pound you. And he's grumpy and hungry since he hasn't gotten his chili or donuts. It's never good to get on the wrong side of a hungry hellhound."

Fire Fang growled out his agreement.

Chance's shoulders slumped. "You don't believe me. I'll prove to you I'm innocent."

"Just prove you can walk in a straight line to my car, and I'll be happy."

I tucked money under the till for the magic I'd used, and then we headed out. I kept a tight grip on Chance's elbow to make sure he didn't get any dumb ideas and escape, but the fight had left him. He was dragging his feet, and his head was down. He kept wiping his eyes and muttering to himself.

He must have regrets over killing his best friend. Although, it was more likely he was having regrets about getting caught.

Once we were in the car, the doors locked and cruising back to Witch Haven, I relaxed. This case was almost solved. Laris would get justice for Gaian, and this criminal would be off the streets.

Fire Fang was squashing Chance on the back seat of the car. He kept shifting around and looking out the windows.

"Don't even think about jumping out," I said to Chance. "If you do, I'll reverse over you."

"It's not that. I think we're being followed."

"You're paranoid."

"It's hardly a surprise, given someone tried to kill me. I'm telling you, when you changed lanes a moment ago, that black car moved with us."

"Where is this suspicious vehicle?"

"Three cars back. They're discreet, but I always know when someone is watching me. It was a skill Micky had, too. We could sense trouble and get away before things got sticky."

"That wasn't the case when Micky got poisoned by that pie."

Chance grabbed the back of my seat. "That's not nice. Is she always like this?" He looked at Fire Fang.

"Most days, goblin nobble."

I glowered at both of them in the mirror, not appreciating a discussion about my mood.

Chance looked over his shoulder again. "That car is still following us."

"And you're still keeping secrets. What skills do you have with magical poisons?"

"I already told you the extent of my powers. Poisons aren't my thing. But my charming smile more than makes up for my limited power."

Fire Fang growled at Chance. "Stop sleazing on my witch."

I headed off the main road, keeping an eye out to see if we were followed. At first, no one took the exit, then a car swung off. Maybe Chance was right and someone was tailing us. Could it be the guy who'd attacked him coming back for another try?

"You saw that, right?" Chance said.

"I did," I muttered.

"I knew it. It's the guy who killed Micky. He tried to get me but failed, so he's chasing us to finish the job."

"That's what I was wondering." The car kept back, so I wasn't overly alarmed. "Why do they want you dead so badly?"

"I've no idea. I'm a nobody. Someone who plays tricks and bedazzles people with my endless supply of charm and compliments."

"You're a goblin nobble pond scum," Fire Fang said.

"Cute pond scum, though." Chance's smile faded as Fire Fang bared his teeth. "This hound is trained, isn't he?"

"Trained to know a cheat and a liar when he sees one," I said. "You'll have to do better than that. If the person in that car is following you, there's a reason."

"I... I don't know what it is."

"You cheated the wrong person, most likely. And that car looks expensive. You haven't been messing with the magical mob, have you?"

"No! I steer clear of the really bad guys. It's not the mob. They can't want me." Chance turned around and stared at the car. "Although it does look like a mob vehicle. The windows are blacked out, so I can't see the driver. They're speeding up! Put your foot down."

The car was closing in as I drove the quiet road heading into Witch Haven. If they were planning to make a move on this vehicle, this was the perfect spot to do it.

I sped up, and the car behind us matched my speed.

"Keep going. Don't let them get me." Chance whacked the back of my seat.

"Quit doing that. You're distracting me."

A flash of light shot out of the driver's side window of the car behind us. I tugged the steering wheel to the left just as a spell shot past.

Chance squeaked and ducked.

"Be useful! Keep a watch for more magic coming our way. We're only five miles from Witch Haven. Once we're there, they won't try anything."

Chance peeked through his fingers. "If we get out of this, I'll mend my ways. No more stealing. I'll be a good guy from now on."

"You'll be a dead guy if you don't keep your sour slug mouth shut," Fire Fang grumbled.

"More spells incoming!" Chance yelled.

I jerked the car left and right to avoid a volley of magical blasts. The last one skimmed a back tire, and the car shuddered. I steered into the skid, but the road was narrow and I hit a pothole, sending us flying into the air.

Chance yelped as we landed with a tooth rattling thud.

The back of the car slid out, but I regained control after a few seconds of gritting my teeth and holding on tight, resisting the urge to yank the steering wheel in the wrong direction, and letting the car stabilize.

"Are we almost there?" Chance said. "I don't think I can handle any more attacks like that."

"Three miles to go. Just keep watching." My eyes shot from the road to the mirrors, checking to see if our mysterious attacker was planning any more assaults.

Fire Fang growled. "This looks bad."

"What can you see?" I said.

"Just drive. And fast. We don't want to be under whatever they're about to shoot at us."

"I can't see anything," Chance said. "What is it? How bad are we talking?"

The sky overhead lit up like a firework. Dozens of tiny white balls floated down. The second they touched the car, the engine groaned and metal shrieked.

I lost control of the steering, and the car shot off the road and came to a shuddering halt in a ditch.

"I'm so done with this." I yanked off my seat belt and forced open the door, having to kick it to get it to move. "Fire Fang, stay with Chance. Don't let him out of your sight."

"I'm staying with you. I wouldn't stand a chance against that maniac behind us." Chance went to pet Fire Fang's head, then withdrew his hand as a warning growl rumbled through the car.

I planted my feet, opened my magic, and conjured a huge tornado, swirling both hands in the air and whipping the wind into a frenzy. I slammed the tornado into the path of the car. The driver swerved at the last second, but the back end of the car was caught, and they were spun around several times.

The car skidded to a halt, the engine still rumbling. My hands were poised with more magic, but that giant tornado had taken it out of me. I desperately needed a magic recharge. I couldn't remember the last time I'd taken a break and focused on juicing my magic. When I didn't look after myself, my powers suffered. But I had one more powerful blast of magic in me. I had to hope that would be all I needed to bring down our assailant.

The car's engine roared, and it shot toward us. I spun my fingers, brought down another tornado, and slammed it into the car. The car was whipped away, but that last blast of energy wiped me out, and I sank to my knees, unable to stand.

My heart raced, my vision was blurry, and I had no magic left.

A warm, solid, furry presence stood over me.

"You always push things too far," Fire Fang muttered in my ear. "One day, it'll catch up with you."

"But not today?"

"Not today. Don't worry, I've got you."

I tried to speak, but the only words coming out were nonsense. Fire Fang shouldn't be worrying about me. He needed to stop Chance from sneaking off.

"Relax. I'll get us somewhere safe."

My eyes fluttered closed as I leaned on my furry friend and passed out.

Chapter 9

I became aware of bright sunshine as my eyes flickered open. I'd expected to find myself on the side of the road, but this was a bedroom. And it looked like a bedroom in Odessa's farmhouse.

As I rolled over, I came face-to-face with a snoring Fire Fang. Lying next to him was the stray black cat. What had he called her, Betty? How did she always know where I was?

I was tempted to prod Fire Fang awake and ask him how we'd gotten here, but he looked peaceful with his head on the pillow and a blanket tucked around him. Whatever he'd done last night to get me here must have taken it out of him.

Rather than getting answers, I eased out of the bed, careful not to disturb him or the cat. I felt like I'd just gotten back from a three-night non-stop dance party. Everything ached. But I was alive, thanks to Fire Fang.

I was still wearing last night's clothes, although my boots had been set at the bottom of the bed. I picked them up, tiptoed to the door, and slipped out, closing it quietly behind me.

It was only when I was out of the bedroom that I realized there was no sign of Chance. I gritted my teeth and scowled. Of course, the trickster would escape the second he could. He most likely took advantage and snuck away as Fire Fang stayed with me to keep me safe.

After using the bathroom, I paused at the top of the stairs. There were voices in the kitchen, and Odessa was laughing. She must be having breakfast with Sol or her scarecrows.

I hobbled down the stairs, taking my time, feeling like an ancient goblin and not the all-powerful witch I knew I was. When I made the effort.

I stopped in the open kitchen door. Chance sat at the table, a plate of muffins in front of him. Odessa sat opposite him, along with Tuffin, her familiar. And from the looks on their faces, Chance had utterly charmed them. Idiots.

"What's going on in here?"

Chance jumped in his seat, then his easy smile reappeared. "I was just telling your lovely friend about our adventures. And complimenting her on how soft her guest bed was. I haven't slept that well in years."

"I figured you'd made a run for it," I said.

Odessa hurried over and caught hold of my arm. "How are you feeling? I was worried when Fire Fang brought you here last night. You were muttering, and your injuries took time to heal."

"I'm feeling... alive. This looks cozy. Are you sure you know who you're having breakfast with?" I allowed Odessa to lead me to the table and settle me in a seat. She liked to mother hen me when she thought I needed looking after. Which was most of the time, according to her.

"I have breakfast muffins and some amazing English breakfast tea. Eat up. You need your strength. Chance was telling me you used your tornado magic more than once yesterday."

"It's not such a big deal." I grabbed a muffin and tucked in. Unsurprisingly, it was pumpkin, but there was a sweet cinnamon taste too and delicious chunks of dark chocolate. That just about made up for the pumpkin tang.

Odessa poured me a huge mug of tea. "It wouldn't be a big deal if you looked after yourself."

I slid her a warning look, then nodded at Chance. He didn't need to know about the limits of my magic.

"Don't worry about him. He's charming. I've been enjoying hearing about his adventures."

"Did Chance leave out the cheating part of his adventures?"

"The cheating part?" Odessa grabbed a napkin and placed it on my lap.

"Stop clucking around me." Movement outside caught my eye. There was an unusually large number of scarecrows lurking around the farmhouse. "What's going on out there?"

"They're protecting us," Odessa said. "After you arrived in such a state, I thought it was best to be safe. I set a dozen of my best scarecrows to guard us and placed a magic ward around the farmhouse."

"Bit dramatic," I muttered around my mouthful of muffin.

"We wouldn't have to be dramatic if you'd asked for help. You could have been killed by whoever was chasing you. I've had your car towed here. It's a mess. It's covered in toxic magic. You're lucky to be alive."

"I didn't know I'd need any help when I set out yesterday. And I didn't expect Chance to be chased by the magic mob." I finished my muffin. "How bad is the car?"

"Probably a write-off."

"It wasn't the mob," Chance said. "At least, I don't think it was. Micky and I always steered clear of serious criminals."

"Perhaps not all of them." Odessa finally sat and allowed me to get on with polishing off my second muffin. "From what you've told me, you've become a target for someone important."

"I'm still going with the magical mob theory. That attack was smooth and came out of nowhere," I said.

"Whoever was chasing us, they were professionals. Trained killers," Chance said.

"The magical mob are professionals. Professionals at killing people and making them disappear."

Odessa added a handful of berries to my plate. "Even if it was the mob, you'd have been better able to protect Chance if you looked after yourself."

"We're not talking about that in front of strangers," I said.

"I'm not a stranger. I'm just a friend you haven't made yet," Chance said.

I groaned while Odessa giggled.

"You're pushing too hard and running on empty." Odessa went back to hassling me. "You've got that hollow look under your eyes, and you've lost weight again."

"Now I can gain it all back thanks to your muffins. I'm doing fine. Some days are just rougher than others."

"No day needs to be rough. Do I need to get Luna and Indigo over to speak to you?"

"Leave them out of this."

"Who are they?" Chance said, looking like he was enjoying watching me get browbeaten.

"None of your business. Besides, we're not focusing on me. We're focusing on Chance and who wants him dead." I glared at him.

He shook his head and raised his hands. "If I could think of anything that would help, I'd tell you. I'm as confused as you are."

"Be gentle with him," Odessa said. "Chance told me what happened to his best friend."

"Which I'm not sure he didn't have a hand in," I said. "Chance could be a double murderer."

Odessa pulled the plate of muffins away from Chance. "Is this true?"

"No! Storm, I'm hurt by that accusation. You can call me a trickster or a con artist or whatever you like, but I'm not a killer. I'd never hurt Micky. Without him, I'm nothing. I can't see any future. And I have no idea what I'll do for money. It was always the two of us against the world. I wouldn't destroy that. I killed no one."

Odessa shot me a filthy look and pushed another muffin his way. She was so gullible. "Of course you wouldn't." She patted his hand. "Would you like pumpkin pancakes with maple syrup? They always cheer me up."

"That would be great, thanks." Chance gave her a sunny smile.

I grunted and ate more muffin. Chance was tangled up in this mess, but I wasn't sure if he was the master criminal behind it or simply an unintentional victim and as ignorant as he made out.

Fire Fang appeared in the kitchen doorway. Stray Cat was riding on his back, looking as pleased as punch to be there.

"Has that cat moved in with you?" I said to Odessa.

She glanced over her shoulder and smiled. "No, she arrived after Fire Fang translocated you here. I heard a noise at the door and found her pawing to get in. She raced up the stairs and straight to you."

"You can do translocation magic?" I raised my eyebrows at Fire Fang as he mooched into the kitchen.

"I guess I can. After you passed out, I needed us gone quickly. The tornado whipped the car away, but I had a feeling they'd be back."

"You're full of surprises." This was the first time Fire Fang had ever done such an intense spell.

"Tell me about it. I'm awesome." Fire Fang sank to the floor to allow the cat off his back.

She hopped off, looked around, and selected an empty seat, which she jumped into and curled up on, looking like this was a home away from home. Not that she had a home.

"She likes it here. You can keep her," I said. "We have work to do and don't need a cat tagging along."

Odessa shook her head. "She's all yours. And I have a good feeling about that little cat. You know how sensitive I am to these things. She's important to you. Perhaps she could be your second familiar."

"Second familiar? I don't have any familiars."

Fire Fang grumbled under his breath, not looking happy at my comment.

Footsteps approached the front door, and a second later, Sol came in. "Hey, Storm. Good to see you up. How you doing?"

"I'm on top of the world," I said.

"She's not. She needs a long weekend of doing nothing and a magic spa," Odessa said.

"You'll never drag me to a spa, magic or not."

Sol kissed Odessa on the cheek. "I went out with the scarecrows, and we checked the pumpkin patch. There haven't been any disturbances."

"What were you looking for?" I said.

"Chance told us his friend was poisoned with a pumpkin pie," Odessa said. "I was worried someone stole one of mine. The magic in those pumpkins is powerful. Mix it with the wrong dark spell and you'd have something toxic on your hands. A poison no one could survive."

"It wasn't one of ours," Sol said. "All pumpkins are accounted for."

"It wouldn't have been your average pumpkin used in a spell like that," Odessa said. "I can ask at the suppliers, see if anyone's been looking for something special to use with poison."

"That would be good," I said. "But only if it's no trouble."

"It's no trouble to keep you and Chance safe. The poor lamb's been devastated by what happened to his friend."

Chance jutted out his bottom lip and widened his eyes. He didn't fool me. I knew the truth. There was nothing innocent about that trickster. Unfortunately, he'd pulled the wool over Odessa's eyes good and proper.

"We should get out of your way," I said.

"You stay there and eat until you can't move," Odessa said. "Then you're having a long hot bath, resting, and letting me look into where that pumpkin came from."

"There's no need for any of that."

"There is a need. Have you seen the state of your hair? And whatever you fell in last night doesn't smell sweet." Odessa marched to the kitchen door. "You're having a bath."

I'd paid no attention to my appearance since I'd rolled out of Odessa's guest bed, but maybe I did smell ripe. I'd definitely stood in something wet and boggy when I'd gotten out of the car last night.

"I'll run your bath. Sol will finish making the pancakes, and you can recharge," Odessa said.

I was going to protest, but a glare from Odessa silenced me. "I could do with a break. But only a short one."

"Excellent. So it's agreed. You sit here and chat with Chance. I'll be right back. I've got some amazing pumpkin infused bubble bath you'll adore." Odessa hurried out of the kitchen.

I sank back in my seat and drank my tea. I wasn't chit-chatting with Chance, but I did need to do some thinking. These murders had me stuck, and I wasn't happy about it.

There were two murders, possibly related, possibly not. One trickster sitting opposite me munching yet another muffin, a trickster who could be lying about all of this. And me with zero clue about what to do next.

Chapter 10

I never knew I liked bubble baths. But after spending the morning at Odessa's, surrounded by her smothering love, excellent food, and pumpkin scented bubbles, I felt better. She'd even laundered my clothes while I'd been in the bath, fed Chance so many meals I almost had to roll him out of the farmhouse, and been an all-around, amazing friend.

"Are you sure this visit is a good idea?" Chance sat in the passenger seat of the truck I'd borrowed from Odessa, since my old car was toast.

"I'm not letting you out of my sight, so it's your only option. Besides, Laris is civilized. He won't attack you unless you say something stupid."

"But he thinks I killed his friend."

"He does. So you'd better get your story straight or make a confession now. I can take you straight to the Magic Council. You won't have to meet Laris."

"You really think I did it? After everything you've seen? Someone is after me. Maybe that same someone killed Gaian and Micky."

I turned in my seat and studied him. Chance was nervous. His hands were clenched, and that usual charming smile was nowhere to be seen. "Tell me why. What's the connection between Gaian Grimm, you, and Micky?"

"Other than the fun we had at the casino, nothing. Gaian didn't say much about his connections, but everyone knew he was an influential guy. I'm not influential. Neither was Micky. We were regular guys. And as your fine hellhound said, I'm basically pond scum. I'd float around and get what I could out of people and then move on. I'd have loved to have the kind of connections Gaian had. And his money."

"Jealousy is a powerful motive for killing someone."

"Please stop saying I'm a killer. It doesn't suit me." Chance looked at the large red brick office we'd stopped outside. "Let's get this over with, shall we? Maybe Laris will believe me."

I climbed out of the truck and guided Chance into Laris's office, Fire Fang behind us. Laris was waiting for us as we walked through the door. His usually warm gaze vanished as he focused on Chance.

"It's good to see you, Storm. I was glad to hear about the progress you've made in finding my friend's killer."

"We've been making some progress, but we need to talk. Is there somewhere I can stash Chance? He's a wily one, so it needs to be somewhere secure."

Chance pouted, but said nothing.

"I could call a Magic Council contact and have Chance immediately arrested for murder."

Chance gulped. "I know you won't believe me, but I didn't kill your friend. I also didn't kill my friend. I really am sorry for your loss. I'm still coming to terms with what happened to Micky. It's hard to lose someone you care about."

Laris simply glared at Chance. He turned his attention to me. "We have rooms where we interview clients. You can leave him in one of them."

"Perfect. And Fire Fang will watch over him."

"Do I have to? This goblin nobble never stops talking."

"It won't be for long. I just need to go over a few things with Laris."

"I don't mind listening in," Chance said. "I could have useful information to share."

"Like confessing to a double murder?" I said.

He sighed. "Show me to the room. I'll wait with your hound."

Fire Fang grumbled unhappily but accepted his unwelcome task.

After Chance was settled, Laris led me into his plush office. The wealth on display was tasteful, but it was clear he had expensive tastes.

I settled in a red leather chair, and Laris took the seat next to me.

"When you told me what happened last night, I was worried about you. I don't want this case to put your life in danger."

"It's not unusual for that to happen," I said. "Whoever was chasing us is powerful. They had strong magic and knew how to use it."

"It sounds like it. You didn't get a good look at them?" Laris poured me a glass of water from the decanter on his desk and passed it to me.

I nodded my thanks. "No, but I suspect it was the same person who attacked Chance in the shopping center."

"You mentioned the magical mob when you called earlier. Any evidence to show they could be involved? I've had a few of their guys cross my path during criminal investigations. They thrive on intimidation tactics."

"Nothing other than that they had serious magic clout, drove an expensive, flashy car, and had no scruples about trying to kill us. It's just a theory, though." I leaned forward in my seat and rested my elbows on my knees. "Laris, something is off with this investigation. I don't think it's as simple as it seems."

He was quiet for a few seconds. "To begin with, it seemed Gaian had gotten on the wrong side of Chance and Micky. But with Micky showing up dead so soon afterward and then an attempt on Chance's life, what do you think is going on?"

I contemplated the question, not certain I had a good answer. "Did Gaian ever talk about Chance and Micky? Could there be a connection between them outside the casino?"

"Not that I can think of. Gaian was a sociable guy, so he had lots of friends. I think he mentioned Chance and Micky in passing, but it seemed they were more casual friends than anything else. I can't imagine why the same person would want them dead."

"I don't suppose Chance and Micky were Gaian's secret love children? Maybe it was a secret that needed to be hushed up."

Laris smiled. "There's a thought. No, Gaian never had children. He doesn't have any family left alive, and he never married. I suppose that's fortunate, in a way. He hasn't left behind any grieving children. Small comforts."

"It could be a money connection. If the only way they knew each other was through the casino, that has to be the link." I shook my head. I wasn't convincing myself with that line of inquiry.

"But..." Laris prompted me to continue.

"Maybe Gaian overheard information he shouldn't while he was with Chance and Micky? Something serious enough to get them on a hit list."

"What information is worth killing over?"

"You'd be surprised. People panic when they think their secrets are about to get out."

"We must keep Chance alive so we can learn more about this connection," Laris said. "If someone wants him silenced, for whatever reason, they'll come after him again."

"That's what I was thinking. The guy who wanted Chance dead was determined. He was pulling out the magical big guns to get to him." I sat back. "The best thing for Chance is to turn him over to the Magic Council. They can pull apart his background, find a link, and lock him up if they need to. He'll be safer behind bars. And then he can be their problem, not mine."

Laris's mouth twisted to the side. "I don't agree. You need to protect him. You've already proven you can."

I raised my hands. "I've spent enough time with Chance."

"I have a feeling he's an important part of this mystery. The Magic Council has its place, but they're slow to react and may not take the threat to Chance's life seriously. They could let the wrong person slip in while he's in their care. Then Chance's life would be over. He'll take his secrets to the grave."

"Is that your subtle way of saying the Magic Council is incompetent?"

Laris gave a quiet laugh. "I know I'm pushing my luck by asking you to continue with this investigation, but you never stop until you get results. I have to know what happened to Gaian. If Micky or Chance didn't kill him, who did? And why is someone after Chance? I think you're right. This investigation isn't as straightforward as it first appeared. And it's the kind of case that'll have the Magic Council running in circles for months. In your hands, you'll resolve it quickly."

"You mean I'm a blunt instrument?"

"You're an effective, intelligent, hard-working, blunt instrument."

I tapped my fingers on my knees. Laris was pushing his luck, but if I resolved this case in its entirety, my obligation to him would be over for good. "I'll watch over Chance and make sure no one kills him. At least not until we've got the information we need."

Laris chuckled. "I can always rely on you to cut to the pertinent point. Although when you did it with those werewolves—"

"We don't talk about the werewolves."

"Of course." His smile lingered. "I still recall the look on the alpha's face when you described his j—"

"No! Not ever."

Laris poured his own glass of water, still smiling. "I know this isn't your usual kind of work, but I trust you to find out what happened to Gaian. And since Chance seems to be of the slippery persuasion, he's best suited in the hands of someone who takes no nonsense."

"Which brings us back to me being a blunt instrument."

"There's nothing wrong with that. And your track record speaks for itself. I believe in you. You can solve this mystery. Storm, please. I know you have an obligation to me, but I also consider you a friend."

Urgh. The friend card.

Looking after a whining trickster would never be on my top ten list of fun things to do, but keeping him close would be the quickest way to get this solved.

"Do I have to get on my knees and beg?"

I raised a hand. "Don't do that. You're so old, you might not get back up."

"There's life in this old hound yet. What do you say? Finish this?"

"I'll dig into Chance's background, see what I can find. He stays with me while I do that. Perhaps there's a connection in his past that led to him becoming a target, along with Micky and Gaian. Something must tie them together."

"Which suggests you don't think Chance is the killer."

"I'm fifty-fifty on that. He had no idea Micky was dead. And so far, other than the casino link, I can't find anything else that connects him to Gaian. Chance is also terrible in a fight. He's more likely to run than attack. I suppose, if he killed Gaian, it could have been an accident."

"You see, you're already figuring things out."

"More like I'm putting out questions I don't have answers to."

"Yet. But you will. I can always rely on Storm Winter."

Laris was a good guy, but possibly also deluded.

I collected Chance from the interview room and we left Laris's office.

"Does your friend no longer hate me?" Chance said.

"He's on the fence."

"And you?"

"I'm on the wrong side of the fence. My hate grass is getting overgrown."

"Do you want me to mow it?"

"Stop talking."

"I just—"

A glare from me silenced him.

Chance hurried along beside me and hopped in the back of the truck with Fire Fang. "What do we do now?"

I turned to him before I started the engine. "Let's be clear on this. There is no we. You're in my custody until I figure out who killed Gaian and Micky."

"But you don't think it was me?"

"You've yet to convince me otherwise."

"I will. You can guarantee it. I can convince people of anything." His smile was a touch on the smug side.

"Let's head to Odessa's. We'll collect our things and get out of her way. I don't want my friends tangled up in your mess. You can stay at my place."

"Only if you bake muffins as great as Odessa."

"I don't bake. If you want food, you find it yourself."

"Oh. Well, I guess that's okay."

"It's the best offer you'll get."

I drove back to Odessa's in blissful silence, and we headed inside.

"We're not staying," I said, as Odessa switched on the kettle and pulled out mugs.

"You can stay for a late lunch. I expect neither of you have eaten. Fire Fang looks famished." She tossed him a handful of Tuffin's snacks, which he gobbled down.

"We're still full from breakfast." I jerked a thumb at Chance. "I'm looking after this one for now. I'm taking him to my apartment."

"You're welcome to stay here. I have the room."

"And I have a couch. When Fire Fang's not sleeping on it. That'll do for Chance. Or the floor."

"Odessa's guest bed is comfortable. We should stay. You don't want me getting under your feet." Chance shot me a hopeful smile, but he was wasting his time.

"You'll get under my feet, however much room we have. Besides, Odessa doesn't need this mess in her life."

"I don't mind a little mess. And if Chance is at a loose end, I can find him work on the farm."

"Are we talking manual labor?" Chance didn't look impressed.

"It's a farm. It's all manual labor," I said. "And her scarecrows bite if you don't watch your back."

"We still have pumpkins to sort. That's fun," Odessa said. "I can find you some of Sol's old work clothes to wear. It's no trouble."

Sol hurried through the kitchen doorway. "Odessa, two scarecrows are running riot in the lower field. They could do with your attention. I've tried commanding them, but they're ignoring me."

"Oh! I was just setting Chance and Storm up. I was thinking they could stay for a while."

"No, we're not doing that. We're good. My apartment is perfect. And I have all my things there," I said.

"What things?" Odessa said.

"Odessa! The scarecrows." Sol gestured out the door. "And don't forget, we've got our date night tonight. We missed last week because of the scarecrow conference."

"Exactly. You don't want us cramping your romantic style," I said.

Odessa sighed. "If you insist. But at least take food with you. Chance, hold out your arms." She loaded him up with three plastic containers of food, kissed me on the cheek, and dashed out of the farmhouse with Sol to deal with her marauding scarecrows.

Chance looked longingly around the kitchen. "I could get used to a place like this. It's homey.

Nothing like where I grew up. Is your apartment like this?"

"It's the opposite. Let's get out of here. If Odessa comes back and finds us, she won't let us leave."

With obvious reluctance, Chance followed me out of the farmhouse and loaded the food into the back of the truck.

As I headed away from Odessa's, I glanced at him. "Let's start at the beginning. I need to know everything about you if I'm going to solve these murders and keep you alive."

Chapter 11

I didn't bother to stifle a yawn as I blinked my gritty eyes. Chance had been talking for hours. It was dark outside, I wanted my bed, and he still had more to say. Other than a couple of breaks, when I'd gotten takeout food and walked Fire Fang, I'd listened to dozens of Chance's inventive stories and was struggling to pull the fact from the fiction.

His life had been a series of mistakes and tragic fumbles. From a lack of a stable upbringing, poor school attendance, and a series of unfulfilling jobs that led him to his current career as a thief and mid-level trickster. Chance had a history no one would envy.

He rooted around in the almost empty bag of cookies I'd brought back from the store. "We never got treats like this when I was a kid."

I finished the last of my coffee. "You said you were raised by an aunt."

"Aunt Edith. She was a stereotypical spinster. And she never liked having me around."

"What a shocker," Fire Fang mumbled. He was half-asleep on the rug, the stray cat flopped over him. It looked like she was staying and being encouraged by Fire Fang's willing acceptance of her presence. I let her intrusion slide. After all, she had helped save my life not so long ago.

"Your aunt doesn't like you?" I said.

"I was the burden she didn't want. I used to ask about my parents all the time and hoped she'd send me to them, but Aunt Edith refused to talk about them. Then I found out the truth." He emptied the crumbs from the cookie bag into his mouth.

"What was the truth?"

"I drove Aunt Edith to distraction one day. She got so angry with me that she revealed my parents were dead. Well, one dead and one who might as well be dead. He probably is by now." Chance settled into his seat. "My mother died young. I was less than a year old when she died. I was sent to Aunt Edith after that, since she was my only living relative."

"What happened to your mother?"

"It depends which story you believe. Some say she died of a broken heart because the man she loved didn't want her. My aunt said she lived a lascivious lifestyle, so of course, she would die young and full of shame."

"Doing what? Wait. What about your dad?"

"I've no clue about him. I never met him. I don't even know his name."

"You must have seen your birth certificate. Everyone has one. His name could be on that."

"I tried to find it, but it doesn't exist."

I sat forward. "That's impossible. Everyone has a birth record. Unless you were birthed in secret, so there was no official entry of your birth. But why do that?"

"Maybe my mother never got around to filling out the right form to register me. She was a busy woman."

"What did she do?"

"Have you heard of Rose Starlight?"

I tilted my head back. "The name's familiar."

"That was my mother. She was a famous medium who worked the royal circles. Not only was she wildly popular because of her talents, but she was extremely beautiful. Apparently, men fell over themselves to spend time with her. My aunt enjoyed telling those tales, mainly to prove to me how fame and showing off led to ruin. You can look Rose up online. See for yourself how stunning she was."

I typed in her name on my phone, and dozens of pictures of a beautiful blonde woman with brilliant blue eyes appeared. "I remember now. She had a talent for being able to speak to anyone who'd died. She could drag souls back even if they didn't want to come. Rose must have had some crazy power going on."

"She was a strong bridge between the living and the dead. Influential families used her talents to talk to lost loved ones. Sometimes it was something as simple as needing information so they could access bank accounts or locked safes. Other times, grieving widows would ask her to help them communicate with their husbands and give them a chance to say a final goodbye. My mother helped them all. That meant she had little time for anything else."

"Rose had a stage show, didn't she?"

"She used to hold four shows a year. They'd always sell out, and there'd be standing room only. She'd be on stage for hours, helping people talk to the dead. It was her gift."

"How do you know all this, if she died when you were so young?"

"I read everything I could about her. Even though I have no actual memories of her, I feel like I was there when she performed."

I studied another picture of Rose and then looked at Chance. "You have her eyes."

He smiled warmly. "I think that, too."

"But you didn't inherit her medium ability?"

"No. I can only assume whoever my father was, he had little power, and I got my abilities from him. Nothing passed on from my mother."

I kept flicking through the pictures. Rose had a liking for long floaty cream dresses and sparkle in her hair. "It sounds like Rose moved in influential circles."

"She did. There were even rumors she was romantically linked to a king."

"Which one?"

"Several. But they were all married, and she wouldn't mess with anyone's marriage. Although I don't remember her, I think she was kind to all. She helped people who suffered loss."

"For a price."

Chance's smile faded. "Why not? She had a talent people were prepared to pay for. That's not a crime."

I threw him the last mini chocolate bar. I was tired, and my brain wasn't working properly, which made me snappy. But I wouldn't be able to sleep if I went to bed. I had too many thoughts churning. "What about your aunt? We could speak to her. See if there's something in your past that led to a target being put on your back. A target linking you to Gaian and Micky."

"Ah. You'd need my mother's talent to do that. Aunt Edith is dead. I have no living relatives. I'm all alone." His mouth turned down, and he ate the chocolate bar in two bites.

I set down my phone. "When did she die?"

"Four months ago."

"What happened to her?"

"The doctor said old age. Apparently, it was a peaceful death. I wasn't there when it happened. But I inherited all her things. Not that she left much. Aunt Edith was a make do and mend person."

"Where are those things?"

"In storage. I haven't bothered to go through it. It's mainly old lady stuff. Nothing interesting."

I pulled myself to my feet and rolled my shoulders. "Don't be so quick to discount old lady stuff. There could be information in there that tells us why you're being targeted."

He wrinkled his nose. "I doubt it. Why would Aunt Edith be involved in me becoming a target for mask wearing assassins?"

"We have to start somewhere. Even if there's nothing in there to make the connection we need, there could be information that leads you to your dad. Wouldn't you like to find out who he is? You could still have a living relative."

"Huh! I guess. I hadn't thought about that. But surely Aunt Edith would have told me how to find my father if she knew who he was."

"Not necessarily. Your aunt had old-fashioned ideas about family and proper behavior. Were your parents married?"

"I don't know. I don't think so."

"If Rose gave birth to you and she wasn't married, I doubt your aunt would have approved."

"You can guarantee she would have hated that. She was a traditional lady." He stood and collected the cookie crumbs off his shirt, looking around for somewhere to dump them.

"Give them to Fire Fang."

Fire Fang raised his head off the rug and opened his mouth.

Chance cautiously tossed the crumbs in. "Okay. I'm game. Let's see what Aunt Edith left me. There's nothing else to do. Although..."

"Scared the assassins are waiting for you?"

His eyebrows shot up. "I wasn't until you suggested it. But it's getting late. You really want to go now?"

"As you said, there's nothing better to do."

"We could sleep."

"We'll sleep when we're dead. Show me where the storage place is."

We took a drive to the river. The night was cold and crisp, and the storage facility was quiet as I parked.

"It's good to make a start on sorting through this stuff. I only leased the storage unit for three months, and the money runs out at the end of the week," Chance said.

"And let me guess, you were planning on charming your way into getting a free extension?"

"There's no harm in trying." He flashed me a smile. "Although my charm doesn't seem to work on you."

"Funny that. I'm good at picking up when someone is being fake."

Hurt flashed across his face. "I'm not fake. I enjoy making people happy. Charming someone makes them happy."

"Does lifting someone's purse also make them happy?"

"I don't always do that. It's important to me that other people have a good time. That was why I used to go to the casino with Micky. It was party central. We'd add to the party atmosphere. A little flirt, some banter, a few jokes, maybe a handful of coins taken. No harm done."

"Sure you did. Let's get a move on. Fog is rolling in across the river, and I need to see to drive us home."

We all climbed out, and Chance pulled a key from his pocket and headed to a storage unit at the end of a long row of bland gray doors. He unlocked it and rolled up the door.

The smell of mothballs and wood polish drifted out. There were a few items of dated looking furniture stacked up, and the rest of it was boxes and crates.

"Is this it?" I said.

"My aunt believed in minimal living. She threw nothing away. She'd just patch it up and keep using it. She once told me proudly she'd had a dress for over forty years. The thing was threadbare, but she still wore it. She even darned stockings. She was a funny old thing. Not easy to love, but I tried."

After a quick check around, I returned to the entrance. "Fire Fang, keep watch outside."

"Got it."

Stray Cat had also tagged along.

I glanced at her. She was watching me with bright eyes. "You, too, fuzz ball. Think you can handle a little guard duty? You've got to earn your keep if you're staying with me."

She flicked her tail and walked away.

I looked back at the two dozen boxes. There wasn't much here to show for an entire life. "Let's see if we can find anything useful."

"What are we looking for?" Chance opened a tatty brown box and peered inside.

"Anything your aunt kept that could connect you to Gaian and Micky. Since someone is after you, it suggests you know something they want kept quiet. Something you shared with Gaian and Micky."

"Like what?"

"You tell me. But maybe your aunt kept information about what it was. Since she never tossed anything out, your secret could be in here, too."

"She wouldn't hide something from me if she knew it would put me at risk. Aunt Edith could be a mean old thing, but she'd never intentionally hurt me."

"Maybe she didn't know it was important. Or kept it quiet because she thought she was doing the right thing. Your aunt could have believed no one else knew this secret, so you were safe. Perhaps if she was still alive, she'd pass the information on to you. Then everything would make sense."

"Aunt Edith didn't know anything important. She filled her days with attending the local coven, making homemade jam that was as sharp as a witch's elbow, and knitting blankets for the local homelessness shelter. That was her life. She preferred things simple. She wasn't hiding some deep, dark secret about me that led to my best friend dying and someone I gambled with being killed."

I was sorting through the second box. "Everyone keeps secrets. And we all have pasts."

"What secrets have you got?"

"If I told you, they wouldn't be secrets."

He laughed. "You remind me a bit of my aunt."

"A bitter spinster, you mean?"

"No! I meant you live a simple life. How long have you lived in your apartment?"

"A while."

"Are we talking months or years?"

"Years. Why is that important?"

"It's just there's nothing there. Some photographs, but the rest is all make do and mend. That was how my aunt lived. She cared nothing about material things."

"And that's bad? People who get obsessed with buying the latest phone or purse are usually broke and unhappy. They're filling a void in their lives with things."

"Maybe that's true for some people, but you don't seem happy living the life you do."

"You don't know me well enough to pass judgment." I thumped down a crate and sorted through the contents. It was mainly books and old receipts.

"You should be happy. You've got a great friend in Odessa, and Laris likes you. And you have your hound and that skinny cat. They seem loyal to you."

"What's your point?"

"Well, I was wondering, is this secret you keep the reason you're so unhappy?"

"You don't know what you're talking about." I spoke through gritted teeth. It was none of Chance's business whether or not I was happy. My job was to keep him alive until I figured out if he had anything to do with these murders.

"I'd just like to know what makes you tick."

"Keep looking. Focus on your problems, not mine."

"So... you have a problem?"

"You're my most recent problem." I started on the next crate. This was full of framed pictures, most of them countryside watercolors.

Chance had stopped his search and was focused on me. His unwanted attention made my skin itch.

"I noticed a lot of pictures of a young girl in your apartment. She looks like you."

"Funny that."

"A relative?"

"Sister."

"Where is she now?"

"Minding her own business. As you should be."

Chance didn't speak for a moment. "She's your secret, isn't she?"

I dropped the picture I was looking at and turned to him. "Why do you care?"

"Storm, I know you think I'm a smooth talking idiot with no prospects, but I understand loss. I'm still processing what happened to Micky. I keep expecting him to come through a door, laughing and telling me this was a scam, and he got me good. Of course, that'll never happen. But when you lose someone you care about, it affects you."

"What makes you think I've lost someone?" My hands clenched, and my heart beat too fast.

"Did you lose your sister? Is she dead, too?"

"No."

"What was her name?"

"You need to stop asking questions. It's bad for your health."

"It's what I do. I find out about people. I learn what makes them smile."

"You find their weakness and exploit it."

"I won't do that to you. You're helping me."

I turned away, not liking the haze in my eyes. "She's not dead. Her name's Eden. She went missing when she was a kid. Someone took her from her bed in the middle of the night. I'm still looking for her."

Chance's hand rested on my back, making me jump. "That explains it."

I moved away. "What does it explain?"

"Your anger. And your unhappiness. Of course you'll feel like that if you've lost your sister."

I yanked out a framed picture and glared at it, not seeing the subject. Chance had no right to bring this up. He was only doing it to find my weak spot.

"Hey, I remember that picture."

I snapped out of my musings and stared at the picture of a young Chance dressed as a prince in velvet pants and a smart white shirt. A small crown sat on his head.

"Aunt Edith made me dress in that ridiculous outfit. She said I looked like royalty." He shook his head. "It was humiliating. I wanted to dress as a pirate, but she wouldn't let me. It was the only time we ever had a formal family picture taken."

"Shouldn't your aunt be in the picture, too?"

"She refused to be involved. That picture was up in her living room until she died. I took it down. Fortunately, we didn't have many visitors who'd laugh at it."

I turned the picture and heard something slide inside the frame. I flipped it over and found the backing loose. Carefully, I pried it off and discovered folded paper hidden behind the picture.

"What have you got there?" Chance said.

The lights went out before I answered. Fire Fang yelped, Stray Cat shrieked, and there was a crash. Something hot moved close to my face, making me jerk back.

I tucked the paper inside my pocket and conjured a light ball. Chance was missing. I raced out of the storage unit. Fire Fang was gone, too, and there was no sign of the cat.

There was another yelp in the distance. I raced away from the storage unit and almost collided with

Fire Fang. He was staggering about and shaking his head.

"What happened?" I grabbed him and checked him over for injuries.

"Someone crept up and slammed me with a donkey helmet spell. I didn't hear them coming."

"Storm!" Chance yelled.

"We need to get to Chance. Are you okay with running?"

"I'll be fine. No goblin nobble will disable me." After another shake of his head, Fire Fang ran along beside me.

"Where's the cat?"

"She fled. She got hit with a spell, too. I think she's okay. Just scared."

We turned the corner to see two burly guys dressed head-to-toe in black, dragging Chance away.

I thrust out my hands and conjured a lightning bolt, slamming it into the ground near their feet.

They shrank away but regrouped, grabbed Chance, and tossed him into the river. With their hands free, their attention focused on me and Fire Fang.

"I'll take the one on the left," I muttered.

"I've got the sour slug on the right."

I slammed down another lightning bolt, sending the guys scattering.

Fire Fang raced after his target while I focused on the other guy. A black mask covered his face, just like the guy who'd attacked Chance. This wasn't the uniform of the magical mob. These guys were organized and professional, especially if they could sneak up on Fire Fang and disable him.

My target dodged my next bolt of lightning and stood his ground. He was either fearless or stupid. Maybe he'd never gone up against a weather witch before.

I tried to hit him with another bolt, but he was fast and dodged my magic. I conjured hailstones and smashed them on him. He cast his own spell, and a protective bubble formed around him so the stones didn't hit.

He glanced at his friend, who was tussling with Fire Fang, then made a move toward them, but I cut him off with a blast of icy wind.

I peered into the gloomy depths of the river but couldn't see Chance. I hoped he could swim.

My attacker thrust out three spells in quick succession. I dodged the first two, but the third wrapped around my arm and froze me in place. The magic crept across me, icing my skin.

The guy watched for a moment and then advanced. Idiot. I may have one arm disabled but could still call upon the elements.

I feigned being injured and unable to cast spells, encouraging him closer. When he was almost within touching distance, I lunged, thrusting out a solid spike of ice. It slammed into his shoulder, causing him to yell and stagger back. I jumped on him and grappled for the mask on his face.

He slammed me back with a spell, and I flipped in the air, but not before I saw a symbol on his sleeve. I was so shocked that I didn't move for a second. It was a Magic Embassy symbol. I was dealing with a high order magic user. What was the Magic Embassy doing trying to kill Chance?

"Storm, look out!" Fire Fang yelled.

His warning was a second too late, as a tingling spell hit the side of my head. It skimmed off me, and I was able to jump to my feet with no new injuries. But I wasn't quick enough to stop the attackers from escaping. The one I'd been after grabbed his colleague, and they disappeared in a flash of light.

I staggered over to Fire Fang. "Did you see their faces?"

"No, but the one I was after was strong."

"I know who we're dealing with." I looked at the river. "But first, we have a drowning rat to save."

Chapter 12

I tossed a towel to Chance, then headed into my bathroom to change clothes and dry off. My hair stank of rank river water, and one ear was waterlogged.

I'd just wriggled out of my clothing and was standing in my damp underwear when Chance tapped on the door.

My hand shot out, and I held the door shut. I'd never bothered to put a lock on this door. "I'm busy."

"And I'm scared. Why are Magic Embassy henchmen attacking me?"

I grabbed dry clothing and pulled it on, using one hip to stop Chance barging in. A shower would have to wait, since my unwanted apartment guest was so spooked. "You must have the answer to that. Give me a minute and make sure you're not dripping on my floor."

"You're sure it was them? It was chaotic out there. Maybe you saw an emblem that looked like they worked at the Embassy. You could have made a mistake." There was a yelp and a thump.

"I've sat on the goblin nobble so he stops hassling you," Fire Fang said.

"Appreciate that." I ran the hot water, grabbed a handful, and rubbed it through my hair and over my face before drying off.

There was another tap on the door. "Storm, what if they come after us here? Are we safe?"

I yanked open the door and glared at Chance. He'd stretched out his arm, the rest of him squashed under my giant hellhound. "If they do, we'll deal with them. But no one followed us here. Fire Fang, you can let him up now."

I left the bathroom, and Chance rolled to his feet and followed at my heel.

"Storm! What should we do? I'm terrible at dealing with danger. I run from it. I like fun and laughter. Danger is... well, dangerous."

"Sit down and stop bothering me." I shoved him onto the couch.

"I thought I was a goner when they threw me into the river." He grabbed the towel he'd abandoned and roughly dried his hair. "You're a strong swimmer. All-around strong, since you dragged me out so easily."

"I'm not that great. And it's lucky you can swim. It's also lucky I bothered to jump in and get you." I made us coffee and out-of-date cheese sandwiches and headed to the couch.

Fire Fang was looking out the window.

"You see anything good?" I said.

"I'm looking for Binky. I'm worried about her."

"That cat would survive a nuclear holocaust. She'll find her way back here, eventually." I hopped off the couch and peered out the window with him for a moment. Although that cat was a nuisance, I didn't want her in the dark on her own and scared.

"I should go look for her," he said. "Those donkey helmets terrified her."

"Her homing beacon is set to here. And you said she wasn't injured. She'll come back when she's ready." I petted his head and fed him a large meaty chew stick.

"Did either of those guys say anything to you?" Chance said.

I returned to the couch and took a bite of my sandwich. Out-of-date cheese wasn't so bad. "Nothing. I tried to get the mask off one but got whacked with a spell." I could already feel a bruise developing. That would be fun to sleep on.

"This makes no sense. The Magic Embassy doesn't even know I exist. Now they're trying to kill me."

"You must have done something to come to their attention if they've set their assassins on you."

"Assassins! I didn't know the Magic Embassy even had assassins."

I tried to rub the sore spot on my back but couldn't reach around far enough. "Neither did I, but everyone who works for the Magic Embassy has the same red winged bird symbol on their uniforms."

"She's back! Binky is outside. I'll go get her." Fire Fang raced to the door.

I let him out and only had to wait a short time before he returned, Binky riding on his back. I gave her a visual inspection. She didn't have any injuries, although she didn't look happy.

"What happened to you?" I said. "It's no good getting scared while on jobs. You'll have to get used to situations like this if you hang out with us."

The cat's gaze ran over me. She leaped off Fire Fang's back and landed on my shoulder. Rather than scratching me for making a sassy remark, she settled around my neck and licked the skin. A second later, a warm plume of heat traveled down my back, wiping away the ache. She licked my cheek and then jumped off.

"Huh! You're a healer." I rolled my shoulders. I felt like I'd had a two-hour massage, not something I usually enjoyed, but it felt great to be pain free.

I had no cat specific food to feed her, so I cut up one of Fire Fang's larger chew sticks and gave it to her. She didn't look impressed with my offering, but eventually ate it.

"Storm, what are we going to do? Those guys will keep coming for me until I'm dead." Chance jumped up and paced across the apartment.

I shoved him back to the couch. "You should hand yourself in to the Embassy. If they've assigned people to get you, there must be official paperwork to back it up. They always play by the rules. They're as bad as the Magic Council."

"I'm not giving myself to the enemy. Once they have me, they'll make me vanish."

That wasn't such a bad idea. Then he'd be off my hands. But this case had changed direction. I no longer thought Chance was the killer. He'd gotten himself tangled in something complex and dangerous. Something so important, the highest magic organization in the land needed to keep him quiet.

I grabbed my jacket and pulled out the piece of paper I'd retrieved from the back of the picture. I opened it. It was blank.

I dropped it on the table and sank back into my seat. "There I was, thinking your aunt Edith had written your deepest, darkest secrets on this and then hidden it. It was a waste of time going to the storage unit."

"Maybe not. And we didn't go through all the boxes. There could be something there to give me a clue about why the Magic Embassy wants me dead. We could go back."

"It's too risky to keep taking you out. Every time you're in public, someone tries to kill you."

"It hasn't always been this way. I used to be a popular guy." Chance leaned forward and picked up the piece of paper. He yelped and dropped it. "What's on that? It burned me."

I stared at the paper as words appeared. "It must have a spell on it. It activated when you touched it."

"I'm not touching it again." Chance rubbed his fingers together.

"It's an address. And a reference number. I don't know what it's referencing, though." I grabbed the paper. It did nothing when I made contact, so I studied the numbers. There were three letters, followed by a series of numbers. It meant nothing to me.

Chance blew on his fingers and then sat on his hand.

"Do you recognize the address?" I held it out for him.

He looked at it cautiously. "I've never been there, but it's in a well-to-do area. You only get the rich magic users spending money there."

"What about the reference number? Does that mean anything?"

Chance took a moment to study it. "It does look familiar. I've seen that kind of reference before."

"How about we go see who lives at this address?" I said.

"You just told me going out in public is dangerous."

"This information was so important your aunt hid it in a picture of you. Only you were meant to see it, which means the information is relevant to you. At this address, we could find the reason everyone wants you dead."

"Not everyone," Chance muttered.

"I do," Fire Fang said. "You've made this place smell like a dank river. And you scared Binky." He swiped his tongue over the cat's head, knocking her over.

"I'm sorry about scaring you, Binky," Chance said. "I didn't know we'd be attacked."

The cat blinked at him and flicked her tail in the air before turning her back and settling against Fire Fang's side.

"I'll translocate us," I said. "That way, we'll only be in the open for a couple of minutes. We'll get to the house, figure out what this reference relates to, and then come back here."

Chance didn't look thrilled with that idea, but nodded. "I do want to get to the bottom of this. I want to get back to living my life, not hiding from Magic Embassy henchmen."

I finished my cheese sandwich and stood, tucking the paper in my pocket. "Shall we? Fire Fang, you and... Binky coming with us?"

"Sure. Just in case you try to get yourselves killed again."

I placed a hand on Chance's arm and rested my other hand on Fire Fang's head. Binky sat on his back so we were all connected when I performed the translocation spell.

We arrived outside a smart red brick townhouse. The windows were dark, and the curtains left open.

"It looks like nobody's home." I hurried to the front door and knocked softly. There was no response.

I tried the handle, but it was locked. A simple spell solved that problem. I ushered Chance, Fire Fang, and Binky inside and eased the door closed. We waited in the hallway for a few seconds to see if anyone would appear.

We crept around, checking the rooms, before I was convinced no one was hiding in the shadows.

I risked a small light ball, so it was easier to see where we were going, and headed into the study at the back of the house. The decor had a masculine slant. There was lots of wood, dark colors, and a large pair of tartan slippers sat to one side of a chair.

I pulled out the piece of paper and looked at the reference number again. KFD. 401. A5H65. My gaze went to the wall covered with books. "I wonder if our home owner was a book nerd."

"You know what those numbers mean?" Chance said.

"It could be a book catalog reference."

"Oh! Of course. I think you're right. Aunt Edith used to drag me to the library when I was a kid. We'd spend hours there. She said there was never a reason to buy books, when there were plenty of free ones in the library. I'd spend my afternoons sorting through the catalogs. It's no wonder those numbers looked so familiar."

"Not all these books have reference numbers, but these do." I ran my finger along the spines until I came to the right number. I pulled it out, but the book only came so far. There was a click, and a side panel next to the bookcase popped open.

Chance hurried over and looked inside. "There are more papers in here."

"Let's see what our mysterious homeowner is hiding."

He hesitated, his hand hovering over the papers. "What if I get stung again?"

I shoved past him and grabbed the bundle. Nothing happened. There were two dozen letters in white envelopes and a slightly bigger document tied up with a ribbon. I was about to undo the ribbon when a sound at the front door had me looking up.

"Whoever lives here is home." Chance grabbed my arm. "We need to hide."

I stuffed the papers inside my jacket. "Let's get out of here. We don't want to deal with any more Embassy assassins." I checked along the hallway. A figure loomed outside the front door. Chance was still clinging to my arm, so I hustled him to the back of the house and into the kitchen. Fire Fang and Binky were behind us.

Chance tried the back door, but it was locked.

"Use a spell to open it," I said.

"I don't know how. I've never done that kind of magic."

I cast an unlock spell. The door didn't budge.

"Hurry! The front door is opening," Chance said.

I did another spell. "There must be magic preventing it from being opened. Out the window." I shoved Chance to the kitchen window. It was also locked, and magic wouldn't make it move.

"We can hide. We'll wait until they've gone to bed and sneak out," Chance whispered.

"Or I could just eat them," Fire Fang said.

"It's too late for us to hide." Footsteps were hurrying toward us along the hallway. "Stay behind me."

Chance was happy to oblige, while I stood with Fire Fang and Binky, magic primed on my fingers.

The kitchen door flew open to reveal Laris.

Chapter 13

"Storm!" Laris's eyes were wide as he stared at me. "What are you doing at Gaian's house?"

I lowered the spell on my fingers. "This is his house?"

Laris flicked on the light and stepped into the kitchen. "Yes. I'm taking care of it. How did you know he lived here?"

"I didn't. We found information in Chance's aunt's belongings. She'd written this address on a piece of paper, along with a reference to a book in Gaian's collection."

His head tilted, and confusion crossed his face. "Why would your aunt do that?"

Chance looked just as perplexed. "I can't tell you. Aunt Edith didn't have friends in high places. She didn't really have any friends."

"When we found the book, it was a fake. It opened a panel in his study. We were taking a look at what was inside when we heard you. We thought you were coming after Chance, so we ran," I said.

Laris's forehead wrinkled. "A hidden panel?"

"Did you know this house has hiding places?"

"No. What was in it? And why would Gaian have anything that would be of interest to you?" He addressed the question to Chance.

"I'm as much in the dark as you are."

"How did you know we were here?" I said.

"I set magic wards around the house. They alert me when anyone enters the property. I was worried the house would get broken into if it stood empty. Gaian had expensive tastes, and people might take advantage of that." Laris gestured to some nearby seats set around the kitchen table. "Let's take a moment to process this. And I need a strong drink. Translocation magic takes it out of an old warhorse like me." He opened a cabinet and took out a decanter, pouring himself a whiskey.

I declined the offer of a drink, but Chance happily accepted.

Once we were seated, I took out the bundle of papers and set them down. "Gaian must have hidden this information. Unless there was a special someone who lived with him who concealed these papers."

Laris shook his head. "His work kept him too busy for anything serious. He lived alone."

I opened the ribbon, and the letters dropped out. "Chance, this must be relevant to you since your aunt knew of their location. Do you want to look at them first?"

His hands hovered over a letter. "I'm not sure. What if it's bad news?"

"Better you know now and try to fix it."

"You should read them," Laris said.

Chance opened a letter and pulled it out. He took a few seconds to read through it. "It's a love letter. And it's signed by my mother."

"Who happened to be Rose Starlight," I said to Laris.

"The famous medium!"

"Did Gaian know her? Is that why he has her love letters? Perhaps they dated."

"He never mentioned knowing her, but it's possible their paths crossed. With the work he did, Gaian would attend the same events as the diplomats he looked after. And Miss Starlight worked in the royal circles, didn't she?"

Chance nodded as he read the second letter. "She was popular with many of the families. She traveled the world to entertain them."

"Are those love letters for Gaian?" I said.

Chance shook his head. "No. They were sent to someone called Valdey."

"Did Gaian know anyone by that name?" I said to Laris.

"He had lots of friends. He could have known a Valdey. Is there a surname?"

"No. Take a look at this." Chance handed me the letter he was reading.

I opened it.

My darling Valdey,

I know you'd never abandon me. This is your family's doing. You love me and this child. And I know we'd be blissfully happy together. I understand how hard this is for you, and I wish you didn't have to make the choice between your family and me. If only they'd accept us. But we know that'll never happen. Being with a woman of the stage isn't acceptable to someone of your status.

I hope you find a way to be with us and make peace with your family. We both love you and want the best for you.

With my undying love, Rose.

"Whoever this Valdey was, his family didn't approve of their liaison," I said.

"Do you think I was the child?" Chance said.

"You must have been. Unless Rose had more children."

"Aunt Edith never mentioned any siblings. I think I was an only child." Chance stared into space. "My dad wasn't allowed to stay with my mother because his family didn't approve. It seems so old-fashioned."

We all looked through the letters. Rose's tone became increasingly desperate as it seemed Valdey decided to remain with his family and not support her.

Laris pulled out the last two documents. He opened one, and a choked sound came out of him. "This can't be right."

"What is it?" Chance said.

"It's a record of your birth." Laris handed me the birth certificate. His face was pale.

My mouth dropped open as I read the details.

"Storm, what is it? Does it say who my father is?" Chance leaned forward.

I nodded and handed it to him. My gaze met Laris's, and the disbelief and shock were clear in his eyes.

Chance laughed as he stared at the document. "This has to be fake. There's no way this is my dad."

"It looks legitimate to me," Laris said. "And I've seen plenty of birth certificates in my line of work."

"But that means... It can't be. My father is Lord Valdemar Grimlow?"

"It would appear you're the oldest son of the Grimlow ruling family. Lord Valdemar's firstborn. Do you understand what that means?" Laris said.

"I only understand this can't be real. I'm not royalty." Chance turned desperate eyes to me. "Storm, this can't be true."

"If this turns out to be genuine, then you are."

"And when your father succeeds to power, which will likely happen in the next eighteen months if the rumors are true, you'll be next in line for the throne," Laris said. "And all the fortune and responsibility that goes with it."

"Hold on. Not if Chance is illegitimate," I said. "It'll change nothing since Rose and Valdemar didn't marry."

Chance leaped from his seat. "Right! I'm not a member of any royal family. I can't have a claim to the throne. And I don't want to. I like my life simple. I don't want to be the center of attention. That family is always hounded by the media and involved in public disputes."

"The legitimacy may not be important. Just the fact Chance is alive will cause a scandal. It could ruin that family," Laris said. "And they've been in a long dispute with the Fagan clan. I can imagine how they'd manipulate this situation if they discovered you."

"Of course. The Assault on Green Lane," I said. "The Fagan clan almost knocked the Grimlows off their seat of power."

"Those families have been battling over who should rightfully sit on the throne for decades. If an illegitimate eldest son is revealed, the Fagan clan will pull the Grimlows apart. They'll use Chance as proof the Grimlows can't be trusted to rule. They're cheaters and liars, and they've hidden Chance to avoid a scandal."

"They didn't hide me. No one knows about me," Chance said. "I didn't even know about me. These documents are fake. Someone's idea of a bad joke."

"Someone figured it out," I said. "And Grimlows have power. If they've worked out there's an illegitimate oldest son floating around, they'll want you out of the picture."

He went still. "That's who's trying to kill me?"

"Maybe it's not them. It could be the Fagan clan. But they'd want evidence of Chance's existence for different reasons. They'd want to hold him up as a symbol of everything that's wrong with the Grimlows," Laris said. "You'd be a poster boy for corruption."

"No, no, no! I don't want any of that. Let's put back the information. Pretend we never found it. I want nothing to do with any royal lineage or chance to grab a throne or any of that. I want my life to be what it always was. I want Micky back and Aunt Edith sniping at me and telling me I'll amount to nothing. And I want your friend alive, too, Laris. I wish none of this had happened."

"It gets worse." Laris was studying the final document in the pile.

"How could this get worse?" Chance said.

"What's on that document?" I said.

"It's a marriage certificate. It shows Rose Starlight married Valdemar Grimlow. And he married her before his current wife, Lady Arabella." Laris flashed his eyebrows up.

Chance slumped back into his seat and hid his face in his hands.

"Which means your birth was legitimate," I said.

"And Lord Valdemar illegally married Arabella," Laris said. "The Fagan clan will be beside themselves with glee to learn of this."

"They won't learn about it. Not from me." Chance still hid his face.

"This also means you have a genuine claim on the throne when your dad steps aside," I said. "No wonder they want you dead."

"I don't want it. Destroy that. Throw the papers into the fire."

I left Chance to his mutterings and turned to Laris. "I still don't see why Gaian would have this information. What was his involvement?"

Laris passed me the document, a sorrowful look on his face. "Gaian was a witness to the marriage. He knew about the legitimacy of Chance's birth."

I took a moment to process this information. Gaian was dead because he knew this secret. Magic Embassy henchmen were hunting Chance. And Micky had been murdered, and an attempt made to cover it up.

I studied Chance's partially concealed face. "The first time I saw you and Micky together, I thought you were brothers. You looked so alike. It was spooky."

He ran his hand through his hair. "People always said that about us. We played up to it. Two cute looking brothers hanging out together was appealing to some. Especially the ladies."

"Did you ever get mistaken for each other?"

"Sometimes. From people who didn't know us well. Why do you ask?"

"Because Micky was never meant to die. Whoever killed him got it wrong. All this time, they were after you. You were supposed to be the one poisoned by a pumpkin pie and dumped in the river. The killer messed up and picked the wrong trickster."

Chance stared at me, his mouth open. He snapped his jaw shut, and his tongue whipped across his bottom lip. "Micky died because someone thought he was me?"

"I think so. Somehow, your secret is out. Someone powerful has learned of your existence and that Rose married Lord Valdemar, which makes your claim to the throne legitimate. They've decided to wipe out the problem. But whoever they used to do the job, they killed Micky by mistake."

"And I suspect it's not the only person they've killed," Laris said. "Gaian knew about this marriage and the baby, then his magic unexpectedly misfired and he's dead. I never believed that was true."

I nodded. "It was another coverup. Micky's murder was a case of mistaken identity, but Gaian was targeted because he knew too much."

"What does that mean for me?" Chance said.

"It means you're still a target. But we also need to find out if any other people connected to this secret are still around to talk. And if so, we have to get them talking before they're killed next."

Chapter 14

The shamanic center–Enlighten Veil–looked like a basic, single story building on the outside. The windows were small and the walls dark brown and roughly finished. I was waiting outside with Chance, and we had an appointment to speak to someone about Rose and Valdemar's marriage ceremony.

"It was such a long time ago. How can you be sure this shaman will remember conducting the ceremony?" Chance shifted from foot to foot, his gaze flashing around.

"He'll remember this one. He married a member of royalty in secret to a famous medium. That's got to stick in the memory, no matter how many ceremonies he's performed. Besides, they must keep records of all the ceremonies. Even if it slipped his mind, there'll be documents to show when it happened to prove it was legitimate."

I was about to press the bell again when the door opened. An elderly, stooped man in a red velvet robe appeared. His head was shaved, and his black eyes regarded us with suspicion. "We've already made donations to the poor and needy for the day. You'll have to come back tomorrow."

"We're not here for a handout. We have an appointment with Shaman Goody," I said.

"Then you're two months too late." He tried to shut the door, but I pressed my hand against it.

"Too late? When we called earlier today, there was no problem with making an appointment to visit him."

The man tutted. "That would be the idiot boy we've just hired. He can't remember anyone's names. He probably thought you meant me."

"And you are?"

"Not Shaman Goody."

"I gathered that. Where can we find him?"

"In the cemetery down the road. We buried him two months ago."

I exchanged a glance with Chance. "What happened to him?"

His black eyes narrowed. "Who did you say you were again?"

"I didn't. I'm Storm Winter. We had questions for Shaman Goody about a marriage ceremony he performed thirty years ago."

"Then you've had a wasted journey all around. We perform hundreds of ceremonies every year. And one from such a long time ago wouldn't be something he'd have remembered. He was getting old, and his memory wasn't what it should have been. That was why his magic went wrong."

"What happened to his magic?" I said.

"We're not certain. No one was there when it happened, but he must have used the wrong ingredients in a potion. He blew himself up." The grumpy shaman suppressed a grimace. "Left a terrible mess behind. Guess who had to clear it up?"

"There seems to be a lot of misfiring magic going around," I muttered to Chance.

"What was that?" the shaman said.

"Was there any investigation into what happened to Shaman Goody?"

"A brief one, but it was obvious what happened. He always was a stubborn man and insisted on putting together his own potions. I don't know why. That's what we have assistants for. But he liked to do everything himself. Look where that got him. Now, go. I have a full meditation class waiting for me." The shaman shut the door.

"I wouldn't like to take a meditation session with him. He probably yells at people to stay calm and think bright thoughts," Chance said.

"Let's take a walk to the cemetery."

"This isn't a coincidence, is it?" Chance hurried along beside me. "Gaian is dead, Micky is dead, my mother is dead, and we've just learned the shaman who married my mother to Lord Valdemar has also been wiped out."

"There's definitely a pattern. We may never know if Rose's death was an accident because it happened so long ago, but someone is going to great lengths to wipe out all evidence of your existence."

"And they'll keep coming for me until I'm dead." Chance stuck to my side as if we were glued together.

"Not if we get them first." I inspected the cemetery plan and located Shaman Goody's grave. It was a simple affair, just his name and date of birth and death on the headstone. No mention of what kind of man he'd been. One who could keep secrets would be a solid guess.

I stood beside the grave with Chance. "You said your aunt died from natural causes. Was there much investigation when she died?"

Chance blinked rapidly several times. "Not really. She was found dead at the kitchen table. It was believed her heart gave out."

"You don't think that was true?"

"I didn't question it. She was old. And the last time I spoke to her, she said she was having chest pains. I told her to see the doctor if it was troubling her. When she died, I figured she must have had some underlying health condition she hadn't treated properly. Aunt Edith preferred her home remedies. She didn't trust doctors."

"We need to get your aunt's death looked into again. Since she left the information about how to find your birth certificate and those letters, she knew the truth about your father marrying Rose. If someone found out, they'd want to silence her, too."

"Aunt Edith was murdered?"

"I reckon so. What was her surname?"

"Osman."

"From your mother's side of the family?"

"Yes. At least, I think so."

"You said she was a spinster."

"That's right."

"So why the different last name?"

"Err... I don't know. Maybe she did marry, and he left her. I was tempted to at times." He lifted a shoulder. "She could be spiteful."

"Or she wasn't even your aunt."

"I... wow! I'd never thought to question that. Why look after me if we weren't related?"

"Money? Obligation for a past debt? Duty? Could she have been in your mother's employment?"

He shook his head. "No clue. Maybe that was why she was always so sharp with me. We didn't have any real connection. She could have regretted taking me on, but owed it to my mother not to abandon me. I'm shocked. Aunt Edith wasn't my aunt. I need a minute."

I sent a message to Olympus Duke while Chance took his minute, asking him to re-open Edith Osman's case file and check any medical records for suspicious symptoms.

"It's not definite she was murdered, but it's another one of those odd coincidences that keep popping up," I said.

"Poor Aunt Edith. I didn't have much love for the old girl, but if someone killed a defenseless spinster, that was cruel."

"Let's head to my office. We'll regroup and get the next step underway." I cast a translocation spell, and we appeared outside my office. Although casting spells all the time got tiring, using magic to move us around was the safest option.

We went inside, and I checked on Fire Fang and Binky. I found them asleep in a heap on the rug. They'd developed a strong bond in a short amount of time. Maybe I could re-home them together. Surely someone would take on a hellhound who was secretly a mortal and a cat who could magically heal people. It was a neat trick. Although the being mortal thing, not so much.

I grabbed snacks and drinks and was heading back to the office when I heard male voices. I hurried in to find Olympus and Laris had arrived. Chance sat in a seat, looking a little concerned a high up member of the Magic Council was in the same room as him.

Olympus didn't look happy when he turned to me. "Lord Brack has been keeping me informed about what's going on in this investigation. I wish you'd show me the same courtesy."

"I have. I sent you the message to re-open Edith's case. It could be another murder connected to this investigation."

He sighed. "That's not enough information for me to re-open an old case. Without being kept in the loop, I'm powerless to assist."

"That's my fault. Don't blame Storm," Laris said. "We've learned so much in such a short amount of time, thanks to her excellent work, that it's all taking a while to process. I should have been in touch sooner."

Olympus looked at Chance. "Your father is really Lord Valdemar Grimlow?"

Chance shifted in his seat. "It looks like it."

"Extraordinary. I've heard the rumors about his wandering eye, but they've always been silenced before evidence surfaces. Then he makes those grand public appearances with Lady Arabella, all seems well, and the rumors die down."

"The Grimlows are known for their public appearances to ensure everyone believes they live an idyllic life," Laris said. "But Gaian told a different story about what went on behind closed doors. Most of those families bicker and fight. The Grimlows are no different."

My office door opened, and a hunched man of around forty with a milk white face and a sweaty top lip, wearing the uniform of the Magic Council, appeared. "Sorry I'm late. I was held up in a meeting." He nodded at Olympus and everyone else in the room.

"Thanks for coming, Pepin," Olympus said. "This is Pepin Flowerbottom. We need a liaison with the Magic Embassy on this case. Someone who will be our link to the Grimlow family. That's Pepin's specialty. He has years of experience at the Magic Council before moving to focus on diplomatic relations." He introduced the rest of us to Pepin.

I grimaced. A double whammy of bureaucracy was the last thing I needed slowing me down. "We don't need more help. We've already found the connection between the murders. Now we just need the evidence to assign guilt."

"Storm, the royal families are almost impossible to access without going through the right channels. You can't simply walk into a palace and demand answers," Olympus said.

"I could try. Just because they're royalty doesn't mean they're above the law."

"If I may, diplomacy and tact is always the best route to these families." Pepin's hands were clasped in a show of deference. "There are ways to do things in order to gain access to them. They don't appreciate heavy-handed measures."

"I won't be heavy-handed, but I will get straight to the point. If someone in the Grimlow family is killing people to hide a secret, they must be held accountable."

Pepin cleared his throat. "I don't disagree, but we need to go about this subtly."

"This isn't open for debate, Storm," Olympus said. "And with cases this sensitive, I must have all the information. It's only thanks to Lord Brack I'm up to speed on the deaths linked to this situation. You need a tactful liaison, or this won't work."

"What would you have me do, report to you every half an hour about what I'm doing, or solve this mystery?"

His scowl deepened. "Perhaps not every half an hour."

"Reports and red tape cost lives. More people could die to keep Lord Valdemar's secret."

"An alleged secret," Pepin said.

"If you call a marriage certificate, a birth certificate with Lord Valdemar named as the father, and love letters showing he spurned the woman he married because his family forced him to, sure, I'll go with the alleged secret concept."

Pepin's face paled, and he tugged at his collar. "The evidence does sound convincing."

"As do all the people who keep dying. I've just come back from trying to meet Shaman Goody, the individual who married Rose Starlight and Lord Valdemar. And surprise, surprise, he died two months ago. Apparently, a potion he mixed backfired. He blew himself up."

"Goodness. Well, that changes things." Pepin looked imploringly at Olympus, as if hoping he'd be able to rein me in. Good luck with that.

Olympus looked almost as uncomfortable as Pepin as he squared off with me. "I know you have a certain way of doing things, but we must follow protocol. There is too much at stake."

I wanted to tell him where to stick his protocol, but I looked at Laris and bit my tongue. He appeared haggard. I'd promised I'd help solve his friend's murder, so I'd toe the line. I'd probably snap it a few times, but I'd do my best to behave.

"What's our next move?" I said.

"The Grimlow family can be reached," Pepin said. "I've dealt with them many times, so I'm certain I can get access to whoever you need to speak to."

"Including Lord Valdemar?"

He gulped. "If it should come to that."

"That'll do for a start," I said. "But we need to move fast. There's still a target on Chance's head. And my babysitting days need to be over."

"Storm, you're not thinking about abandoning me," Chance said. "I've been helpful, haven't I?"

I didn't bother to reply, but tossed him a snack bar.

"Everything we do from now on must be discreet," Olympus said. "We can't have a royal scandal."

"Why not? They caused the scandal and are wiping out the evidence. The truth needs to be revealed," I said.

Olympus pressed the bridge of his nose. "I beg you not to stomp all over this. These families have huge influence over all areas of our lives."

"You mean they'll make your position in the Magic Council difficult?"

A flush spread up his neck. "That's not the important thing here. So much goes on behind-the-scenes with these families. Negotiations for peace, trade, prosperity. Destabilizing one family will cause chaos with the others. There could be a power grab. There's even a potential for war to start if the Grimlows are exposed. I know you want this resolved swiftly, but we have to make sure whatever steps we take are done methodically."

Methodical meant slow and time wasting. I was more of a go in with magic blazing kind of witch, but I could be discreet for a few hours.

"Do we have a deal?" Olympus said.

"Sure." I looked at Pepin. "I'll get you up to speed on what's been going on. Then we'll go have a chat with Lord Cheater, shall we?"

Chapter 15

The next day, I was up early and in my office. I'd spent most of yesterday afternoon with Pepin, and he'd been politeness personified. He hadn't once interrupted me as I'd told him about the connection between Lord Valdemar and Chance.

He studied the letters and the certificates and agreed the situation was serious and we needed to act fast. And while I was happy to go along with his plans, I wanted to make my own.

I leaned back in my seat and waited for my call to connect to John Smith, my favorite sleazy warlock with connections in all the wrong places.

"Storm Winter. I'm happy to hear you're not dead."

"Not today, John."

"You never told me how that screaming skull case rounded out. The curse didn't get you, then?"

"Not unless you're talking to a ghost."

"Boo! Ha!"

"I got the skull, with a little help from some friends. It won't be back to bother anyone else."

"I knew a cursed skull wouldn't stop you. What can I do for you?"

"I need an in with a royal family. Specifically, the Grimlows. Can you help?"

A burst of laughter shot along the phone line. "Do you now? Trading up?"

"You have connections, so I figured you'd know a back way in."

He chuckled some more. "I may be able to help. For a price."

"Of course. What's your connection to them?"

"Details first. Who are you looking into?"

There wasn't much I could tell John without revealing the secret royal baby connection. "Someone was poisoned. We think the poison was concealed in a pumpkin pie."

"Poison. Interesting. And funny you should mention pumpkin pie."

"What's funny about that?"

"It's Lady Arabella's favorite dessert. She insists on having it at least once a week."

"How would you know that?"

"Because of my connection. I dated a kitchen servant at their home in Greenville. That girl was as cute as a button, but she loved to talk. She'd tell me all about the food she made, who enjoyed it, and how much they ate. And she was always going on about Lady Arabella demanding pumpkin pie."

I tapped my fingers on the desk. Had Lady Arabella found out about her husband's first marriage and the baby? She'd sent someone with that poisoned pie with the intention of getting Chance. She wouldn't have delivered it herself but could have used one of her aids to get the poison to the right person. Or rather, the wrong person. It was her calling card. A sign to her husband that she knew the truth and wasn't playing nice anymore.

"I need to speak to this girl you dated. You still friendly?"

"That won't be possible. She hates me after I ditched her. All that talking was giving me a headache."

"You need to un-ditch her. She could have useful information in a murder investigation."

"It's not worth my while. I don't want her getting the wrong idea and thinking we're getting back together. No amount of money is worth that."

"Then find me another way to talk to other people in the kitchen. Someone could remember something useful about a pumpkin pie being made and sent. Maybe the poisoner was seen slipping something into the pie."

"I'll see what I can do. But no promises. And if that girl gets wind I'm poking around, I'm out of there."

"I know. You never promise anything."

"You got it."

I ended the call and was heading up the stairs to freshen my coffee when the door to the main office opened. I stepped back down and poked my head around the side of the doorjamb. Pepin stood there, his hat clasped in his hands.

"I was just getting coffee if you'd like one," I said.

"Sure. Coffee would be great." He hurried up the stairs behind me. "Do you live here?"

"Sure do. It makes for an easy commute to work." I headed to my kitchen.

He chuckled. "It must. Have you just moved in?"

I flicked on the kettle. "No. I've been here a while."

Pepin walked around, inspecting my things. "I see you're practicing a minimalist lifestyle. Or is this shabby chic?"

"It's neither. I just don't waste my money on buying things I don't need."

His cheeks flushed. "Oh! Of course. It's lovely what you've done with the place."

I made the coffee and passed him a mug. "I've got us a possible back way in to learn more about the Grimlows. Someone has a connection with a kitchen server. And she loves to talk."

"Well, that's admirable you've done your research." Pepin cleared his throat. "But I have a front way in. I've made an appointment to meet with the head of security in one hour."

I arched an eyebrow. Maybe Pepin wouldn't be useless after all.

***

The leather chair I sat on squeaked as I shifted around. I was in a waiting chamber with Pepin. Lots of official types scurried about with paper in their hands, trying to look important.

Delicate china teacups were set beside us, alongside a plate of tiny cookies. They'd been provided by the smartly turned out receptionist when we'd arrived for our appointment with Fritz Goon.

"What does everyone do here?" I muttered.

"They all look after the royal families. This is the central Embassy hub, much like the Magic Council has a headquarters and then smaller outreach offices. And the families keep us busy. Most of them travel or host numerous social events. It needs careful coordination," Pepin said.

"It sounds exhausting."

"Perhaps. But it's necessary. You may have noticed in the news the growing tensions reported between certain families."

"I don't follow the news closely. The media doesn't tell the truth."

"Well, pay attention to those stories. I'm one of a dozen liaisons the families use, and we've been kept on our toes for months to ensure diplomatic negotiations don't break down." Pepin leaned closer. "And you didn't hear this from me, but the Grimlows aren't easy. They're stubborn. They think they have a right to be here."

"And they don't?"

"Some say not. Some would even say a change is long overdue."

"What are your thoughts on that?"

He raised a hand and leaned back. "As a diplomat, I remain impartial. I focus on ensuring safe and stable negotiations. Whoever rules has my support."

"Spoken like a true diplomat who wants his fat pension when he retires."

"The benefits help, but it's more than that. I've been doing this job for years. I see value in making sure those who rule are content. When the powerful become unhappy, everyone pays the price."

Several members of the Magic Embassy hurried past, displaying their red bird badge.

"Does everyone who works for the Embassy have to wear that bird symbol?" I said.

"Yes. It's how we're identified. I have both. Magic Council and Magic Embassy. The Council keeps me on a retainer." Pepin lifted his lapels to show a white badge and a red badge. "They basically act like a pass to get you through doors without questions. They're handy to have."

"When Chance and I were attacked at the storage unit by the river, I saw a red bird badge on one of the attackers."

Pepin jerked back in his seat. "You're certain it was the emblem of the Magic Embassy?"

"The fight was intense, but it caught my eye. Our attackers were dressed head to toe in black and wearing masks, but they still kept their Magic Embassy badges on. Something they were proud of, perhaps?"

"It can't have been anyone from here."

"Why not? Surely, an organization of this size must have corrupt members."

"No, that's not possible."

"Or maybe they were following Lord Valdemar's order to murder Chance."

"It would be too risky for Lord Valdemar to order anyone's death. As you mentioned with your connection to the kitchens, things slip out. Servants overhear confidential conversations, and they gossip. Gossip gets around. It would be impossible to hide such a thing."

I wasn't so sure. "What if whoever ordered Chance's murder and the other murders did it on the quiet? They bribed an enforcer from the Embassy to do the job for them."

"We don't have snakes working here. Bribery is never acceptable."

"People's circumstances change. An enforcer might have needed money quickly, and someone from the Grimlow family exploited that need."

"Everyone is vetted before they join the Magic Embassy. I had to go through four rounds of interviews and three assessments before my position was confirmed. They don't let just anybody in. And if there's even a hint of corruption or bribery, that person is dismissed without question. We all know the thin line we tread. Dealing with such powerful individuals comes with responsibility."

"Storm Winter and Pepin Flowerbottom." The receptionist sitting behind a large black desk at the end of the room looked at us. "Fritz is available for you now. He's in conference room four."

We followed her directions and discovered a tall, broad-shouldered man with a sharp crewcut and a crooked nose studying a map spread across a table.

He glanced up when we appeared in the door and gestured us inside. "Pepin, good to see you again." He shook Pepin's hand, then turned to me. "We've not met."

I shook his outstretched hand. "Storm Winter." From his perfect posture, I had to assume Fritz was a former military man.

"Very good. I don't have long. There's a dispute on the northern border out on West Ridge we need to deal with."

His brusque manner wasn't putting me off. "Multiple murders may take time to discuss."

Pepin cleared his throat and stepped forward. "What Storm means is we're looking for information on a sensitive situation. It's possible it could involve the Grimlow family. Your cooperation in this matter would be appreciated."

Fritz's sharp gaze shifted away from me. "I don't like where this is going. Pepin, explain."

I shrugged. Fritz was clearly a man's man and didn't want to hear what I had to say. That didn't mean I wasn't going to speak my mind.

"A young man was found dead in Serpent Lake. Initially, it was believed he'd drowned after a night of exuberance, but further investigation revealed he'd been poisoned," Pepin said.

"By a pumpkin pie," I said. "Do you know anyone around here who likes to eat pumpkin pie?"

Fritz's attention returned to me. "No. Of course, any death is unfortunate, but I don't see what this has to do with the Grimlow family, or me."

"Whoever put poison in the pie killed the wrong man. Since that death, we've uncovered the murder of a shaman—"

"Possible murder," Pepin said.

"The *possible* murder of an elderly witch who knew too much, and the murder of Gaian Grimm."

Fritz paused for a heartbeat. "I heard about Gaian. I met him a number of times. Decent man. But his death was an accident. A spell gone wrong, so I was led to believe. I still don't see the relevance."

"Gaian's death wasn't an accident," I said.

"This is all conjecture at this stage," Pepin said. "But we have concerns there is a connection to these deaths and someone in the Grimlow family. That's why we needed to speak to you."

"I can't help you."

"You've not overheard any conversations about a problem that needs taking care of?" I said.

"No. I don't eavesdrop."

"As head of security, you must encounter tricky situations all the time. The families get in trouble and need a problem to vanish. Is that where you step in?"

"I can't comment. They're confidential matters that are dealt with discreetly."

"How do you deal with them?"

"As I just said, discreetly."

"Does that discretion include killing people who threaten to reveal an unwelcome truth?" I said.

Fritz crossed his arms over his broad chest and continued to glare at me.

I glared right back. I wasn't intimidated. If Fritz did the dirty work of the Grimlow family, I needed to find out.

"Don't take offence, Fritz," Pepin said. "But we need to get to the bottom of this. If there's anything you've overheard, it could be helpful in solving what happened to these people."

"I wish you the best of luck, but I have no information to share."

"Because you don't know anything, or because you've been sworn to silence by a Grimlow? Was it Lord Valdemar or Lady Arabella?" I said.

He didn't reply.

"It must be hard being given orders to follow that you don't agree with. Or do you have no scruples about murder?"

"Everything I do for this family, or any of the royal families, I don't take personally. It's a job. I receive my orders and carry them out."

"What orders were you carrying out four nights ago between two and six in the morning?" I said.

"I would have to consult my diary."

"I suggest you do that. Unless you want to become a suspect in a multiple murder investigation."

"Storm, I —"

I cut Pepin off with a glare. "We need this information. Someone is carrying out these murders for a member of the royal family."

Pepin's expression was full of apology as he simpered at Fritz. "Any help you give us would be gratefully received. Just to discount you and clear the royal name."

"Give me a moment." Fritz marched out of the room.

"Do you enjoy being a toady to alpha idiots like that?" I said to Pepin.

His mouth twisted to the side. "It's easier this way. Some people prefer to be in charge and enjoy being an alpha. I think you could be one of them."

"And that's a problem?"

"No! I like an assertive woman." Pepin sighed. "But I also like a simple life. Sometimes, you bite your tongue for the greater good."

"I'm hearing that phrase a lot with the royals."

"It's no surprise. They have power. You tread carefully around those who wield such strength."

Fritz returned with a paper diary in his hand. "I was working during that time."

"Do you always work such late hours?" I said.

"I'm available whenever the families need me. I was at the Grimlow household dealing with a private matter."

"What was the matter?"

"It wasn't connected to a murder, but it was of a sensitive nature and involved a young lady who needed escorting off the premises."

"Can anyone else confirm that?"

"Private matters such as that are handled discreetly. You have my word. That is good enough."

"Of course it is. Thank you for your time," Pepin said.

Fritz's expression was firm as he watched me. "Be careful in making accusations of murder in connection to the Grimlow family."

"If I don't, will I be on your hit list, too?"

"Thank you. We'll leave you to your business," Pepin said.

"One more thing." I shrugged Pepin's hand off my elbow. "Do you know the name Rose Starlight?"

Fritz was already walking away. "Good day, Miss Winter. Pepin."

Pepin tugged me out of the room. "You shouldn't goad Fritz. He's a highly decorated military man.

I once heard someone say he knows how to kill people in twenty-five different ways."

"And I can conjure lightning bolts from the air and blow someone apart. He's not that impressive."

Pepin choked out a laugh. "You really are quite extraordinary, Storm."

"Thanks. I wasn't convinced by him. What's to say Fritz wasn't following orders? He wouldn't blink if he was told to kill everyone connected to Chance."

"I... I don't know about committing multiple murders for the Grimlow family, but he's always been a loyal employee. I can't believe he'd go as far as to murder anyone, though."

"You heard him say he carried out his orders to the best of his abilities. And he didn't deny killing for the family."

Pepin adjusted his collar. "I don't know what to say to that."

"A diplomat lost for words. Things must be terminal." I walked along the corridor and out of the building with Pepin beside me. "We need to speak to the person giving Fritz his orders."

"You want to speak to Lord Valdemar?"

"Not yet. I want to tackle our pumpkin pie loving Lady first."

"Oh! That's impossible. Lady Arabella is a private person."

"Nothing is impossible when you have the right mindset. Let's make it happen. How can we get a private audience with her Royal Pumpkin Pie without anyone noticing?"

Chapter 16

"I don't like this idea. It's risky. Too much could go wrong." Pepin's lips were pink from where he kept chewing on them like a toffee apple.

I resisted the urge to snap at him. I had to expect this level of sniveling caution from someone who worked for both the Magic Council and the Embassy. And he had brought me and Fire Fang carrot cake when he'd arrived two hours ago.

"You don't have to be involved." I'd been studying the route the royal procession was taking tomorrow and had been most of the previous night. Carriages loaded with different noble families would work their way through a dozen towns and villages as part of the centenary celebrations. It was to highlight the stability and peace provided by the ruling families.

And the timing couldn't be better. Tomorrow, the Grimlow family was taking part in the procession, and that included a public showing from Lady Arabella.

"What if we get caught?" Pepin cantered about the apartment, almost tripping over Fire Fang.

"No reward is without risk."

"They'll think you're trying to kidnap Lady Arabella. They might think I am!" Pepin had been fretting over this idea ever since I'd suggested it.

"So I'll get arrested and take the blame. If your name gets mentioned, I'll say I forced you to help."

He turned his startled gaze on me. "Do you want to go to jail for the rest of your life?"

"It won't come to that. If I get caught, which I won't, I'll play dumb and pretend to be an obsessed royal fan. They're always doing insane things, like breaking into the royal residences or sending bits of themselves through the mail, aren't they?"

Pepin grimaced. "There have been occasions when bodily items have been dispatched to certain family members."

"Really? I thought that was an urban myth. What are we talking? Did someone slice off an ear and send it to Lady Arabella?"

"No! Not an ear."

"But something got sliced and sent?"

He shuddered. "Let's focus on this impossible task. You may have friends in the Magic Council—"

"I wouldn't go that far. I know a few people. We're not best buddies."

"It doesn't matter who you know. An attack on a member of the elite families will be punished severely." Pepin was wringing his hands as he paced.

He was making me nervous just watching his jitters ratchet to ten. "Grab a coffee and relax. This is the quickest way we can get to Lady Arabella. We need to know if she has revenge on her mind after finding out what her prince charming did all those years ago."

"Oh, dear. This is terrible. What if it is someone in the family? Lady Arabella could be getting rid of the evidence. It's... ruthless. It's very her."

I was warming to the possibility of a vengeful wife issuing kill orders. "Lady Arabella is wiping out everything connected to her husband's shady past."

"And she thinks she'll get away with it because no one would ever connect the deaths." Pepin glanced my way. "Except you did."

"Thank my suspicious mind. It's useful when working these kinds of cases."

Pepin paced some more. "The family name is the most important thing to these people." He stopped by a window and looked out. "And you didn't hear this from me, but Lady Arabella is difficult. I've done my best to avoid her over the years, after she almost had me fired."

"What did you do to annoy her?"

"My record is exemplary, but... she doesn't like my chin." He rubbed at his normal looking chin.

"What's wrong with it? It does its job. Although what job does a chin have? To have something to rest your hand on? To gesture at things when your hands are full? To scratch an itch on your shoulder when you're too lazy to use your hands?"

Pepin simply looked more worried. He didn't add to the point of a chin debate I was having with myself. "Lady Arabella wanted me gone because she didn't like the way I looked."

"She sounds charmless."

"She has her moments of charm, but there's always frost beneath the smiles. Lady Arabella is almost as intimidating as her grandmother. Since

I learned she thought me unattractive, I've stayed out of her way. There are so many of us employed in the diplomatic service, it's not difficult." Pepin turned from the window. "You must be careful. Lady Arabella is dangerous and powerful."

"I'll be in and out of her carriage before anyone realizes what's going on. And I won't hand out business cards or give out my name."

"She will still track you down."

"Perhaps. But a disguise will help. We'll get the juicy inside information about her fake perfect life, and if she makes trouble for me, I'll take her down. Trust me, it'll be messy. She won't come out of it well. It'll get the gossip wheels spinning."

The hand wringing continued. "Have you ever been inside a royal carriage?"

"Yeah, I lounge about in them all the time."

"Really?"

I resisted the urge to eye roll. "I don't mix in those circles. But they can't be that difficult to access."

The worry lines on his forehead deepened.

"Or maybe they are. Give me the lowdown on what to expect."

Pepin finally settled on the couch. "Lady Arabella always travels with her entourage of security."

"Anyone would think she was unpopular since she surrounds herself with so much security."

He shifted around in his seat. "The unmentioned body parts are usually delivered to her."

"Got it." I grinned. "Was it a finger?"

"Please stop asking. The carriage driver will be trained in defensive magic, as will the assistant beside him. Don't be fooled by their size. Everyone working royal protection duty is a higher magic user. And they have permission to use kill spells. There'll also be two guards riding the back of the carriage."

"Also trained to kill?"

"Correct."

"Anything else?"

His eyes widened. "The carriage won't be unlocked. You'll have to force your way inside."

"I can do that. What about Lady Arabella's ability? Any special skills I should be worried about?"

"Fortunately, not. Once you're past the security and magic, you should be fine. Lady Arabella is a lazy magic user. Her line is descended from the water nymphs, so there are no special skills other than her great beauty. I can't remember the last time I saw her cast a spell."

"Which is good for me. Her powers will be sluggish, so she'll be easy to subdue."

The lip chewing started again. "How do you plan on subduing her? You're not going to hurt her ladyship, are you?"

"Only if she puts up a fight. I'll start with some questions. If Lady Arabella is innocent, she'll want this matter cleared up quickly."

Pepin looked far from convinced. "What about the crowds? Thousands of people will watch the procession. Someone will spot what you're up to. They could stop you."

"They could try to stop me. But if you all cause enough distractions, there won't be any attention on me."

Pepin tugged at his collar. "You want me there?"

"I do. How's your yelling?"

"I... I can yell."

I tilted my head, almost feeling sorry for this downtrodden drone. "Do you want to yell?"

He looked away. "Yes. I want to help. What do you need me to do?"

"Kick up a stink about a dark magic threat. Yell about seeing dark spells being performed, then set off flares to create panic."

"Flares!"

"Sparkle, light, lots of distraction. Maybe a few bangs. You can do that, right?"

"Of course. But... what if I'm caught?"

"Plead ignorance. Say you saw something dodgy and wanted to keep the public safe. You're a trusted member of the royal diplomatic team. They won't think it weird you're going out on a limb to save the royal families."

He scrubbed at his chin. "I suppose I could try."

"No supposing about it. You're in, or you're out. If you can't help, you're no use to me."

Dots of color blotched across his skin. "I could lose my job."

"Not if we make a plan and stick to it. So long as we don't deviate, everything will go smoothly. And it won't just be you messing things up. Fire Fang will get the crowds scattering. He's great at terrifying people and making them run." My gaze went to my bedroom, where Fire Fang and Binky were snoozing. Those two did nothing but sleep.

Pepin shuffled to the edge of his seat. "I have another option. One that'll guarantee no one gets scared or chased, loses their job, or risks jail time."

"I'm listening."

"I've submitted a form requesting a meeting with Lady Arabella. We should wait for that."

"And how long will that take to process?"

"Well, a lot of people like to meet her Ladyship. It could be a couple of months. No more than three. Maybe four."

"Which is too long. We've got everything we need to make this work. Fire Fang's ferocity, your distracting skills, and my weather magic. I'll bring down a dense fog over the crowd and the procession. No one will be able to see a thing. I'll sneak up to the carriage, get rid of the guards, and get inside. While order is restored, I'll ask the questions. Even if I don't get any answers, it'll give me a chance to see how guilty Lady Arabella looks when I reveal all the murders and the love child to her."

Binky darted out of my bedroom. She headbutted my leg and glared up at me.

"You can't be hungry. I fed you and Fire Fang two hours ago."

"She wants to be involved," Fire Fang said as he appeared in the doorway. "And she is part of the team now. What job can you give her?"

I peered at the slightly less skinny cat. "I'm not sure. What skills have you got that could be useful?"

The cat puffed out her fur and a shower of sparks shot out of her. They were bright enough to dazzle for several seconds.

"Wow! Binky has skills. That'll work. Shoot out dazzling sparkle magic, and we can add even more chaos into the mix. You're on the team."

She nodded and strutted away, looking like she knew she was already on the team, and I was the one slow on the uptake.

"I'm still not sure about this. Is there anything I can do to change your mind?" Pepin said.

"You know where the door is if you don't agree with this plan." I threw him a tiny bone to give him a get out. "I know Olympus is forcing you to work with me, so no hard feelings if this isn't for you."

"It's not that. I can deal with stressful situations. I once single-handedly placated a horde of rampaging ogres."

"Impressive. How did you do that?"

"Lots of ale and the promise of a hog roast feast. Sometimes, the simple things work."

"It'll take more than a greasy ham hock to make Lady Arabella happy."

His shoulders sagged. "What if you learn she was involved in killing all these people?"

"She'll be arrested and charged with the murders, the same as everyone else. Her sparkling tiara won't get her out of this."

Pepin was quiet for a moment as he resumed his pacing. "You're right. I'm being timid. If there is a Grimlow family connection to these murders, it can't go unpunished. I'm with you. I'm still terrified, but I want to do the right thing."

"I'm glad to hear it. Tomorrow, we're going to the parade. Make sure to wear your best chaos making clothes."

I was up early the next morning and outside, checking the route the royal procession would take through Witch Haven. A few eager people were already laying claim to the best spots, so they'd get a prime view of the carriages as they went past. Bunting had been strung across the roads, and the stores were already open to maximize the extra sales they anticipated.

I grabbed a coffee for me and savory bacon butter muffins for Fire Fang and Binky to share.

Binky sat on my shoulder, having claimed the spot before we left the office. I still wasn't sure what to make of this cat's insertion into our lives, but I didn't hate it. And as she'd shown more than once, she could be useful. There were good reasons to keep her around. Not forever, but I could handle for now.

Fire Fang ate his muffin in two bites, and I broke small pieces off the other one and offered them to Binky. She ate a few, but then shook her head, so Fire Fang got the rest.

My coffee was hot and my mind focused as we strolled along the route. In a few hours, this place would be crazy crowded. I had to pick my spot carefully, so I had minimal eyes on me. I needed to be able to bring down a fog weather spell discreetly, without anyone noticing. And I could guarantee there'd be security agents walking among the crowds, making sure people weren't up to mischief.

On the whole, they wouldn't be. The magical elite were respected and left alone, but there were always a few dissidents looking to cause trouble at events like this. I suppose I'd be classed as a troublemaker today. But they'd have to catch me to prove anything.

"This could work," Fire Fang said. "We hit them on this bend. The carriages will have to slow, and you can only get a couple of rows of people on the tight corners. Fewer eyeballs and less speed."

I walked the route one way, then crossed over and walked back. "This is perfect. If we hide behind those trees over there, we can blend in and hit Lady Arabella's carriage at the right time."

"Where do you want us?" Fire Fang said.

"You and Binky stay at the back of the crowd just before the bend. When you see the carriages start causing chaos. But make sure the crowd heads away from the road, not toward it. I don't need them blocking the route so the carriage can't get through."

"How about we cause our diversions as the carriages pass?" Fire Fang said. "That way, even if people run into the road, it won't matter. It could even help. Security will have trouble getting through to Lady Arabella. You'll have more time to question her."

"That will work. Fire Fang, you go on the left. Binky, you're on the right. Got it?"

She nodded and curled her tail around my neck. Binky liked being a part of the gang.

I spotted Pepin hurrying toward us. I deliberately hadn't brought him along this morning because I was tired of his stressing. He wasn't a bad guy, but his fretful jitters didn't help the situation. Of course, he had a lot to lose, but he'd agreed to be involved.

"When I didn't find you at the office, I thought you'd be here," he said. "Not having second thoughts?"

"The opposite. Everything is in place. You work the left side of the crowd with Fire Fang. He'll start scaring people, and you yell about dark magic. It'll be enough to get people moving and leave the way clear for me."

Pepin did several quick, bird-like nods. "Yes, yes. Right, right. We're really doing this?"

I patted his shoulder. "Need a stiff drink for courage?"

"No! I... actually, maybe. But I'll stick to coffee." He looked along the road. "What do we do now? It's four hours until the carriages are due."

"We grab snacks and wait until it's our moment to put royal noses out of joint."

I sent Pepin to get the snacks and drinks, and we set ourselves up on a bench for a couple of hours. We were just your average excited Witch Haven residents, looking forward to the royal procession. Once the snacks were gone and the crowd getting bigger, we casually retreated behind the trees. Nothing suspicious going on, just a couple of people and their animals relaxing and enjoying the atmosphere.

"Storm! I thought that was you." Odessa appeared around the tree we were using as cover. Her eyes widened when she saw me with Pepin. "Oh! This isn't a date, is it? Have I interrupted a romantic moment?"

Pepin's cheeks flushed. "No, this isn't romantic. This is—"

"Business. Odessa Grimsbane, meet Pepin Flowerbottom. And I'm on a case, so scram."

"It is her!" Luna appeared next, alongside Indigo. "What are you doing skulking around behind these trees? You hate nature."

"I like nature well enough. It's the quiet I prefer. And you shouldn't have been able to see us." Maybe this hiding spot wasn't as good as I'd thought.

"Fire Fang said you were here. What's he up to? He looked suspicious," Luna said.

"Storm is on a case." Odessa's whisper was conspiratorial. "And this isn't a date. Although, Pepin, you're cute. Are you single? Storm is."

His blush deepened.

"Don't answer any questions. Odessa is always nosing about in people's personal business. A place she has no right to be in," I growled out, giving my friends an evil glare.

"What case has got you hanging out by the procession?" Indigo arched an eyebrow. "What are you up to?"

"Keeping out of people's way. Which means we don't need a crowd. Get out of here."

"You won't see much from here," Luna said. "Join us. Cole has a great spot picked out. He's guarding it in typical alpha werewolf fashion."

"And Albert's got a pop-up stall out for his bakery. People can't get enough of his brownies," Odessa said.

"He's even iced brownies with the royal crests on them. He had to get approval from the families before making them, but he's already sold out of three lots," Luna said.

"Sounds great, but we'll pass on the snacks. Although save us some for later," I said.

"We should get going. We don't want to lose the spot. And I want another one of those brownies before the greedy well-wishers buy them all," Odessa said. "You sure you won't join us?"

"Sure. Have fun. But be careful out there. Things could get hectic," I said.

"Hectic how?" Indigo settled a hand on one hip. "You're not planning on messing with this procession, are you?"

"A tiny bit of mess may occur. If you see Fire Fang and Binky racing around blasting magic, don't stop them. They're doing it for a good reason."

"You're doing it again," Odessa said.

"Doing what?"

"Leaving us out."

"I may be leaving you out, but I have a team in place. I've got Fire Fang, Binky—"

"Back up a step. Who's Binky?" Luna said.

"Oh, that stray cat. Fire Fang named her. Maybe she'll find a home sooner if she has an actual name. And she's got power. She could be useful to someone."

"It sounds like Binky is already being useful if she's helping with some devious plan involving the procession," Indigo said. "Are you sure you can't tell us what's going on?"

"The less you know, the better. I've got the fluffies and Pepin as my team. I've got all the hands I need."

"We could still help," Luna said.

"Storm doesn't want us helping, because she knows it wouldn't be on her terms," Indigo said tartly.

"It's a bad thing I have boundaries? This is my career."

"It's also a you thing," Indigo said. "Be careful if you're messing with this event. These royal families don't play gently. Get on the wrong side of them, and it'll be your head on the chopping block."

"They stopped doing beheadings fifty years ago. The worst thing that'll happen to me is a lifetime of imprisonment," I said.

Odessa squeaked, Luna chuckled, and Pepin cleared his throat and tugged at his collar.

"She's joking," Indigo said. "You are joking, aren't you? You're not planning on getting arrested, right?"

"Go. Have fun. Remember, don't mind the chaos. It'll be over soon."

My friends finally left, and I checked the time. "We need to get into position. The carriage will be here soon."

Pepin bit his lip and began that annoying hand wringing again. "Maybe we should have gotten your friends involved. I sensed their power."

"No way. They have busy enough lives without trying to hijack a royal carriage. Remember what you have to do?"

"Yell a few times and then vanish?"

"Exactly. You've got this." That was about as good as my pep talk got.

"Yes! I have." Although Pepin attempted to look confident, I wasn't fooled. The shaking hands and sweaty top lip were a giveaway.

I checked Fire Fang and Binky's positions. They were exactly where they needed to be. I led Pepin to a suitable spot and gave him a final warning glare not to mess things up, then a shoulder pat, and headed around the bend on my own.

The crowd was noisy and excited, and I had to do some less than gentle shoving before I could get into position. But I was finally where I needed to be.

I climbed a lamppost to look over everybody's heads. In the distance, I spotted the first royal carriage. Lady Arabella would be in the final carriage. They were well spaced out, which was ideal. I didn't want to enter the wrong carriage in the confusion and fog. But hers was impossible to miss. It was the biggest, shiniest, and most over the top carriage I'd ever seen. Not that I spent much time geeking over carriages, but this one was a picture of opulent over-indulgence.

I gave a cheery wave over my head, making out I'd spotted a friend in the crowd. It was a signal to the others that we were about to start the chaos making.

The first carriage passed slowly. It was open topped and had three members of the Winnibug royal family in it. They were waving and smiling cheerily, occasionally throwing out gift bags full of treats, which the crowd pounced upon like starving animals.

The second carriage had a closed cover and contained some of the Mayweather family unit, who looked happy to be gliding past their loyal admirers.

Finally, the ornate gold carriage containing Lady Arabella moved slowly toward me. Just as it reached Fire Fang and Binky's position, I gave another wave. That was the cue to unleash the magic.

It only took a few seconds before the crowd churned and people yelled. There were dazzling blasts of magic shooting in all directions from Binky. I even heard Pepin yelling, although it sounded strangled and pitchy. I was proud of him. I didn't think he'd have the courage to go through with it.

I slid off the lamppost and was heading to the trees to perform my fog spell in private, when my eyes widened, the world stopped turning, and I forgot how to breathe. Eden was in the crowd.

Chapter 17

I was frozen to the spot as I stared at my younger sister. My stomach plunged to my feet and bounced up so hard I choked. Eden was here. In Witch Haven!

My attempt to get through the crowd failed. People either didn't want to move as the carriage grew closer or were staring at the increasing number of people fleeing from the chaotic magic going on nearby.

I barged through, stamping on toes, getting yelled at, and being shoved. But I couldn't care about any of them. Eden was here. How? Where had she been? She must be looking for me.

My head spun with so many questions I got dizzy, but I kept moving.

As I got closer, she vanished in the crowd. I kept shoving and barging, my desperation making me sweat and cuss. "Eden! Stop."

She was moving away from me. Why was she running? Hadn't she seen me? Eden must have heard me calling her name. Why wasn't she stopping?

The crowd surged forward, and I got a glimpse of Fire Fang snapping at people and growling. I shoved through to the place I'd seen Eden, but she was gone, and I couldn't see her as the crowd surged around me. But she had to be close. I had to get to her.

"Eden!" I yelled at the top of my voice, causing several people to back away from me.

The chaos Fire Fang, Binky, and Pepin were causing wasn't helping me. People were running onto the road to avoid the magic and the snarling hellhound. I got slammed into several times.

I conjured an icy blast of wind and spun it around me, knocking people out of my path. There were more cries of alarm, but finally the route was clear.

In my haste, I almost missed Binky. She looked up, her expression one of confusion. She cocked her head and flicked her ears.

"I know! This isn't the plan. But did you see Eden? My sister is here. She must have run right past you."

Binky's ears flattened, and she hissed before sparkly magic shot out of her, causing more people to stagger away, blinded by her light.

"Storm!" Pepin was waving at me from across the street. "What's going on?"

"I've seen my sister." I didn't have time to explain. I scanned the crowd. Where had Eden gone?

"Storm!" Pepin pointed at the road, where Lady Arabella's carriage was well around the bend. If I didn't move now, I'd miss my chance to question her.

I took another desperate look around the crowd. My eyes hadn't been playing tricks on me. That was

Eden. Sure, an older version of my missing sister, but she was family. I'd know her anywhere.

"It has to happen now," Pepin said. "You won't get another chance like this."

My thoughts were as scattered as my magic as I shoved my hands out, fingers splayed and palms flat to the ground. There was no time for subtlety. An intense, drenching fog descended on the crowd in seconds. It was so thick, I couldn't see where I was going, but I found the road and soon the bend. I had to get on that carriage.

Still, I hesitated. What if Eden didn't stick around? And if she was back in Witch Haven, why hadn't she come to see me? She must be hiding for a reason. Was she ashamed of something she'd done?

I turned back, took a step, and stopped. None of this made sense. Should I chase the potential murderer and get answers or find the woman who looked like my sister?

No, that was Eden I'd seen. But what if I'd made a mistake? I'd done it before, chasing young women who looked like Eden, only to be disappointed. Was this another one of those times?

A shove from a panicking person got me moving, and my brain flipped out of freaking out mode. "Fire Fang! I need you."

He was by my side in an instant. "What's wrong?"

"Look for Eden while I deal with Lady Arabella. I think... no, I know I saw her. Can you sniff her out? She's here."

His eyes glowed through the fog. "I'll hunt for her. I won't let you down."

I was too choked to talk, so wrapped him in a hug. Then I sprinted after the carriage. This diamond wearing diva had better not waste my time, or she wouldn't be so sparkly when she got to the end of this trip.

Dodging past the almost rioting crowds, I saw the back of the carriage dimly through the fog. As Pepin predicted, two members of Lady Arabella's security team rode on the back, their hands wrapped around sturdy poles and their feet on narrow steps.

I took one guard out with a fierce blast of wind, sending him sailing to the side. The other guard tensed, his gaze narrowed as he peered through the fog. He fired out a spell, which I ducked, but another followed.

My hands spun, conjuring more wind, which I directed at him. But he was fast and bolted off the carriage, hit the ground, and charged me.

A tornado spell flew from my whirling fingers, capturing the guard and knocking him down. I raced past him, the carriage almost within my grasp.

My feet were smashed out from under me, and I hit the ground. Strong hands gripped my neck.

"Stay down, witch, if you value your life," an angry, rasping voice growled in my ear.

I pressed up off the ground, twisted, and slammed hailstones into the guard's face.

He yelped and batted them away with his magic.

My gaze shot to the retreating carriage. I had to speak to Lady Arabella. She couldn't get away.

From out of the fog, Pepin appeared. He clumsily thumped into the guard and sent him sprawling.

I snorted out my shock. Pepin was handy to have on my team.

"What are you doing, idiot?" the guard yelled at Pepin.

"You were hurting someone."

"A witch attacking the carriage. I'm protecting Lady Arabella. I'm part of her security detail. Get off me!"

I was off and running. I glanced over my shoulder. Pepin was doing an amazing job of looking like he was helping the guard up, but tripped and they went down again. I'd buy him a cookie if we got out of this mess in one piece.

My hands gripped the carriage door. I checked the driver and his companion. They were hunched over, intent on getting Lady Arabella to safety.

Spikes of protective magic flickered off the door, warning me to back off if I didn't want to get hurt. I pulled a scarf over my mouth and nose to conceal my face. I frosted my fingers with an ice spell, numbing the pain from the magic, flung the door open, and leaped inside.

"What is going on... Oh! Who are you?" Lady Arabella shrank back in her seat, her mint green eyes wide. She was a stunning older woman, her skin pearly with barely any lines and her mouth full. Nymphs aged slowly and always looked regal and elegant.

"Names don't matter. I need answers." I eased the door shut and sealed it with a locking spell, just in case Lady Arabella decided to be a heroine and throw herself out.

"How dare you!"

"I have no choice but to dare. Do you know Gaian Grimm?"

Her heart-shaped face scrunched up, and she sucked in air.

Before she could scream, I thumped her with a silence spell. "No need to make this unpleasant. I'm not here to hurt you, abduct you, or steal your jewels. I need answers about multiple murders. Murders you could be involved in."

Those pretty green eyes grew even larger. She tried to scream, but nothing came out.

I shrugged. "You can talk when I say. But listen, first. Gaian Grimm, Micky Cox, Edith Osman, Rose Starlight, and Shaman Goody are dead. These deaths are connected, and the connection comes back to your family. Maybe even to you and your love of pumpkin pie."

Her mouth opened and closed several times, but the anger in her gaze had lessened. It was replaced by curiosity and caution. She pointed at her gloss painted lips.

"No screaming. Or yelling."

She nodded, so I released the silence spell.

Lady Arabella cleared her throat, one hand on the sparkling blue gems around her neck. "Who are you?"

"Not important. Did you know any of the people who have been killed?"

"Why would I?"

"We can keep asking questions and not answering each other, but you won't like the outcome. I ask the questions. You answer them."

Bright spots of color flashed on her cheeks. "You impertinent witch."

"No, just a busy witch on a schedule. This carriage journey will end soon at your royal residence, and I don't want to injure more of your security while I escape."

Her small forehead wrinkled, and she straightened in her seat. "You're not here to harm me?"

"So long as you answer my questions, we'll get along fine. This was the quickest way to get to you."

Her lips pursed back and forth several times. "What do you need to know?"

"Let's start with Gaian Grimm."

"I'm acquainted with him."

"He's dead."

"I heard."

"His murder was set up to look like a spell he cast went wrong. He was murdered."

She blinked once and settled her gloved hands in her lap. "Continue. You mentioned others."

"Micky Cox?"

"I am not familiar with that gentleman."

"Also dead. Initially, it looked like he drowned. He was poisoned by a substance put in a pumpkin pie. Isn't that your favorite dessert?"

"One of them." She adjusted the cuffs of her gloves. "Why is that important?"

"We'll get to that. What about Edith Osman?"

"I don't know her."

"Shaman Goody?"

"Nor him."

"How about Rose Starlight?"

"The medium?"

"That's the one."

"Her death happened a long time ago. The royal circle still talks of her talent. I would have liked to know her."

"I doubt that."

That neat little forehead puckered again. "This is most perplexing. You steal my carriage and accuse me of murder. Why? It makes no sense." She sucked in a breath.

Before Lady Arabella could scream, I hit her with another silence spell.

"Nice try. People are being killed to hide a secret involving your family. Are you responsible?" I said.

She glowered at me, but shook her head.

"It involves your husband. On a scale of one to ten, how faithful is he? You can use your fingers to show me."

She held out all her fingers and thumbs.

"Does that mean you don't know about his first marriage or the child he had with Rose Starlight?"

More color flooded her face. She pointed at her mouth.

I arched an eyebrow. "No screaming."

She nodded, so I released the silence spell.

Lady Arabella drew in a slow breath. "My husband is loyal to me. He would never betray the family."

"A son proves otherwise. And I have the evidence to show your husband married Rose and they had a child together. A child who's now a grown man and a threat to your future. I think you've been erasing anyone who had knowledge of that union."

Several expressions crossed her face in quick succession. "I will admit my husband has his... lapses."

"Does that mean you knew about his marriage to Rose before you were together?"

She dismissed my question with a waft of her gloved fingers. "I want to meet this child."

"That's a terrible idea. You'll only try to have him killed again."

"Again! Someone has made an attempt on his life?"

"Keep up. Several, but they keep messing up. You should speak to your security about that."

"My security team is impeccable. If I had ordered these deaths, which I haven't, they would have been executed perfectly."

I cocked my head. "Is your security impeccable? You currently have a witch sitting in your carriage, questioning you about multiple murders. How did that happen?"

That cold glare settled on me again. "You must be powerful. Let me have your name. We could be of use to each other."

"Or you can use that information to come after me, too. You're missing the bigger picture. You've been linked to this investigation, and it won't be long before the Magic Council comes knocking. You won't be able to hide behind your security and title then."

She settled in her seat, not bothered by the murder word I kept shoving out. "Why do you assume I had anything to do with these deaths?"

"I've outlined why. Your husband married a woman before you, and she gave birth to a son. He's the eldest son. I'll let that sink in for a second."

Her glossy lips pursed a fraction. "If what you're saying is true, then he has a claim to the throne."

"Bull's-eye. Gold star for you. A mother would do anything to protect her children. If this claim turns out to be legitimate, which it is, it'll mean none of the children you've had with Lord Valdemar will sit on the throne. Unless, of course, the eldest son dies."

A sharp tut shot out of her. "I'm aware of protocol and lineage entitlements. Although my husband can be a foolish man, he wouldn't keep this from me. It's too important."

"He has. But you found out. How?"

"I know nothing about this affair or the child. Even if I did, I wouldn't order people's murders because they also knew about it."

"Everyone knows the Grimlows are fiercely proud of their reputation. You cover scandals as thickly as I spread cherry cream on a scone. You don't want anything to tarnish your reputation. If that happened, there'd be someone waiting to fill the void once your fingers slipped off the greasy power wheel."

Lady Arabella was silent for a moment, her gaze shifting to the window of the carriage.

I slid a glance that way, too. The fog was thinning as my control wavered. It took a lot to hold a powerful weather spell in place for any length of time, and I wasn't operating on full strength. My thoughts were also scattered as I kept thinking about Eden and whether Fire Fang had found her.

Lady Arabella returned her attention to me. "I can see, if you were looking at this situation from the outside, perhaps I have a small motive for keeping this unpleasant matter quiet."

"A matter that would shatter everything you've known and boot your cheating husband off his royal seat, taking you with him."

"Yes." She hissed out the word. "But I didn't kill those people. We have methods for ensuring silence. People always require things, money, or a new situation. Those are within my power to grant. I prefer the carrot rather than the stick method. Whipping someone into submission never keeps them silent for long."

"Murder would, though."

Lady Arabella smoothed her silk dress over her knees. "It would, but if I'd discovered my husband's betrayal, I would have ensured the people involved had an incentive for keeping quiet. Perhaps I would have gifted the shaman his own sanctuary or Gaian a privileged royal placement."

"This must be the biggest secret you've ever stumbled across. You couldn't risk it ever being revealed."

"Yet it has been revealed, which means I knew nothing about it until you told me. And I'm still not sure I should believe you. Give me a reason to trust you."

"I risked my life to get in this carriage and question you. I'm not doing this for a dare."

"It is risky going up against me and my family." Her gaze traveled over me. "What do you get out of this?"

"I owed someone a favor. This is me repaying the debt. And I don't like killers getting away with their crimes. No matter their status, everyone needs to play by the rules."

"Something I think you don't do. You wouldn't be inside my carriage, risking everything you have, if you did."

My thoughts flashed to Eden. I was risking losing her by being here, but I had to trust my friends. If she was out there, Fire Fang would find her. He wouldn't stop looking for her until he did.

"Ah! I've hit a nerve. You are taking a risk by being here. What do you have to lose?"

"We all have nerves that don't like being tickled. Just like we all have secrets. You found out your husband's dirtiest secret, didn't you?"

Irritation flashed across Lady Arabella's face. "No! When did these people die? Was it a freak accident that took them out?"

"Aside from Rose Starlight, they've been picked off one by one over the last few months. Edith Osman was first. Apparently, a natural death, but the Magic Council is re-opening her case to look at what killed her. Then Shaman Goody, apparently by a misfiring spell. The same with Gaian, and that was only a few days ago. Then Micky Cox was pulled from Serpent Lake. The autopsy revealed he was poisoned by a pumpkin pie."

"You keep coming back to this pie."

"Is it your calling card? You sent a signal to your husband that you knew what he'd done, and you were responsible for murdering his eldest son."

She drew in a sharp breath, one hand pressing against her stomach. "This Micky Cox you speak of was my husband's secret child?"

"That must have been what the person you sent to kill him thought, but they didn't get it right."

"You've lost me. Is the young man still alive or not?"

"You know he's still out there. You keep sending people to get him. Fortunately for him, they failed. And they'll keep failing while I'm involved."

Lady Arabella huffed out a tiny snort of indignation. "You can't possibly connect me to any of this. And it's clear from what you've told me, other people are involved in these murders."

"Of course. I don't expect a Lady to bloody her hands by ending another person's life. But you give the orders, and they get carried out. And I've spoken to your head of security. Fritz demonstrated that's exactly what he does every day. The rest of your team will be the same. I expect you pay well for loyalty and silence."

"Which means you can prove nothing. I could give half a dozen alibis, and it wouldn't help you in this situation."

"How about, instead of an alibi, you give me a confession? This has gotten messy, and everything will spill out soon. It can be done discreetly in negotiation with the Magic Council and the Embassy, or it can be splashed over the tabloids for the world to see what kind of lady you really are. It'll ruin your reputation, get you put in jail, sully your children's reputations, and your husband will look like an unfaithful, disloyal ruler. I know what I'd do if I was in your situation."

I got another tiny snort at that statement. "You have no understanding of what it takes to maintain this position."

"I'm guessing murder."

"No! Stop saying that. You barge in here and accuse me of scandalous things, you throw around accusations about my husband and a ridiculous lie about some child with a dead medium, and I'm expected to take it? You want me to raise my hands and beg for mercy? I'm a Grimlow. We do not grovel."

"Maybe you will when you figure out a plea bargain." Lady Arabella was a tough cookie, but there must be a chink in her silken armor. A way to get her to break. "Let's start with your alibi for Gaian Grimm. He died eight days ago. What were you doing then?"

A glint of satisfaction lit her eyes. "I can tell you precisely where I was. I was giving back to my loyal subjects. I'd planned a weekend of supporter events. A public dinner, a series of processions, much like this one, and a formal meet and greet with a few fortunate individuals. They got to be in the same room with me and ask me a question. I was the star of the show. Thousands of people witnessed me there."

"What about your security team? The ones most loyal to you? Who was missing?"

"No one. My team stays with me the whole time. Partly to ward off situations like this. You really are wasting both of our times, Miss..."

"Nice try. You don't get my details. I know what you're like when someone gets on your wrong side." I slid a finger across my throat.

She tutted at me again. "It appears we've hit an impasse. You think I'm guilty, I know I'm innocent, and you have no evidence to show otherwise."

"There are multiple murders I'm certain you're involved in," I said. "And I will find the evidence to make sure you pay for your crimes. I may even start with pumpkin pie. Someone made that pie with the poison in it and made sure it got into the victim's hands. You wouldn't have made it, and I doubt you slipped in the poison yourself. Although maybe you did, to make sure the dose was strong enough. I'll work back to the source of the pie. I'll ask about the order and if you showed any special interest."

Lady Arabella glanced out the window again. "This dreadful weather has ruined the procession. As has your presence."

"Happy to oblige. Think of me the next time you eat pumpkin pie. It may be your downfall." Sweat slid down the side of my face. I was losing my grip on the fog spell, but I was done with Lady Arabella.

I checked the guards driving the carriage weren't paying any attention, unlocked the door, and leaped out. I'd only made it a few steps before Lady Arabella screamed. I intensified the fog to cover my tracks and dashed away.

I needed to check her alibi, but that still wouldn't clear her name. I didn't yet know how to prove she'd given the orders to kill Chance with a poisoned pie and dispatch everyone else, but there had to be a way through.

This was one tangled, murderous mess Lady Arabella was mixed up in, but there'd be a loose thread. If I tugged on it long enough, all the dirty secrets would tumble out.

But first, I had to get back and find Eden.

Chapter 18

As planned, I returned to our designated meeting spot, my office. Pepin was there, along with Binky and Chance, but there was no sign of Fire Fang. My heart lurched. He must still be looking for Eden. That wasn't a good sign. If he hadn't found her, maybe she'd disappeared again.

"What happened out there?" Pepin marched over, blocking my way to an enticingly empty mug that was begging to be filled with coffee. "You didn't follow the plan. You said to follow the plan, and we'd be fine. I had to fight. I don't like fighting. And lie. Who were you chasing in the crowd? Did you even get to the carriage?"

"Cool your heels. It worked out. I got to Lady Arabella, and we had a chat."

"It was chaos out there." Pepin looked like he wanted to shake me. Wisely, he didn't.

"Which was exactly what we needed." I edged past him and grabbed my mug. "Binky, where's Fire Fang?" Why was I talking to a cat who couldn't talk back? My synapses were fried.

"Storm! Why were you running away from the carriage?" Pepin followed me like he was my shadow.

I eased into a seat and shooed him out of my personal space. The coffee would have to wait. "It's a complicated story."

He paced the room. "We shouldn't have done this. The guard I tackled was suspicious, even when I explained that I thought he was attacking an innocent person."

I rolled my shoulders to ease the tension in my back. "I appreciate the save. Lady Arabella doesn't mess around with her security. The guy I tackled had powerful magic and was planning to use it on me."

"Of course he would." He chewed on his bottom lip. "When I saw you were in trouble, I couldn't abandon you. It was scary, though. The guard questioned me for several minutes. I eventually pulled out the diplomacy card and made up nonsense about a threat being called in at the last second, and I overreacted. And of course, the fog made it difficult for me to see clearly. I acted muddled. It wasn't difficult to do. I was muddled."

"Since you haven't been arrested, it looks like you've gotten away with it," I said.

He tugged at his shirt collar. "I hope so."

"Did you find out if Lady Arabella wants me dead?" Chance said.

Before I answered, Fire Fang loped through the door, a sorrowful look on his fuzzy face.

I jumped up. "Did you find her?"

He shook his head. "If she was here, she's already left."

"It was her. I don't get it. She must be out there." I walked to the door.

"Who are you talking about?" Pepin said.

I glanced at him but shook my head. He'd saved me once or twice, but I didn't know him well enough to share my struggles.

"Storm, if this involves the investigation—"

"It doesn't. It's a private matter. A family matter. I thought I saw someone I knew, but maybe I was wrong."

"I'd have found her if she was here." Fire Fang nudged me back to my seat. Once I was settled, he rested his head on my lap.

I took several deep breaths. "I need to take a break from this."

Pepin and Chance exchanged worried looks.

"Should I get food?" Pepin said. "We're all stressed after what happened. We'll eat, debrief, and—"

"No. I mean, from this investigation. I have other things in my life I must focus on. If I hadn't been distracted by this case, I wouldn't have messed up with Eden."

"You're giving up on me?" Chance's bottom lip trembled.

"I might have to. And you know about Eden. This is everything to me. I was stupid to chase that carriage. I messed up."

"You didn't mess up," Fire Fang said. "And if she's back, she'll find you. Eden knows you're here, and even if she doesn't know where you live now, all she has to do is ask around. Everyone knows where your office and apartment are."

Pepin cleared his throat and shifted his weight from foot to foot. "Eden Winter? Your sister?"

I shot him a glare. "What do you know about her?"

Sympathy fizzled across his face. "I'm aware of your loss. I heard your younger sister vanished one night. I'm sorry."

My hands formed into fists. "Who have you been talking to about my private business?"

Pepin backed away. "Don't take offence, but in my line of work, it pays to run checks on anyone I have dealings with. Working in the diplomatic sector, it's common for people to exploit you. They know of my connections with influential figures and fake a friendship or pretend they can help me. Then suddenly, they're wanting access to contact lists or a meeting with an influential individual. Olympus asked me to step into this role and told me who you were, and I acted on automatic pilot. Of course, there are records of your sister's disappearance at the Magic Council. It came up when I ran my search. I wasn't snooping."

"And I expect Olympus told you all about it, too."

"He mentioned it. But only because he wanted me to have the full story. We weren't gossiping about you. It's a terrible thing to happen."

I nodded, too lost in my thoughts to contribute anything valuable to the conversation. I'd been too busy, not recharging my magic as often as I should, sleeping odd hours, and this was the result. I'd made a terrible choice.

"We'll find her," Fire Fang grumbled.

Had I made an error and imagined Eden in that crowd? I was so desperate to find her, my brain was playing tricks on me. I needed time to think, but I didn't have that luxury.

"If I may ask, how did you know it was Eden you saw?" Pepin said. "I believe it has been some time since you last saw her."

"It's been more than a decade. And I can't explain how I knew, but it was like a whack to the head. It was her. At least, I think it was. I'm not so sure anymore. If it was Eden, why did she run? I yelled her name several times. She must have heard. And then she just vanished. It must have been a magic trick."

"Have you changed much in appearance over the years?" Chance said. "Maybe she didn't recognize you."

"I've gotten taller. My hair's shorter. That's about it."

"It was crowded on the streets, and with Fire Fang and Binky stirring up panic, maybe she simply didn't hear you," Pepin said.

"It could be that. Or it could be, I should follow my friends' advice, take time off, and have a couple of weeks at a spa retreat. Recharge the batteries. Then I wouldn't keep slipping up." My nose wrinkled. If I did that, I'd die of boredom.

"While you go get a spa, I could be killed," Chance muttered.

"Then you should learn to take better care of yourself."

He looked down at his hands. "Yeah, maybe I should. If I survive."

"I'm sorry I snapped at you," Pepin said. "I was surprised when you didn't follow the plan. But I understand now. I'd be exactly the same. And... I know how you feel."

"You've had a sister abducted in the middle of the night and never heard from her again?"

"Not quite. But when I was a teenager, a good friend, Billy, went missing one day. We'd been out on our bikes, riding around aimlessly as you do when you're kids. We split up to go home, but Billy never made it. His bike was found at the side of the road, but there was no sign of him. His dad searched for him for ages, and we all helped, but it was as if someone scooped him up and he was gone. I never found out what happened. I sometimes wonder about it. You always do, don't you, when something that shocking happens?"

My anger and frustration faded. We all had twisted, unhappy messes in our pasts. "I know I do. I think about Eden every day. I wonder what she's been through and the struggles she's faced. She was young when she was taken, so I even wonder if she remembers her early years. Remembers me."

"With such an amazing sister, she'd remember you." Pepin gave me a nod of encouragement. "You have a bond. She'd know you'd never give up looking for her."

I rubbed my hazy eyes. "I hope she does. And thanks, I appreciate that. I didn't mean to abandon the plan, but at least I got to speak to Lady Arabella."

A hopeful look entered his eyes. "Did she tell you anything useful?"

I was about to respond when my phone rang. It was Laris. I answered it and put it on speakerphone. "Your timing is perfect. Everyone's here. And I just got back from speaking to Lady Arabella."

"She granted you an audience?" Laris said.

I smirked at Pepin and winked. "In a way. It was more of an informal meeting."

"And how did she react to your no doubt blunt questioning?"

"I had to silence her a couple of times. Lady Arabella is a screamer, but she admitted her husband has lapses. Though she wouldn't admit to knowing he married Rose and they'd had a child together."

"Did you sense she was lying?"

"I got a sense she'd do whatever she had to do to protect her family and their reputation. And I wouldn't like to be Lord Valdemar when she gets home. If she didn't already know about Chance, she'll be livid. It'll take more than a few diamonds to make up for this indiscretion."

"You didn't mention Chance, did you?" Laris said.

"I didn't mention his name, but I brought up Micky and the poisoning. Besides, she knows Chance is still alive, since people keep trying to kill him. Lady Arabella admitted to knowing Gaian and being aware of Rose Starlight's reputation, too. She claims not to have known Edith, Micky, or Shaman Goody. But of course, she'd only have to have heard of them and realized they knew her husband's secrets to organize their murders. She'd never have needed to meet them to get the deed done. The life of the privileged."

"All of which makes it difficult to pin anything on her," Laris said.

"It does. I checked her alibi for Gaian's death. She claimed to be on a fan retreat."

"She loves those," Pepin said. "Lady Arabella adores nothing more than people fawning over her. She insists on having one every month. She books an exclusive venue, hires an entire floor for herself and her retinue, sits on a pearl glazed throne that's brought to every event, and lords it over her wide-eyed fans."

"It'll be easy to check if she was there, but we also need to get to her security. If she gave orders to have Gaian and everyone else killed, it must have been to someone from her inside circle," I said.

"Lady Arabella handpicks her security," Laris said. "And she is quick to remove anyone who even hints at disloyalty."

"Can we get to them? Would Fritz order them to tell the truth?"

"His loyalties are with the family. If he thinks a member of the security team is planning to reveal a secret Lady Arabella needs keeping, he'll order their silence. You won't get anything out of them."

"I need to check her alibi, anyway, and then figure out if she's lying."

"Did she seem shocked when you told her about Lord Valdemar's marriage to Rose?" Laris said.

"She did. And she was angry. She could be covering, though. I need to keep digging. But... we can't overlook other avenues. An associate of mine said the servants love to talk. They overhear things.

Maybe a chat with servants closest to the family will uncover something new."

"You could try, but most of them are fearful of the family. They won't say anything to risk their jobs and potentially their lives," Pepin said. "I... err... I have another avenue we may consider exploring."

"Other than the Grimlows?" I said.

His face was pale as he nodded. "I've been thinking about this ever since I learned what was occurring, but hoped it wasn't true. Because if it is, it could mean war."

"War! This is serious. Go on," I said.

"There are rival factions keen on removing the Grimlows from power and taking their seat. A royal baby scandal would give them the ammunition to plant doubt in other ruling families' minds, cause public unrest, and strengthen their position. The Grimlows would fight back, and the unrest would grow. If it wasn't dealt with swiftly, well, the outcome would be unpleasant for a lot of us."

"Who most wants to get rid of the Grimlows and take their place?" I said.

Pepin chewed on his bottom lip. "The Fagan clan."

Chapter 19

"It's confirmed. Lady Arabella was at the event just like she said she was. I've spoken to three people who were there, and they told me the same story. She arrived in her golden carriage, swept into the hotel, and spent the evenings with her loyal following." Laris was perched on a seat in front of me.

He'd joined us after our earlier conversation to help with alibi checking and scouting other suspects in this mess of a mystery.

"I'm still not sure about her innocence. Lady Arabella must have had an opportunity to pass on orders or check in with whoever she sent to poison Chance." My feet were up on my desk in the office.

"Possibly, but she stayed out of the actual business of murder." Pepin hovered by my desk like a nervous fairy. "Those I spoke to said Lady Arabella behaved normally during the event. Surely, if she anticipated receiving a report about whether her husband's secret love child had been killed, she'd have been on edge. Snappier than usual."

"Not if she makes killing people a habit." I kicked back in my seat and sighed. I was tired, and hunting for clues about Lady Arabella's guilt was getting us nowhere. "She has a loyal following who would lie about her behavior."

"Also true," Pepin said.

"And I expect if anyone ever says anything bad about her, they find themselves out of a job and blacklisted everywhere." I still had an inkling about Lady Arabella's guilt, but I couldn't lose sight of the other suspects. "She isn't the only one interested in silencing Chance, though."

"Which means it's still not safe for me to leave." Chance was hunched in a seat in the corner, looking morosely into a box of out-of-date crackers he'd found in my kitchen cupboard.

"You can leave any time you like. I don't reckon your chances out there on your own, though," I said.

"I know you don't want to keep looking after me. You've made that clear." He was still sulking after I'd snapped at him.

I studied the picture of Eden on my desk. "My life would be easier if you weren't around." Still, I took pity on the sad-faced idiot. "But I owe Laris, and I hate having a puzzle I can't solve. I'll see this through to the end. But the end had better come quickly."

A sunny smile lit his face. "Thanks, Storm. I don't know what I'd have done if I hadn't met you."

"You'd be dead, goblin nobble," Fire Fang growled from his position by the office door. Binky was sprawled next to him.

Fire Fang had been moping ever since the royal procession debacle. I could tell he felt guilty about not finding Eden. The more I thought about it, the more I realized I was the one at fault. I'd been so shocked at seeing that woman, my brain had malfunctioned for a second. I'd added up the clues and arrived at the wrong answer.

It couldn't have been Eden. There was no way she'd return to Witch Haven and not find me straight away.

"I... err... I've been doing some discrete digging," Pepin said. "And I think you're right."

"I usually am. About what, in particular?" I said.

"The Fagan clan could be involved with this."

"You were the one who mentioned them, not me. Although Laris has also discussed their desire to destroy the Grimlows. I don't disagree with either of you, but I'm not super friendly with high-powered elites, even the rough around the edges ones like the Fagan family. That's why you're here. You know everyone who's anyone."

"Right. And Laris is correct. The Fagan clan causes the most problems for the Grimlows. They've been antagonizing each other for centuries."

"What got the feud started?" I said.

"It began so long ago, no one is certain. But they submitted a proposal to the collective royal families less than a year ago, stating the Grimlows weren't fit to rule. They wanted them removed and would take their place. They claimed they were greedy and corrupt and couldn't be trusted. But the most interesting part was that they said Lord Valdemar was disloyal to his wife. And they said they had proof of his infidelity."

That had me interested. "Did this proof ever appear?"

"Not that I know of. But matters this sensitive are dealt with behind closed doors in the strictest of privacy. The report came through the proper channels, and my department was poised to get involved. As you can imagine, the Grimlows were furious about the allegation and demanded it be retracted."

"If the Fagan clan had proof, they'd have revealed it," I said. "Was it a bluff? Or do you think they know about Chance?" I glanced his way. He was eating a stale cracker.

"I'm not certain. Perhaps we should find out. Or do you plan to focus only on Lady Arabella as the killer?"

"Nope. Since we're getting nowhere with her Royal Ice Queen, let's explore the Fagans. Lady Arabella stays on the radar, but until I can get proof of her involvement, we keep looking. Let's go visit the Fagan clan."

"It's not as easy as that. You don't go to a member of the Fagan clan and have a friendly chat," Pepin said.

My right eyebrow arched. "I never said the chat would be friendly."

"If they learn you're investigating the Grimlows, they could try to turn you. Force you to join them."

"This witch is not for turning. And if they try, they'll regret it. Where do I find the head of the family?"

Pepin worried the cuffs of his shirt. "Sirius Fagan lives in Lonewood Sanctum."

Fire Fang lurched to his feet, sending Binky scurrying away. "Don't go there."

"Why? It's no worse than the places I've been to on other cases. You've been with me for most of them. Remember Bog Valley and the demons?"

He stalked toward me. "I have a bad feeling about that place."

"Have you ever been there?"

Fire Fang hesitated. "I must have, but I don't remember when."

"Pre-hellhound days, maybe?" I still had the thorny issue of telling Fire Fang he wasn't what he thought he was. But right now, I couldn't focus on that.

"Pre-hellhound?" Pepin said.

I waved away his question. "Only criminals and those evading the Magic Council enjoy Lonewood, but if that's where Sirius Fagan spends his time, that's where we're going. We can head there tomorrow."

"Let me make a formal introduction," Pepin said. "The Fagan clan has been attempting to enter the inner royal circle for years, so I have a number of connections. And they enjoy protocol. They'd see it as disrespectful if we showed up uninvited."

"Maybe they deserve disrespect. Especially if they're killing off people to get to Chance."

"Why would they do that?" Chance said. "They can't want me dead, since I'm proof Lord Valdemar was married to Rose, and they had me."

He had a point. Maybe those crackers he was munching on weren't so stale, if they got him thinking. "They could be removing roadblocks.

People who sided with the Grimlows to keep the secret. Or they wanted you to believe the Grimlows were killing off those closest to you, in the hopes it would turn you against them."

"And make Chance side with the Fagan clan," Pepin said. "That would work. If they had Chance on their side, it would strengthen their cause. They want to put him on the throne to act as their puppet."

"I'm no one's puppet," Chance said.

"You look more muppet than puppet to me," Fire Fang said.

"As I keep telling everyone, I want to go back to my simple life. I don't want a throne and all the responsibility that goes with it," Chance said. "I'm not good at being responsible."

"Pepin, set up a meeting with Sirius Fagan. Let's see what he has to say," I said.

Pepin looked unhappy with his task, but nodded. "I'll see what I can do."

I stifled a yawn behind one hand. "Now, I suggest everyone go home, take a break, and get some sleep. We'll tackle the Fagan clan in the morning."

***

I hadn't meant to oversleep, but the previous day's exertions had exhausted me. I'd slept through my alarm, and only Fire Fang and Binky repeatedly nudging me because they were hungry stirred me from my bed.

I felt better after a long sleep, but my magic still didn't feel at its peak. I really was considering a spa retreat. Every time I took a five-minute break here, something came up that needed my attention. Going somewhere where no one knew me and shutting off my phone wouldn't be a bad idea.

"I'm still hating the idea of going to Lonewood Sanctum." Fire Fang padded after me as I filled food and water bowls.

"Maybe we won't have to. We can bring the Fagan clan here. Everyone in Witch Haven would love to meet shady, power hungry magic users like Sirius."

Fire Fang grumbled. "I've been doing my research. They've spent most of their lives fighting with one royal family or another. They're desperate for a royal seat. And the last fight they had got bloody. Lives were lost."

"When did you do your research?" I sipped a welcome mug of coffee.

"While you were sleeping. Sirius Fagan is a donkey helmet. He's been arrested for dozens of crimes but only charged with a couple of minor ones. He's a slippery eel with the soul of a grimy demon."

"When you have the right connections, you can literally get away with murder," I said. "Unfortunately for him, we're on the case, so if Sirius is involved, he won't get away with it."

Chance was still huddled on the couch under a blanket. "Fire Fang made me read through the research, too. I want nothing to do with Sirius."

"Which is ideal, because you're not going to this meeting. It's too risky."

"But I need fresh air. This place smells musty. And you have terrible snacks."

"Then make yourself useful and do some cleaning," I said. "And order in groceries. Get what you like. I have an account at the local store."

His nose wrinkled. "Is there any coffee for me?"

"It depends. If you give this place a clean, you can have coffee. But no touching my stuff. And stay out of my bedroom."

"I'll clean if I get bored."

"You should clean to return the favor of me keeping your sorry behind alive. I'm facing off with some seriously bad people to do it."

Chance shuffled upright, his blond hair messy. "Sorry. I do appreciate it. And I know I'm complaining, but I'm scared and don't know who to trust. Do the Grimlows want me dead, or does the Fagan clan need a puppet to do their bidding? Or someone else? Someone we haven't thought of yet. We should never have found out I have a royal father. I preferred it when it was just Aunt Edith and an air of mystery."

"Do you really want nothing to do with your royal heritage?" I took him a mug of coffee and sat next to him on the couch.

"Would you? Being part of such a family sounds like a nightmare. I wouldn't mind a bit of the money, but that's it. Pepin was right. The Fagan clan is bloodthirsty. They see weakness and attack. The Grimlows are no different."

"Sirius Fagan and his power hungry goons may not even be involved. It's just another avenue to investigate. And I'll make sure they don't know where to find you."

His smile was timid, but at least it was there. "If you do that, then I will clean this place."

"And I'll make sure you don't get killed today." I bumped my mug against his.

After a quick breakfast, shower, and change of clothes, I was ready to go. I was about to call Pepin when he arrived in my office.

"From the anxious look on your face, I take it you contacted the Fagan clan," I said.

He hurried in, hands clasped, top lip sweaty, face pale. "Sirius agreed to meet today. But I couldn't get him to budge on the location. He wants to meet on his home turf in Lonewood Sanctum."

"I figured he would. Let's go see what he has to say about murder."

A quick check of the location and one translocation spell later took us to the boundary outside Lonewood. Magic acted strangely in this place. Spells warped and potions misfired, so I'd need to be careful about conjuring powerful weather spells if things got difficult. It was probably the reason Sirius chose this place. It gave him the upper hand. Or so he thought.

A skinny guy with a crewcut and a green and black tattoo running up his neck appeared by the border. "State your purpose."

"We're here to see Sirius Fagan," Pepin said. "We have a meeting arranged."

The guy checked our IDs and pointed at Fire Fang and Binky. "No familiars. They wait here."

"That's what you think, goblin nobble." Fire Fang advanced but only made it a few steps before a repelling spell knocked him back and he almost slammed into Binky.

"Hey! There's no need for that." I checked Fire Fang was okay, but he was already on his feet, growling menacingly at the guy.

"That's the rules. None of us have our familiars in here."

"Don't do this," Fire Fang said to me. "You need me by your side."

"We're just going in to talk. You stay with Binky. We won't be long. If there's any sign of trouble, I'll conjure a lightning bolt. That'll be your cue to move."

Fire Fang growled his unhappiness, but then settled in beside Binky.

The tattooed guy led us a short distance across the border to a gray building with a sagging roof and an air of hopelessness drifting from its dank walls. He took us inside, through low-ceilinged rooms, and into a back room that was brightly lit with candles. It looked almost homey, with its velvet couch and dried floral wreaths on the walls.

Sitting at a wooden table was a handsome guy, a scar slashed across one cheek, and a twinkle in his dark eyes. He stood when we entered the room. "That'll be all." He dismissed tattoo guy.

I stood beside Pepin, whose nervous energy wasn't enjoyable, and eyeballed Sirius.

He extended his hand. "Pepin Flowerbottom. I've lost count of the number of letters you've sent me over the years. It's nice to meet the man with such fine penmanship."

Pepin hesitated, then shook Sirius's hand. "We appreciate you taking the time to meet us."

"I couldn't resist when I heard you needed to discuss a murder." Sirius's attention turned to me. "And you must be Storm Winter."

I had manners, so I shook his hand. "That's right. I've been hearing about your interest in claiming a royal seat."

"Not so fast. Just because I don't have a royal seat doesn't mean I sidestep the royal hospitality. Please, make yourselves at home." Sirius poured spicy smelling drinks and handed them around. He settled in a seat at the table, and we joined him. "To your good health."

I sniffed the drink and took a tentative sip after he'd drunk from his own glass. It was sweet with a clove aftertaste. Not unpleasant. I set down my glass.

"Pepin was good enough to give me some background as to why you wished to meet. Although the details were light," Sirius said. "I have a feeling I only received part of the story. What did he leave out?"

"I suspect you know the answer to that," I said.

"Perhaps. But I'm interested in your input. A witch with your reputation wouldn't be involved if this wasn't a serious case."

"All the cases I work on are serious, whether it's a familiar being stolen or a lost wallet."

Amusement glinted in Sirius's eyes. "A true professional. But I need to know everything, or I won't be able to help." He leaned back in his seat and rested his hands behind his head.

"How much do you already know?" I knew Pepin had kept things vague when arranging this meeting.

"I'm aware this has something to do with the Grimlows. It's the main reason I let you visit. The more dirt we get about those scam artists, the better."

I looked at Pepin fidgeting in his seat. He wasn't going to be much help. So much for his diplomacy skills. "You recently claimed the Grimlows aren't to be trusted, and you have proof of infidelity on Lord Valdemar's part. You never followed through with that claim. I'd be interested in knowing what your proof was."

A thick eyebrow arched. "Interesting."

"Do you have proof, or were you taking a chance someone would slip up and tell you something they shouldn't?"

"We heard rumors and wanted to see how far they'd take us."

"Who were those rumors about?"

"More like what." Sirius sipped his drink, taking an annoyingly long time to set his glass down. "An affair and a subsequent child. I was intrigued and looked into it, but I kept hitting dead ends. Convenient dead ends."

"Convenient how?"

"Everything was too neat and tidy. Life isn't like that. When someone dies or disappears, I'm always suspicious."

"Whose death did you think was too neat and tidy?"

The thick eyebrow arched again. "Do I get to ask questions?"

"You just did."

Sirius's smile tightened. "I'll share my secrets if you share yours."

"That depends how good your secrets are."

He considered his options. "Do you know the name Rose Starlight?"

I kept my expression neutral. So Sirius had been looking into Chance, following the same path as me, but hadn't gotten as far. "I do. She used to be a medium."

"An acclaimed medium, desired by many members of the royal circle. Her beauty was as coveted as her ability to contact anyone who'd passed over. And it's believed she formed an intimate acquaintance with someone she shouldn't. A child was born and hidden away. Or maybe... disappeared."

"Is that where your rumors led you?"

"Like I said, they led to neat little dead ends tied up with a cute bow, so no one would think to ask anything else."

"Why submit the report with no evidence? It made you look dumb."

Pepin made a raspy cough in the back of his throat. I'd have to get him throat lozenges if it didn't clear up.

"We submitted the report in the hope we'd find definitive proof soon after," Sirius said.

"How's that going?"

He looked away. "We're still searching. And we'll continue to do so."

No one spoke for a long minute.

"What if I told you there was a baby?" I said. How would Sirius react when he learned the truth?

Pepin rapidly cleared his throat again, alarm crossing his face.

Sirius shifted in his seat. "Then I'd want to meet this child. Well, the grown adult. The person ready to take their rightful place."

"And would that rightful place be with you or the Grimlows?"

He inclined his head. "We think alike."

"I don't think like a criminal."

"You must, in order to catch them. Surely, this person, what's his name..."

I shrugged.

Sirius chuckled. "I had to try. This person wouldn't associate with the family that abandoned him. Or her. Can I know their gender?"

"It's not relevant."

"I'll assume male. He'd join us. We could protect him and ensure his rightful role was fulfilled."

"Why would you do that?"

"Kindness begets kindness."

"And favors. Let's assume this individual didn't know of his birthright. He grew up living a free and easy life. A life of simplicity. Why complicate things with royal rules and protocol?"

"He'd want everything available to him. It would be his duty."

"Not to you," I said.

"That would be his choice. This man could choose his family. Find a family that fits his values.

A family that would strive to make him the best he could be."

"If such a person existed, it would be just the scandal you needed to get access to a royal seat. Perhaps not for yourself, but if you had a pliable member of the Grimlows in your pocket, he would give you everything you desire."

Sirius pursed his lips. "He would. But it wouldn't be that simple. The Grimlows wouldn't step aside. They'd have to be forced out. And force involves violence. I don't want a war."

The way he'd lingered on the last word suggested that was exactly what he desired.

"You'd keep him safe?" I said.

"If there was a child, I'd protect him. Pepin will tell you how ruthless the Grimlows are."

Pepin mumbled an agreement. "They demand respect. They expect everyone to conform to their standards. A secret eldest son would be considered an abomination."

"All rightfully ruling families demand conformity." Sirius settled in his seat.

"Different monsters, same tyranny," I said.

He chuckled again. "I see you have little respect for our ruling classes."

"Some aren't so terrible." I sipped more drink. "Maybe the offspring needs protecting from you. If you could, you'd abduct him and brainwash him into your way of thinking."

"He exists, doesn't he? This conversation isn't conjecture." Sirius rubbed his hands together slowly. "I would very much like an introduction. Pepin, will you make the arrangements?"

Pepin jolted upright. "I suspect that wouldn't be appropriate. Storm?"

Sirius cut me off before I could respond. "What's appropriate is for the other ruling families to learn how untrustworthy the Grimlows are."

"I suspect they already know that. But they like to keep their enemies close," I said.

Sirius's gaze flickered from Pepin to me and back again. He shrugged. "Storm, I see you're in charge here. What can I do to convince you to encourage this meeting?"

"Nothing. And we've jumped ahead. I need your alibi."

"To discount me from which particular investigation?"

"A murder. More than one."

A muscle in his jaw twitched. "I have nothing to hide."

"Where were you ten night ago?" I'd start with his alibi for Gaian's murder.

Sirius hesitated, then broke into a smile. "With two hundred of my closest friends, celebrating the ten-year anniversary of my leadership. We hired the bar on Westgate Row. The owner will confirm I was there all night. As will all the guests."

That still didn't make him innocent. Sirius had people who would tidy up any mess he needed fixing. But did it benefit him to kill people who knew the truth about Chance? Maybe he approached them, and when they refused to tell the truth, he murdered them. He must have been worried word of what he was attempting to do could get back to Chance and he'd vanish.

It was pointless to ask for more alibis. He'd have a cover story for all the murders.

"Will you tell me the name and location of the royal heir?" Sirius said.

I shook my head. "I'd be an idiot to do so."

"And you're not that. Unfortunately. I would suggest a payment, but you don't seem motivated by material things." His gaze flicked over my dirty boots and fraying jeans.

"I'm not." I glanced at Pepin. "Anything to add?"

He chewed on his bottom lip. "Thank you for your time."

There was another round of handshaking, Sirius squeezing my hand for a second too long, his sharp gaze on me.

I pulled away. Glares, veiled threats, and a show of strength wouldn't steer me off course. I was done with the information gathering. It was time to regroup and put together the pieces of this mystery. Someone out there was a murderous trickster, but I still had no idea who they were or how to prove it.

Chapter 20

I was up early the next morning. There was only the barest hint of pink in the sky as the night reluctantly gave way to a new day. I was on my second mug of coffee, a plate of toast crusts sitting beside me, and Binky tucked under the bend in my knees, where I'd hunched up my legs so I'd fit in the window nook.

I never enjoyed times like this. When I kept busy, I had no space for unwelcome thoughts to seep in and question me about what I was doing. Not about the case. I was certain I had the pieces to solve these murders. I just needed to get them in the right order. But in these quiet times, before the business of the day drove away the questions, my thoughts turned to Eden. And even more so since she'd appeared at the procession.

Every time I settled on that fact, tiny doubts crept in. Was I losing my mind? Had I imagined seeing her? We'd created bedlam to make people confused and panicked and report to the Magic Council they'd seen fictional bad guys running amok. Had I fed off that energy? I'd conjured the image of someone who couldn't have been in that crowd.

But Eden had to be somewhere. Why not here? Why not come home to be with me? I was the only family she had.

I picked up my coffee mug and realized it was empty. Just as empty as the well of hope in my heart. I'd been searching for such a long time and always promised myself I'd never give up on my sister. But if I was seeing things that couldn't be real, was that a sign that I had to draw a line under this and say goodbye to Eden?

My nose wrinkled, and I shook my head. I'd give up on Eden the day I stopped breathing. Even then, I might come back as a ghost and keep looking for her. I'd make an excellent ghost. Maybe I'd be a poltergeist.

Binky shuffled out from under my legs and settled herself next to me on the window ledge. She raised her head and blinked at me slowly.

"What do you think? As the newest member of this weird little team, do you have an opinion on my missing sister?"

Binky reached out a velveteen paw and rested it on my foot for a second.

"You're right. Never give up. Just like you. It took you long enough, but you got your way. You moved in, and all it took was months of howling, sneaking, and tricking me."

Her claws flashed out in a warning to my sass. Then she turned her back on me and flicked one ear.

"And I actually surprised myself. I don't hate you being here." I risked a stroke of her soft black head, and she leaned against my hand. "I'm not big on asking for assistance, but I know some people who'll help me figure out the next move with Eden." I lifted my phone and dialed Indigo's number. It rang and rang and then went to voicemail. I didn't leave a message. I tried Odessa and Luna next, but neither of them picked up.

Given the early hour, I could hardly blame them for not answering. I wasn't even sure what I'd say. I'm thinking of giving up on my baby sister. I know I promised my parents I'd always protect her, but it's gotten too hard.

And there was that tiny voice in the back of my head that whispered: *What about you? Don't you deserve a life? Don't you deserve to be happy?*

I always stamped on that treacherous voice. What right did I have to be happy when Eden was gone?

Instead, I texted Pepin and Laris. Finding a murderer was much simpler than dealing with my personal life.

I'm ready to move on figuring out who the killer is. Drop by as soon as you can.

I got a message back from Laris almost instantly.

I'm in court most of today. But call me when you get together, and I'll listen in.

Half an hour later, I got a message from Pepin.

I'm on my way. I'll bring breakfast.

It was probably his way of making up for being such a squashed sweet potato when we interviewed Sirius yesterday. He'd been shaking in his seat. Pepin must have been around plenty of powerful people in his line of work, but I was amazed he'd held down that job for so long, since influential people affected him so badly.

I collected my dirty dishes, freshened up, changed clothing, and was heading back into the lounge when there was a knock at the door.

I nudged a sleeping Chance, who was still huddled on the couch, before going to open it.

Pepin stood outside. He held up three large takeout mugs and a bag full of sweet smelling goodies. "Good morning."

"You're always welcome when you show up with food." I let him in, and once Chance had rolled off the couch and pulled the blanket he'd been sleeping under around his shoulders, we sat down.

When the warm pastries had been distributed and coffee was in hand, I called Laris.

"Storm. Perfect timing. We're starting soon, but I can spare a few minutes."

"Hey, Laris. I'm here with Chance and Pepin. Thought you might like an update on Gaian and the others."

"Of course. Although the gossip mill is already running wild about your visit to the Fagan clan."

I smiled ruefully. Laris had connections almost as good as me, but they were on the right side of the law. Mine, not so much. "You're correct. We went to see Sirius Fagan. He's excited about the prospect of Chance being real."

"He can get excited all he likes," Chance grumbled. "I'm planning on getting a magic disguise and changing my name if we don't figure this out soon."

I studied him for a second. His upbeat manner was being worn away by stress and having to sleep on a lumpy couch. And, of course, the ever looming threat of imminent death.

"What's your next plan of attack?" Laris said.

"I'd still like to dig into Lady Arabella's alibi some more. It's unlikely our dainty lady got her hands dirty by being there when the killings took place, but I want to make sure nothing was missed. Maybe someone overheard her at the event. She'd have to have given orders to confirm she wanted the murder to take place."

"What about her right-hand man in security, Fritz?" Laris said. "You didn't think he laid out all the information when you questioned him."

"Not that we expected him to. He could be guilty. He killed because someone ordered him to."

"But whose orders?" Laris said. "Lady Arabella or Lord Valdemar?"

"Or someone else," Pepin said.

"We need a chat with our philandering lord next. If Lady Arabella isn't pulling the strings, it must be him," I said.

"Ah! Then I have to disappoint you. We can't quiz any members of the Grimlow family," Pepin said. "A red line dictate went out last night. They've gone into a period of seclusion. They're doing no public events or meetings for the next two weeks. Talise Grimlow, the queen mother, ordered it. And what she says goes."

"Did they give a reason?" Laris said. "The last time that happened, the king was unwell. They didn't think he'd pull through."

"We're the reason they're hiding," I said. "The Grimlows are worried their secrets are about to be exposed. They must be scrambling to come up with a way to keep Chance hidden."

"It's not the line they're rolling out, but that makes sense," Pepin said. "They've simply said they need privacy to plan their next round of public events. They're promising their adoring followers something they'll never forget."

"They'll have fewer adoring followers when Lord Valdemar's secret marriage and love child is exposed," I said. "You're sure there's no way in to see him? Lord Valdemar must be curious about the baby he had with Rose."

"Why would he?" Chance said. "He assumed my true identity was a secret, even to me. I couldn't come after him if I didn't know about my background. And that must be why Aunt Edith kept me in the dark. She never wanted me knowing about any of this. Maybe the old girl cared for me after all."

"Perhaps she wasn't quite as unfair to you as you assumed," I said. "When you didn't know the truth, you weren't in danger."

"But Edith must have known there was still a risk. That information she left with Gaian about your birth and your father was kept as insurance. If anyone learned who you were, you could use that to protect yourself," Laris said.

"It's not done me much good so far."

"Because the other parties have the power," Laris said. "If you'd known this information first, you could have revealed it to the world. They would never have dared make a move on your life then. It would have been too obvious why you were killed and who orchestrated it."

"So we're focused on a member of the Grimlow family sanctioning these murders?" Pepin said.

"We've also got Sirius Fagan to consider. He had the most to gain by revealing Chance's true identity. If he'd gotten to you in time, he would have dripped poison into your ear about how terrible your parents were and how the Grimlows would misuse you," I said. "He'd have convinced you to join him, exposed the secret, and have you under his control. Even if he hadn't gained access to the royal circle, he'd have had you doing their bidding."

"Did Sirius tell you that when you met?" Laris said.

"He didn't have to, but he was close to learning the truth about Chance. He's been following the same clues we have. But someone was hiding the evidence. Too neatly, so he got suspicious."

"Now he knows I'm real, do you think he'll come for me?" Chance said.

"I won't sugarcoat this. I think he will. And even if he can't get to you, if he gets his hands on a copy of the marriage certificate between Rose and Lord Valdemar and your birth certificate, he'll achieve his aim. The Grimlows' reputation will be ruined."

"They'd hate that," Pepin said. "They pride themselves on being respectful and following family tradition."

"And by me being alive, it proves they're living a lie," Chance said. "I should vanish. There are spells that disguise appearance. I can get together some money, change my name, and start again somewhere else. Maybe after a while, whoever wants me dead will stop looking."

"Would that make you happy?" I said. "You'll spend your life looking over your shoulder. And these families have connections everywhere."

"There must be some out of the way place I can hide. Somewhere with a small casino, so I can still have fun. Make new friends."

"No fun for you. Casinos are too high profile. You'd draw attention to yourself. You could try something more sedate, like indoor bowls."

"I'm only thirty! I'm not ready for soft shoes and carpet bowls."

I held back a smile. "Do you really want to live under a magical disguise for the rest of your days? That takes work. You could never lose focus. or the disguise would slip."

"Stick with Storm," Pepin said. "She'll get to the bottom of this. And she'll keep you safe while she does it."

I shrugged. "I'll try not to get Chance killed, but that's as far as it goes."

"Storm is one of the few people I trust with my life," Laris said. "You're in the best place, Chance. I understand how difficult this is for you, but we have our suspects. We simply need evidence to convict one of them."

Chance nodded and flung the blanket over his head, hunching under it in a lonely ball of despair.

"Since access to the Grimlows is closed down, let's start at the bottom," I said. "I've been meaning to see if any servants of the Grimlow estate are willing to talk."

"They'll have been warned to keep their mouths shut." Pepin shook his head. "If word gets back to the family someone is still poking around, it'll mean trouble for you."

"I have no problem with trouble. And we need to keep moving forward. Pepin, where do the servants go when they take a break?"

"It varies. Who do you want to talk to?"

"Who's the most gossipy in the household?"

"None of them. They know better than that."

"They must grumble. Serving staff, cleaners, kitchen staff?"

He pondered the question for a few seconds. "There is Matilda. She's younger than most of the cleaners. And she does like to talk. I know she's had a warning about it. I heard her complaining."

"Can you get me in to see her?"

"I have no influence over that part of the household." Pepin clasped his hands together, his forehead wrinkling. "I can show you where the servants go in and out, though. Maybe you could follow Matilda or something. Do your PI thing and get her talking. But don't attempt a bribe. Anyone who offers money to staff of the household in exchange for information is reported. The informant is given a huge pay raise, so there's no incentive to talk for money."

"Got it. No bribery."

We finished the conversation, Laris went into court, Chance remained huddled under his blanket, and Pepin left for work.

That left me with the mission of how to get Matilda to talk. Gossipy girls weren't my forte, but with multiple murders to solve, I had to be flexible.

It was just before noon, and I'd set up a pop-up cake stand outside the back of the main Grimlow estate. I'd borrowed it from Luna's uncle, and it was laden with treats I'd bought from his bakery. Since the financial bribery angle wouldn't work, cake might sweeten up Matilda. Luna used this trick on people all the time. She'd sneak treats from her uncle's bakery and, over a shared love of delicious desserts, she'd pry out the information she needed.

I didn't have to wait long before people trickled out the staff door. They had to pass through security before they were on the street.

"Free samples from the new Candy, Cakes, and Chaos store. Opening soon." I passed the treats to eager freebie hunters. Pepin had told me what Matilda looked like, but she hadn't yet appeared.

A short redhead with curly hair and a scowl on her face stomped out. She turned and gestured at someone behind her to hurry up. "I told you I'd do it. She can't keep talking to me like that."

That was my target. Matilda looked like someone had sat on her favorite sandwich. Her face was pink and her eyes red, as if she'd been scrubbing them or crying.

"You can't quit and walk out. You won't get a reference." The woman behind her hurried along.

"See sense. Go back and talk to the boss. She'll understand. She's been around Lady Arabella long enough to know she has those funny moods."

"I'm not putting up with it anymore. She doesn't pay that well."

I stepped into their paths. "You look like you need a free treat." I thrust the tray of baked goodies at Matilda.

She halted and stared at the desserts. "Why are you giving these out?"

"We've got a new store opening soon. We're looking for feedback from potential customers. No charge. Try one." I attempted a sunny smile. It made my face hurt.

Matilda grabbed three cakes. "I'm stress eating."

Her friend took one, an apologetic expression on her face.

"Help yourself to more. You do seem stressed. Bad day at work?" I said.

"It's all I seem to have these days," Matilda said. "Mmmm, these are good. We should get some for the rest of the staff."

"Does that mean you're staying?" the other woman said.

"I still haven't decided." She pushed half a cherry slice into her mouth.

"Change your mind. Lady Arabella didn't do anything that terrible to you."

"She called me a dumpy slug." Matilda glanced at me, then tugged her friend away a few steps.

I pretended to refill the tray, straining to hear what they said.

"Everyone knows Lord Valdemar cheats, and we turn a blind eye and say nothing," Matilda said. "But I'm done with Lady Arabella's foul moods and talking down to me. And I've never seen her this bad. He must be cheating again to make her so vile. They can sort out their marital problems without me taking the brunt of those moods of hers."

I walked over with a few more treats, forcing a friendly expression to stick.

Matilda glared at me. "Something I can do you for?"

"I'm just about finished. Do you want these cakes? If you take them, it'll mean I don't have to carry them back to the store. I'll only have to throw them away when I get there."

"Don't mind if I do." Matilda grabbed more cakes, while her friend took one.

"Do you think the royal family might put in an order for something like this?" I tried to sound breathless with excitement about the prospect of giving cakes to the Grimlow family. "If I told my boss they were interested, it would be a gold star for me."

"Lady Arabella does have a sweet tooth," the other woman said. "She loves pumpkin pie."

"But she also insists on having those delicate little iced fancies in the carriage," Matilda said. "I'm surprised she's not twice the size she is. And she calls me dumpy."

"They're not for her. They're an incentive," her friend said.

"Oh! Of course. I wasn't thinking."

"Incentive for what?" I said.

Matilda popped the final cake into her mouth. "Lady-I'm-Too-Important-to-be-Civil hates those carriage rides. She tries to get out of them whenever she can. Sometimes, the queen mother insists she does them. But we know the truth." She winked at her companion.

Her friend tapped her arm. "Shush. You shouldn't be gossiping."

"I don't work there anymore. I can talk to whoever I like."

"You've lost me. Why doesn't Lady Arabella like taking carriage rides?" I said.

Matilda glanced around. "She thinks the public are common and smell funny. Sometimes, she does the bigger events, but... here's the big secret. She uses a lookalike for most of them. Even those weekend getaways she's always booking. Most people never get to see Lady Arabella up close, and her lookalike could be her twin."

I wasn't expecting that. "She has someone pretend to be her?"

"Yep. And her stand-in gets well paid and all the treats she can handle, so long as she keeps quiet about doing Lady Arabella's dogsbody work."

That meant Lady Arabella had given me a fake alibi. Why would she do that if she were innocent? She had something to hide.

"We should go." Matilda's friend caught hold of her arm before looking at me. "I'm not sure it'll do any good, but I'll mention your desserts to the housekeeper. Have you got a business card?"

"Um... Let me check." I was fumbling in my pocket for a fake card I didn't have when footsteps marched toward us. Fritz strode out of the service door and looked straight at me.

It was too late to hide, so I brazened it out.

"What are you doing here?" Fritz snapped at me.

"She's no trouble. She's just handing out desserts," Matilda said. "Finding her out here was a nice end to a horrible morning."

"You're up to something, witch." Fritz's gaze narrowed before his glare slid to Matilda. "Have you been talking to this woman?"

Matilda and her friend looked stunned by his sharpness as they shook their heads.

"Fritz, is it bad news? It's not your brother, is it?" Matilda placed a hand on the brawny man's arm. "Everyone's so worried about him. Any sightings?"

Fritz's glare softened a fraction. "No news, but thanks for asking. We're still looking. Plenty more places to try. And when I find Johan... well, he'll have explaining to do."

"We'd better go," the other woman said. "Even if you decide not to go back to work, I still have a job, and we only get half an hour for lunch. Come on."

Matilda patted Fritz's arm. "You'll find him. I'm sure it's nothing to worry about."

The women hurried away, leaving me with a tense-looking Fritz.

"Miss Winter, I hope you haven't been bothering the staff. They know better than to talk to troublemakers."

"Matilda just quit, so she can talk all she likes. What's going on with your brother?"

He stiffened. "It's none of your business."

"It sounds like he's missing. And I know a few things about that."

"Meaning?"

"Meaning, looking for missing persons is a specialty of mine. Maybe we can help each other out."

Chapter 21

"This had better not be a con." Fritz was hunkered next to me in an alleyway. We were watching people go in and out of a crumbling building with a gray front door that stuck whenever anyone opened it.

"I don't know how many times I have to tell you, but I can find your brother. I've found hundreds of missing people since I set up my business."

"I'm aware of your skills. I checked your background when you requested a meeting with me."

"So stop doubting me. Johan's name came up several times in this area. And this is a cheap, discreet, cash-in-hand place. People don't ask questions, so long as you can afford to stay."

"That information was told to you by drunks and idiots. It's unreliable."

"Drunks and idiots who were paid. And they know what'll happen to them if they lie to me. As you know, I have a reputation."

Fritz grumbled under his breath. "I'm just worried about Johan. This is unlike him. He always tells my parents where he's going. And we talk at least once a week on the phone. He's been silent for almost a month."

"Which means something is wrong, but he's alive."

"If your information is correct."

"It will be. Johan's keeping a low profile for some reason. Are you sure there haven't been any family arguments? Something to drive him out?"

"Nothing. We should go in," Fritz said. "Knock on doors. When I find him, I'll drag him out and back to my parents."

"No dragging. If Johan is hiding something, you charging in and yelling will scare him away. He'll hide the truth from you. Let's wait to see if he returns, and then we'll go in. But gently."

He grunted. "From what I've heard of you, you don't know how to do gently."

"That's because I'm usually pressed for time. But when there's a need for it, I use a softly-softly approach. Your brother might appreciate that."

Fritz was quiet for a moment. "I know my parents are worried about him, but they won't talk to me about it. They keep acting as if nothing is wrong."

"Do they know something and are keeping it from you?" I glanced at him, although I also kept half an eye on the door.

"They never talk about difficult subjects. Our parents are experts at putting on a brave face and pretending everything is fine."

"There's a time for that," I said. "It stops awkward emotional moments. They give me the chills."

"Your parents are emotionally cold, too?"

"Literally cold. They're dead."

"My apologies. That must have been a hard loss to bear."

I nodded. It had been, but I didn't think much about my parents anymore. I'd focused my energy on finding Eden. If I hadn't had her disappearance to obsess over, I'd have grieved more. But I lost all three of them the day Eden vanished. My parents retreated from the world, and they gave up on everything. They gave up on me.

Those thoughts got shoved away. "I get by. And I know how to find people who like staying in the shadows. That's what you should concern yourself about, not if I got all the hugs I should have when I was a kid."

He went quiet again. "I didn't mean to overstep. As I'm discovering, dealing with family matters is tricky."

"Are you thinking of forming a family unit with Matilda?"

"Now who's stepping over the line?"

"It was obvious she likes you. And the feeling seemed mutual, since you didn't snap her head off for gossiping with me."

"Staff can't date each other. It's against the rules."

"Matilda just quit. You shouldn't waste time if you're both single and interested in each other."

There was more grumbling. "Johan has never given me any problems before, so I'm doubly concerned about this situation."

"All I'm concerned about is that you don't go back on your word. I find Johan, and you answer my questions about the Grimlows."

His teeth flashed in the gloom before he nodded. "I'll keep my word. My family is the most important thing to me."

I wasn't sure Fritz would have been so quick to agree to this if a Grimlow had given him a kill order, but maybe he genuinely valued his family more than his career. Perhaps Fritz wasn't the career military man I'd initially taken him for.

A furtive figure scuttled out of the shadows and slipped to the door of the house we were watching. He looked over his shoulder, and Fritz tensed beside me.

I grabbed his arm and held on as he made a move out of the alleyway. "No. You'll chase him off. Let Johan get inside and settled. Then we speak to him."

Fritz tried to shake me off, but I held on like an over-friendly limpet. "Let me go. I'll make him see sense."

"You'll terrify him. If he sees you coming, Johan will jump out of a window and escape. He could be ashamed of whatever it is he's hiding. Don't force him to run. You want to be there to support him, not intimidate him."

"I don't intimidate him."

My gaze slow traveled over his muscles and his set-in stone scowl. "You sort of intimidate me, and that takes a lot."

He snorted his disbelief. "I'll support Johan, no matter what he's done."

I dug my fingers into Fritz's arm. "He doesn't know that. I'll go in first, find where Johan is staying, explain the situation, and then you talk to him. But do more listening than talking. Your brother is scared for a reason. It might take some convincing to get him to return to his normal life."

"Are you sure you know what you're doing?" Fritz bristled with tension but had stopped fighting to get away.

"Yes. I'm the expert, and you're the unhelpful panicking family member who's not thinking straight." I knew how that felt, having almost ruined the snag-a-lady-in-her-carriage mission because I thought I'd seen Eden. "Hang back. I'll check the situation inside."

Fritz's hands were clenched into fists and his shoulders tight, but he obeyed me as we hurried across the street and opened the main front door to the building.

The smell of damp and decay hit my nose. Paint peeled off the faded walls in the entrance hall. There were several bags of trash abandoned by the staircase, and a bent bicycle leaned up against the railings leading up the stairs.

"Why is he in a hovel like this?" Fritz said.

"You don't think your parents asked him to leave, do you?" I kept my voice low as I continued to survey our surroundings.

"There's no reason for them to do that. They kitted out the basement just for him. He likes it down there. He even has his own entrance, so he doesn't disturb them if he gets in late. Not that he ever does. Johan is more a computer and books guy than a stay out late and party person."

"People change." I checked the names against the different apartments. There was no Johan listed on any of them. Not that I expected there to be, since he was keeping a low profile.

"Hey, beautiful," a quiet male voice said above our heads. "I got you the ice cream you like."

"That's him. Who is he calling beautiful?" Fritz was charging up the stairs before I could stop him.

We reached the second floor, and I spotted a door closing.

Fritz was facing the wrong direction and hadn't seen the movement, so I headed to the door and knocked.

No one answered.

I knocked again. There was a scurry of movement and then silence. "Johan, my name is Storm Winter. You're not in trouble, but I'd like to talk to you. It's about your brother, Fritz. He's worried about you."

By this time, Fritz had realized I was standing by the door and chatting to it. He charged toward me. "Did you find him?"

I pressed a finger to my lips. "Johan, we're here to help."

The door cracked open an inch, and an eye appeared. "I don't know you. Why would you help me?"

"I'm helping your brother. He says you've been missing."

"Tell him not to worry. But don't tell him where I am."

"It's too late for that." Fritz pressed a hand against the door. "Johan, what's going on?"

I shoved him back. "Give him a moment."

The door inched open a little further. A smaller, round-faced version of Fritz looked out at me. His anxious gaze shot to his brother. "How did you find me?"

"I had help." Fritz shot a look my way. There was an echo of gratitude among the anger and confusion on his face. "What are you doing in this dump?"

"You must know what happened," Johan said.

"No! I've been looking for you. I had no clue where you were." Fritz pressed against the door again. "Let me in."

Johan looked over his shoulder. He took a deep breath. "There's someone I'd like you to meet. You'd better come in."

I walked into the compact studio apartment first. There was a fold up bed in one corner, a small dining table, and a cubicle off to one side that must be the bathroom. The place was clean, but had the same faded air as the main building.

Fritz marched in and looked around. "You said there was someone I should meet. Are they making you stay here?"

"Minna, you can come out," Johan said, his tone betraying his worry. But there was something else. A hint of pride, perhaps?

A tiny woman with jet black hair and large, round blue eyes appeared from the darkened cubicle. She held her hands protectively over her belly. Even if she hadn't been doing so, it was easy to see she was at least six months pregnant.

Johan held out a hand, a genuine smile on his face. "You're safe. I won't let anything bad happen to you."

Minna scurried over and grabbed his hand, her expression defensive as her eyes swept from me to

Fritz. "We're together. You can't stop us from seeing each other. And we're keeping the baby."

Fritz took a step back. His startled gaze flicked from Minna's face to her belly and back again, then he turned to Johan. "Yours?"

"Ours." Johan lifted his chin. "And this is my fiancee, Minna. We're getting married next week. Minna, meet my older brother, Fritz."

She nodded, her mouth a firm line as she held Johan's hand. "You won't stop us."

Fritz rubbed a hand down his face. "From doing what?"

"Marrying. Being happy. Raising this child together." Minna glanced at me. "Perhaps Johan's family believes we didn't do things the right way, but we want this."

"This?" Fritz gestured at the shabby room. "This is what you aspire to?"

"Fritz," I cautioned him.

He ignored me. "And raising a baby here? No, I don't think so."

Johan stepped forward. "If you don't like what you see, leave. I didn't ask you to come."

"This makes no sense." Fritz glowered at his younger brother. The staring continued for several seconds.

I had to admire Johan. He didn't back down from the angry man mountain looming over him.

"Give Johan a chance to explain before casting your judgment. We don't all get paid by a royal family," I said.

Fritz turned his scowl on me, but eventually nodded. He clasped Johan by the shoulders. "I didn't mean to be so... abrupt."

Johan sighed, and some of the tension left him. "You sounded like Dad. When he found out about Minna being pregnant, he kicked me out. They both wanted me gone. So I left. And they cut off my money. I don't make much from my part-time job, so this is all we can afford."

"I'm looking for work, but..." Minna patted her belly. "No one will hire someone who needs to take time off in a few months. I'm already waddling and have fat ankles and back ache."

"I love your fat ankles." Johan stepped back and kissed Minna's cheek.

"You should have come to me," Fritz said.

"I thought you'd be the same as them. We're so traditional. I know I messed up, but I fell in love. I was planning to marry Minna and have a family with her—"

"But we got overexcited and carried away." Minna giggled. It quickly faded. "But I love Johan. And we're going to love this baby so hard. We might not have a fancy home, but we'll do our best to make their tiny life perfect."

"No."

I glared at Fritz. "No? You don't get to tell Johan and Minna what to do. If you're looking for a battle, go start a fight with your parents and yank their ideas into this century."

"If you let me finish, Storm. No, you don't have to stay here." Fritz looked around, not failing to hide his grimace. "Of course, if this is what you want, you can stay. But I have another option."

Johan shook his head. "I'm not giving up Minna and moving back home."

"I'd never ask you to do that. But I have an annex. It's small, but it has everything you need. It's private and clean and doesn't smell like... what is that smell? Rotting mushrooms?"

"There's a little mold in the kitchen. I keep scrubbing it, but it grows back every night." Minna's bottom lip jutted out. "You get used to the smell."

"Your life can't handle the chaos of a newborn baby," Johan said. "You always insist on order and neatness. You yell at me when I forget to put a coaster under my glass."

Fritz slid a glare my way, warning me not to tease him. "I'm not having your child raised in a fleapit. I can adjust. You should have come to me when this happened."

"And shown Minna what a failure I was?" Johan's nostrils flared. Both men clearly had a stubborn side. "This is temporary. I'm looking for a better place and another job. Things will improve."

Minna winced and pressed a hand to her belly. Johan and Fritz were by her side in an instant, arms hovering as if expecting her to faint or need holding up.

Her smile was shrewd. "Relax, boys. He's restless. It's because I'm hungry. But every time I eat, I feel queasy. Ice cream helps."

"It's a boy?" Fritz said. "I'm going to have a nephew?"

Minna's smile was cautious. "You are. But whatever sex the baby is, we'll love him or her just as much."

"Of course. I didn't mean..." A flush crossed Fritz's cheeks.

"He wants someone to teach fighting skills and marching drills," Johan said.

"I don't! And I can teach those skills to a girl just as well as a boy." Fritz's flush deepened. "You could move out right away. It won't take me long to get the annex ready. You can be settled by the end of the night."

Johan still didn't look happy. "We don't take charity. We have to manage on our own."

Fritz held up a hand. "Then pay rent. I don't expect you to, but if that's what it takes to make you move out of here, we can arrange something."

Johan looked at Minna, and she nodded.

"And it'll be good to have company." Fritz continued. "Since I've worked mainly with the Grimlows, I've not been around as much. If I had been, I'd have known about this. And you might have introduced me to Minna before now."

Johan gripped Minna's hand. "It'll only be temporary. Just until we get things settled and I find a better-paid job."

"Whatever you want. Just, please, leave this hovel. Tonight."

"Yeah, okay. Thanks, brother." Johan gripped Fritz's shoulder with his free hand, and they shared a look.

Fritz stepped back after a second, clearing his throat several times. "You'd do the same for me. Get your things together, and we'll leave straight away." He turned to me. "Shall we step outside?"

I followed him into the hallway, and he eased the door shut.

"Thank you for finding Johan. He's my only brother, and even though he can be naïve, I wouldn't change a thing about him." Fritz glared at the door. "I'll be having words with our parents about their treatment of him. It was unfair."

"Even if they don't accept him back, he's got you. That seems like a good solution."

"And I'll soon have a nephew." The hardness of his face softened. "Things will be different from now on."

"Children always change things. Now, you owe me answers."

Fritz's forehead furrowed, but he nodded. "Very well. I'll uphold my end of the deal."

"Tell me about the lookalike Lady Arabella uses."

He jerked his head back. "How do you know about her?"

"Because as you've seen, I'm great at my job. Nothing hides from me for long."

Fritz exhaled through his nose. "There is someone who stands in for Lady Arabella. She undertakes a lot of public engagements and finds them exhausting. Ten years ago, it was decided to utilize a lookalike so she wouldn't be under so much pressure. And it was hoped it would make relations between Lord and Lady Grimlow calmer. It didn't work."

"From what I've heard, Lady Arabella rarely attends any public events. Even the weekend getaways with her adoring fans."

"True. She finds it draining to be amenable to strangers. The family decided it was best if she stay out of the public eye as much as possible. The older she gets, the sharper she becomes. No one wanted her saying the wrong thing in public and causing a scandal."

"Did she use her lookalike at the events she was supposed to be at when Gaian Grimm and Micky Cox were killed?"

"I'd need to check the records, but I'm sure she did. Lady Arabella usually only attends state level events. Sometimes, her grandmother lays down the law and insists she go, though. Talise Grimlow doesn't think it's right to use a stand-in. She has a deep sense of obligation to the public."

"So Lady Arabella has no alibi for the time of those murders. She would have been alone because she'd have needed to be discreet."

"True again. But even though she uses a stand-in, Lady Arabella wouldn't have killed Gaian or Micky."

"You did it for her?"

"There have been times when Lady Arabella has given me orders I didn't agree with, but she's never asked me to kill on her behalf."

"Would you have refused an order to kill?"

Fritz debated that question internally for several seconds. "It's possible I would refuse. It depends on the circumstances."

"If not you, someone else, then?"

"I'm not sure who. Lady Arabella always comes to me when she has sensitive security issues that need dealing with. She wouldn't know who to reach out to, to undertake such a crime."

"But it's possible, if she wanted these people dead badly enough, she'd find a way to make it happen."

"Why do that? You've yet to give me her motivation," Fritz said.

"It's concerning a mistake Lord Valdemar made a long time ago."

"An infidelity? If these killings have to do with Lord Valdemar's inability to remain faithful, she'd have killed many women, not these random strangers."

"These murders have nothing to do with a recent bout of adultery."

"But they are connected to Lord Valdemar's behavior?"

"They are. It's a secret that can't come out, or it'll ruin the Grimlows." I didn't mind sharing this information with Fritz. He was far from perfect, but he wasn't a killer. He was gruff, a bit rude, and cagey, but he cared about his family and had shown he'd do the right thing when it was called for.

"It's well known in the inner circles that Lord Valdemar strays. Lady Arabella has never killed anyone before because of it. The worst she's done is kick him out and make him sweat. She's threatened divorce a few times but would never go through with it. What's different about this occasion? What is the secret?"

"Would a challenge to the royal rule affect Lady Arabella's behavior? Especially if it meant neither of her children could claim the throne."

His eyes widened, and he scrubbed a hand across his chin. "Something that serious would cause ripples throughout all ruling families. It would even affect the Magic Embassy. Are you saying there could be a challenge to the Grimlow family remaining as a ruling elite?"

"They could be knocked off their thrones. I'm thinking Lady Arabella found out this information and is doing everything she can to keep the situation silenced. She's having anyone with a connection to the secret wiped out."

Fritz hissed air through his teeth. "How many deaths are we talking?"

"You already know about Gaian and Micky. A shaman, possibly a famous medium, and an elderly witch could also have been murdered to keep this secret safe."

"You said there was an episode of adultery a long time ago. Is the woman back and threatening to share her secret?"

"Think closer to home."

Fritz's gaze cut to the closed door. "Lord Valdemar got someone pregnant. Has he really been straying for such a long time?"

"Only he can tell you that. He married Lady Arabella when he was twenty. From what I'm learning about him, he hasn't been able to stay faithful from the start. Although, to give him his due, he met this other woman before making things official with Lady Arabella. I think he loved her. Enough to marry her."

"Was the first marriage dissolved before he joined with Lady Arabella?"

"There's no record of that happening. And from a written account by the spurned woman, Rose Starlight, Lord Valdemar's family forced him to give up her and their unborn baby. He was made to marry Lady Arabella."

"Rose Starlight! You mentioned her the first time we spoke. But this is gossip. I've heard similar rumors, but there's no evidence."

"There is. I have it. And it seems other people are aware of this evidence. Which is why so many deaths have happened. Someone, and I was thinking Lady Arabella, is desperate to keep this quiet. She's clinging to her position. Although I've also wondered about Lord Valdemar. He's a secretive guy. I've not been able to catch him for a chat about murder."

"He wouldn't do that to his own child. Lord Valdemar may not be able to keep his pants up for long when there's a beautiful woman around, but he's a family man and adores his children. He wanted more, but Lady Arabella refused him. She gave him a girl and a boy and then, from what the servants say, she shut up shop. He'd have loved a larger family."

"Well, he can add one more child to the list. And I'm sure you're good at doing sums and understand lineage claims. The child I'm protecting was born first."

Fritz shut his eyes and tipped his head back. "Which means he has a rightful claim over the royal seat when his father steps aside. Now it makes sense. And I think you're right. Word is getting around that this child exists."

I tilted my head. "What makes you say that?"

"There have been numerous visits at the royal residence from a representative of the Magic Embassy. One guy has been repeatedly coming back. A pale looking warlock with hunched shoulders and sweaty armpits. Very nervy."

"You don't mean Pepin Flowerbottom?"

"Yes, that was his name. I caught him when he was sneaking out. I scared him so badly, I thought he'd keel over. He showed me his credentials and said he had a private meeting on a matter of national importance with Talise Grimlow. I didn't believe him. The queen mother rarely receives guests, so I assumed he was making himself seem important. Typical Magic Embassy fluff."

My stomach sank. "Pepin's been coming to the Grimlow residence regularly?"

"I've seen him at least five times. And he's always skulking around like he knows he's not supposed to be there. Hey! Wait! Where are you going?"

I was heading for the stairs. "Pepin is with Chance."

"Chance? Is that Lord Valdemar's firstborn?"

"Yep. I've got to go." All this time, I'd been deceived. Chance wasn't the trickster. It was sweaty, nervous Pepin. And his incompetent act had completely fooled me.

Chapter 22

Once I was outside, I cast a translocation spell to my apartment. I raced up the stairs, but slowed as I discovered my door ajar. I shoved it open and stepped into chaos.

What little furniture I had was trashed, and plates and glasses were smashed on the floor. There was a smear of blood on one wall.

"Fire Fang, Binky, where are you?" I stepped over my broken pallet table and picked up pieces of a ruined lamp.

I turned as something small ran along the hallway outside the apartment. Binky appeared in the doorway, her pupils huge and her hackles raised.

"This was Pepin's doing, wasn't it? He took Chance." I didn't know why I was talking to Binky, but she seemed to understand me.

She raced past the broken glass and hopped onto the kitchen counter. She stamped her paws and meowed until I walked over to join her.

On the counter was a piece of paper with several scrawled lines on it.

Binky kept stamping and meowing, dabbing her nose on the paper.

I narrowed my eyes and peered at what I first thought were scribbles. It was actually words. "Did you do this?"

She bobbed her head.

It took me a few seconds to figure out what the shaky words were. *Chan taken. Pep bad.*

I had my phone out and was calling Fritz as I checked the rest of the apartment. Even my bedroom had seen action. Pillows were tossed around, things knocked over, and books scattered. Chance had fought back.

Fritz answered after the second ring. "Storm! What's going on? You rushed out of here so fast."

"I know you've already done me one favor, but I'm calling in another. It's an emergency."

There was silence for a second. "This is about Lord Valdemar's firstborn."

"He's been taken. His life is at risk. I could already be too late to save him."

Fritz didn't hesitate. "What do you need?"

"It's a big ask, but I need you to bring Lord and Lady Valdemar to a neutral location. If I can get them together and lay out the facts, they should turn on each other."

He hissed out a breath. "They're in seclusion. That won't be easy."

"Inform them I have evidence one of them is a killer. Lady Arabella already knows about Chance and her husband's first marriage, so she'll be eager either to blame him or clear her name. And Lord Valdemar, well, if he's guilty, he'll hope to silence me, too."

"I'll make it happen. Where do you want to meet?"

I gave him the details of the storage unit where I'd been attacked with Chance. It was quiet, neutral ground. "I'll meet you there in an hour."

"What about the Magic Council? They need to be involved."

"I know someone. I trust him."

After a few more seconds of deliberation about logistics, I ended the call with Fritz.

Binky headbutted me hard in the arm before returning to the piece of paper on the kitchen counter. She kept jabbing at the snake she'd drawn.

"Does that mean something to you?" I was dialing Olympus's number, only paying her scant attention.

She kept pointing and stamping and meowing, trying to get me to make sense of the image, but it wasn't something I could decipher, just a wavy, wobbly S shape.

I spotted the pencil she must have used, picked it up, and placed it on the paper. "Write it again. Maybe I can... Hey, Olympus. I need to update you on this case."

Five minutes later, and after much grumbling from Olympus about me keeping him out of the loop as usual, he was up to speed with the suspects, clues, and the plan to get them together. He agreed to meet me at the storage unit.

The next call I made would be risky, but I also needed Pepin and Chance at the storage unit for this to work. Hopefully, Chance would still be breathing, so he could be there.

"Hey, Pepin. How's it going?" I forced myself to sound calm.

There was a pause. "Fine. Where are you?"

"I got stuck trying to talk to Fritz again. He's a brick wall and impossible to break down. I don't suppose you know his weakness, do you?"

"Oh. You're not home?"

"Not yet."

"I can't help you. We don't spend much time together. Where are you going next?"

"It's getting late. I thought I'd grab food and head back to the apartment. Chance could probably use the company."

"No! Don't do that. I mean, I could come meet you. We could eat together."

"Sure. What about Chance, though?"

"He won't mind staying in. Your familiars can look after him. And he was just telling me he was tired, so I expect he'll go to bed soon."

"You've seen him?"

"Oh, no. I mean... I called him. I wanted to make sure he was okay. He was glum the last time we were at your apartment."

"Someone trying to kill you would have that effect."

A nervous chuckle came down the line. "Yes, I suppose it would. Where shall we meet for dinner?"

"Before we do that, I was thinking about going back to the storage unit containing Chance's aunt's things. The last time I was there, I got disturbed. But Aunt Edith seemed like a clever old lady, and I reckon she made a backup copy of Chance's birth certificate and the marriage certificate showing Lord Valdemar and Rose married."

There was silence. "Do... do you really think she did that?"

"I wouldn't put it past her. She knew how dangerous the situation was, which was why she hid the originals." While I was convincing Pepin I was clueless about his guilt, I messaged Laris to meet at the storage unit. "And we can't let this information get out before we know who's killing everyone off. It could scare them away, and then we'll never know the truth."

"You're right. I didn't think about that. I'll join you and help in the search."

That was exactly what I hoped he'd say. "That would be great."

"I... err... I just need to deal with something, then I'll meet you there as soon as I can. See you shortly."

"Wait! You need the storage address details. Otherwise, how will you find me?" I'd gotten him. Pepin knew where I'd be, because he'd ordered those guys to kill me and Chance the last time we'd been there.

His laugh had an awkward twinge to it. "Of course. Sorry, I'm not used to dealing with such difficult situations. All these murders and intrigue, it's too much for me."

"It's funny, I always figured working in the diplomatic field, you'd get used to covering up people's mishaps. That must be stressful."

"Yes, of course, but there are mishaps and then there's evidence that'll rip apart an ancient royal lineage because of an indiscretion thirty years ago. This is one-of-a-kind. They don't train us for this."

I gave him the details of the storage unit and agreed to meet him there in just under an hour.

Binky was still obsessed with the piece of paper with the line on it, but I didn't have any more time to spare her. I put food in her bowl and headed out.

When I got outside, I looked for Fire Fang. It was unusual for him to be out of the apartment alone, but he knew I needed him to keep watch over Chance, so maybe he'd tailed him.

I frowned as I hurried along. Pepin had better not have injured Fire Fang. I didn't think it likely, though. Pepin was a wimp and wouldn't have the courage to go up against a hellhound.

Maybe Fire Fang was punishing me because I'd been leaving him behind more often. But he'd understand when he knew the truth. Since he was a mortal masquerading in a hellhound's body, I didn't want to put him at risk. By dragging him into dangerous investigations, I could end up getting him killed.

With no sign of Fire Fang, I hopped in the truck I'd borrowed from Odessa and headed to the storage unit. I was halfway there when I clocked a car following me. I took a small detour, and it matched my movements.

It could be more henchmen from the Magic Embassy. I wouldn't be surprised if Pepin had set them on me. If he thought I was about to discover a copy of the documents, he'd need to take them. Then he'd need to silence me, and he didn't have the brass tacks to do it himself.

I kept watch on the car as I reached the storage unit. It remained some distance back, but the driver pulled in and killed the lights as soon as I parked. Whoever was in the car wanted in on this situation.

Fine by me, so long as they didn't mind a bolt of lightning sending them on their way if they caused me trouble.

Using a light ball to illuminate the passage to the storage unit, I made my way through the gloom. It hadn't been locked since my last visit, so it was easy to get in. I flipped on the lights and jumped when I spotted Pepin sitting on a cardboard box.

"You got here fast. You must be eager to sort through all this stuff." I extinguished my light ball.

"I'm eager for this to be over." Pepin didn't look his usual refined self. There were the beginnings of a large bruise on one side of his face, and his shirt pocket was torn. I pretended not to notice.

"Let's get searching. When I was here with Chance, we went through the boxes on the left, but everything at the back needs sorting."

"How can you be so sure there are other copies?" Pepin said.

"I can't, not for certain. But why keep only the originals of something so important? Chance's Aunt Edith needed to keep him safe. I wouldn't be surprised if there were several copies to find. They could be hidden anywhere."

Pepin muttered under his breath as he rifled through a box. "Of course. Why would we think this could be easy?"

"Storm."

I turned to see Fritz in the doorway. Either side of him was an unhappy Lady Arabella and an uncomfortable-looking Lord Valdemar dressed in a crisp, dark suit. "Perfect timing. Our special guests have arrived."

"I know that voice!" Lady Arabella said. "You ruined the procession and broke into my carriage."

"And you know the reason I did that. It's why you're both here. And I was fortunate your grandmother insisted you be a part of the event. Otherwise, I'd have been speaking to your stand-in."

"I never refuse grandmama." She furrowed her small forehead and looked like she wanted to stamp her feet.

"Storm, what's going on?" Pepin joined me, his shock at seeing the Grimlows clear.

"You! You're the one with the odd face from the Embassy. I thought you'd been dismissed." Lady Arabella jabbed a finger at Pepin.

Pepin stuttered over several words, an accusing look settling on me.

I shrugged. That was interesting. He hadn't been visiting Lady Arabella to get his orders. He must be working for Lord Valdemar.

His lordship was a tall, fragile-looking man with a Roman nose and shifty eyes. His attention was focused on me. "Fritz informed us you have evidence regarding some murders. Murders you believe we are involved in."

Pepin caught hold of my arm. "Why didn't you tell me about this? What are you doing?"

"Solving the murders. I have to know who gave the orders to kill those innocent people. Lady Arabella and Lord Valdemar know the secret that's been kept all these years. They wouldn't have come here if they didn't. One of them is guilty."

"I only came because Fritz said my husband's dirty little secret is about to be revealed," Lady Arabella said. "It doesn't need to happen. We can come to some agreement so you don't talk."

"I'm not interested in keeping your secret, but I'm also not interested in sharing it. This isn't about what I can get from this situation. People are dying because of an indiscretion Lord Valdemar had thirty years ago. It has to stop," I said.

"Hold on a moment. What indiscretion are we talking about? And how am I supposed to remember that far back?" Lord Valdemar's smile was slimy as he looked at his wife.

"You know which one," Lady Arabella spat at him. "And I'm tired of covering for you. Let this witch tell everyone what you're like. See if I care. My fans will implore me to get rid of you and find a real man, not some cheating halfwit who loses his senses when some pretty slip of a thing flashes an ankle. You're a pathetic man."

"Darling, you don't want to do that. We have a happy home. We have everything we desire." Lord Valdemar tried to take her hand.

Lady Arabella stepped away. "Fritz, I don't want my husband near me. If he tries to touch me, knock him out. Then send him to the cells beneath the house."

Fritz simply nodded, but his gaze was on me, encouraging me to speed things up before the royals started a brawl.

"Storm, you should have told me they were coming." Pepin looked deeply unhappy. And so he should. The game was almost up for him.

"And I really would like to know what's going on," Lord Valdemar said. "It appears I have some apologies to make, but I don't know what for."

"Did you love Rose Starlight?" I said to him.

His jaw dropped, and the color drained from his face. "I... who? I don't know her."

"She was your first wife. And the love letters she sent you, begging you not to give up on her and your unborn child, show you knew her intimately."

Lord Valdemar fiddled with his jacket lapels. "It was so long ago. My memory, it's not so sharp."

"You forgot you married Rose and got her pregnant?"

"Storm, this isn't the time or place," Pepin hissed.

"I know what I'm doing," I muttered to him.

Lord Valdemar looked imploringly at his wife, who refused to acknowledge him. He sighed gently. "Yes, I remember marrying Rose."

"And then you abandoned her and your yet to be born baby for royal duty."

Lord Valdemar looked me straight in the eye, but his nervous gulp gave him away. "It was a different time. I was young and easily persuaded. I had to do what was right by my family. I thought Rose would move on and find someone else."

"She didn't. You abandoned her. The child, a boy, had no parents to raise him after she died less than a year after he was born."

Lord Valdemar lowered his gaze. "I was never told."

"You could have found out. You have connections," I said.

"It was a condition made by my parents. I had to give up Rose, never see her again, and cut all contact. It was only fair to my new bride. I had to do the right thing."

"You must've thought about her, though. And you must have realized what the implications were. You never divorced Rose. You married Lady Arabella illegally."

"Rose is dead, so that doesn't matter now," Lady Arabella said. "And my husband has always been foolish around beautiful women. It's something he's never grown out of. One dumb decision when he was barely out of his teens shouldn't ruin my future. Nor that of my children."

"But it does. Because unfortunately for you, there is a firstborn child who'll inherit the royal title when your husband steps aside. Neither of your children will do that. Unless, of course, that firstborn is dead."

Her face flushed. "I have yet to see proof of this other child. You talk about him, but it could be a fabrication. What do you want? Money, title, an estate? You'll get nothing from me. You're a scam artist."

"I don't think she is."

Sirius Fagan appeared in the doorway, and he wasn't alone. He had four guys with him, and none of them looked like they wanted to shake hands and have a friendly drink.

"It was you following me in the car," I said.

He raised his hands. "You can't blame a man for being persistent. I've been tailing you since we talked. I couldn't let you run wild with all that tantalizing information. Since there is a firstborn Grimlow out there, he needs to know his options."

"You're a disgrace. You work with the Fagan clan?" Lady Arabella said. "You want to throw us off the royal seat, too?"

"You can keep your jewel-encrusted seat. But Sirius was a suspect in these murders, as well. I had to learn what he knew about Rose and her child," I said.

"Arrest him!" Lady Arabella looked at Fritz. "He's a criminal."

Fritz didn't move. "Sorry, your ladyship, but we need to get to the bottom of this matter before any arrests are made."

Sirius smirked. "Too much of your past has been smoothed over, Lord Valdemar. No one's history is that tidy. You made everything too perfect."

"I... I didn't. I had nothing to do with it. I kept my word to my family and never contacted Rose again." Lord Valdemar fidgeted with his jacket. "I want no trouble here."

"You keep talking about murders." Lady Arabella swung my way. "I've already told you I didn't do it. Does that mean you think someone here is the killer?"

"I do. But you looked guilty for a while. You lied about using a lookalike at your public events, and you have no alibi for Micky or Gaian's murders. It could have been you."

"I wouldn't kill anyone." She raised her chin. "Well, maybe my useless husband if he destroys everything we have because he can't keep his pecker in his pants."

"My love—"

"No! Not a word from you. And no more of this charade. Even if you aren't the killer, I'm making sure you stay far away from me."

"Let's stick with you for a moment, Lady Arabella," I said. "Maybe you didn't kill anyone, but you could have easily ordered someone else to do it. Maybe with your favorite dessert laced with poison?"

She drew herself up to her full height. "I would never waste a pumpkin pie by using it as a murder weapon. It was my husband. He knew the truth was close to getting out and would blow apart his comfortable little world. It was him!"

I knew it wouldn't take long before they blamed each other. True love on display for all to see.

Lord Valdemar stepped forward. "No! Please, it wasn't me. I know nothing about any of this."

I kept an eye on Pepin as they bickered and pointed the finger of blame at each other. I wanted to see which member of the family he deferred to. Who had given him the orders? It was hard to tell. He was anxious and unhappy about me lying to him, but didn't seem to pay particular attention to either of them.

I remembered what Fritz said when he caught Pepin and he claimed to be visiting Talise Grimlow. Could the queen mother be tangled in this situation? She rarely went out, and she was practically a hermit. How could she have found out?

"Where is this child?" Lady Arabella said. "If he's planning to depose my children from their rightful place, the least I deserve is to look him in the eyes and tell him what I think of him."

"I'd love to meet him, too," Sirius said.

Movement outside the storage unit caught my attention. Olympus Duke had arrived. He gave me a discreet nod but remained back.

"That's out of my hands," I said.

"I knew it! You've been lying this whole time," Lady Arabella said.

"I can't answer the question about where Chance is. But Pepin can." I turned slowly to him and smiled starkly.

"Me! What are you talking about?"

"You know where Chance is. You saw him last. Or did someone else drag him out of my apartment for you?"

Pepin stepped back, chewing on his lower lip. "Chance is missing?"

"You took him. What happened? Did you say something you shouldn't, and he realized you were the snake? All this time, you tricked us into believing you were helping, but you've been taking orders from a Grimlow and waiting for an opportunity to silence Chance for good and destroy all evidence of his existence."

"Storm! We're friends. We work together. I have nothing to do with Chance being taken."

"I saw you," Fritz said. "You've been visiting the family."

"Of course I have. That's my job. I act as a diplomatic liaison for several families."

"You slid in and out like an asp. I can always tell when someone's trying not to be noticed." Fritz pointed at him. "You're hiding something."

"No! That's... that's just how I am. I aim to be discreet."

"I've been to my apartment. Chance isn't there," I said. "You told me he was fine."

"So you think I took him?" Pepin said. "I want these murders solved as much as you do. Order must be restored."

"Whose order?"

He threw up his hands. "Order! No more killing. This is insane! I'm no killer."

"You've been following orders from a member of the Grimlow family. Was it Lord Valdemar or Lady Arabella who told you to remove all evidence of Chance's existence?"

"It wasn't me," Lady Arabella said. "The first I heard about my idiot husband getting another woman pregnant was when you broke into my carriage and told me. By then, all those commoners were dead."

"It was Lord Valdemar?" I said to Pepin.

"No! Not me. Of course, having my past return in such a manner was alarming, but I wouldn't order the death of my own child," Lord Valdemar said.

"Did you know Rose was dead?" I asked.

Lord Valdemar glanced at his wife. "Yes. I had someone keep an eye on her."

"Did you order Rose's death? You were concerned the truth would come out?"

"I'd never do that. But when Rose died, I figured it was for the best. The child was taken to someone who worked for my grandmother. She was paid to look after him. She was loyal and respectable. No one questioned her taking in an orphan. Edith was seen as helping a child in need."

I studied them. Talise Grimlow kept entering this picture. She was a sucker for tradition, had arranged for Chance to vanish, and enforced order in the family.

There was a blast of cold air and a shift in the atmosphere.

"Enough blaming my grandchildren. They are foolish, but not killers." A strong female voice reverberating with power had us looking at the door. The queen mother, Talise Grimlow, stood there, dressed in red silk, her soft gray hair drifting to her waist and a white fur ruff around her throat. She had four guards with her, magic simmering on their fingers as they took in the scene and assessed the threat.

Everyone bowed or curtsied. Even I felt the desire to bend to such power. Talise was immensely powerful, and it was rumored she single-handedly ended the Battle of Laxfield by using a multi-point destruction spell mixed with a tornado turret.

"How did you know we were here?" I said.

"I watch my grandchildren. I have learned not to let them out of my sight for long. And I was curious about the emergency summons from Fritz." Talise remained in the doorway, her gaze traveling over me from top to bottom.

"It was you who gave Pepin the kill order," I said to her. "You learned about your other grandchild and decided to get rid of him."

Talise dismissed her guards, then swept into the storage unit. "There has been a misunderstanding. No kill order was given."

"You know what this is about, though? You're aware you have a third grandchild by Lord Valdemar?"

Her ice blue gaze swept to her grandson. "He always was an impetuous child, led by his emotions from a young age." She returned her attention to me. "I was aware of this other child. I was content to allow his existence, providing he maintain a low profile."

"You knew about this and never told me?" Lady Arabella said.

"Would it have benefited you to know? My grandson gives you enough trouble. Having the burden of knowing there was a risk your children would forfeit their right to rule because of his reckless behavior wouldn't have made for a smooth marriage. Not that your marriage is smooth. Any more bumps and it will explode."

"You should still have told me. It's not fair." Lady Arabella pouted.

"What misunderstanding do you believe has happened?" I said to Talise.

Her gaze settled on Pepin, and she sighed. "I forget how powerful my words can be. A conversation was misinterpreted. I may have suggested the world would be simpler if my firstborn grandson never existed."

"Grandmother!" Lord Valdemar looked appalled.

"Do not pass judgment on me, child. You have thought it yourself."

"I... I wouldn't wish anyone dead." He glanced at his wife.

"And Pepin overheard this conversation and made your dreams come true?" I said to Talise.

Pepin's attention was focused on Talise, an adoring, desperate look in his eyes. "I want to do what's best for the family. It's my job to make you happy. When the family is content, the royal circle operates perfectly."

"You're confessing to the killings?" I said to him.

"I... No! I mean, I had to do what was right for the royal family. They needed a problem solved."

"And you thought by solving it, you'd earn their favor? You're looking for a promotion? Is that what this has been about? You're climbing the slippery pole to a better job."

Pepin's cheeks darkened, but he didn't answer me.

"It is not all his fault," Talise said, her tone softening. "My magic is unusual. I have the power to exert influence over others and manipulate their strengths. If I have a desire strong enough, it affects the behavior of those around me. It is why I keep myself secluded. But there was a time, not so long ago, when I was concerned about Chance's existence. Rumors had been circulating that there was evidence of his birth and that my numb-headed grandson married Rose Starlight. I sent a team to investigate, but they found no evidence. But by then, I'd been dwelling on the issue. It haunted my dreams."

"And Pepin, with his implicit desire to please people, picked up on your longing to kill Chance and wipe out all the evidence," I said.

Talise showed no regret. She simply nodded. "I believe so. By the time I became aware of the deaths and the connection to my own interests, it was too late."

"You could have locked Pepin up. That would have stopped him." I swung toward Pepin. "Is Chance dead?"

Pepin stammered and shuffled, his attention on Talise, seeking her acceptance and thanks.

She spared him a curt smile. "Not that I condone murder, but it would be simpler if Chance was out of the picture. This matter can be resolved this evening, and life will go back to normal."

"Not for Rose, Gaian, Shaman Goody, or Micky. Their lives have been snuffed out because your desire turned a weak individual into a killer. How is it fair you get to carry on as normal, but other people have been destroyed?" I said.

"I simply meant there needs to be no changes. With Chance dead, the family rule remains intact. Pepin, of course, needs to answer for his crimes—"

"So do you."

Talise thrust the full fury of her icy gaze in my direction. "I did nothing but have a few dark thoughts. We all experience those. That is not a crime."

Olympus stepped out of the shadows. "The Magic Council and the Embassy can't allow the agreement you signed to be broken."

She turned toward him, a towering statue of indignation. "I am aware of the agreement, and it has not been broken. I did not explicitly order Pepin to kill. My power was not used with intention."

"You know the power you have over others," Olympus said. "You must have witnessed that Pepin was a people pleaser, determined to ensure your every need was met. All you had to do was think those thoughts when he was nearby. Then you left him to carry out your instructions."

"It is hardly my fault the man has no control. But with Chance dead, this matter is over," Talise said.

"Like heck it is." I gestured at Olympus to arrest Talise.

He gestured back. "You still need to answer some questions to ensure we have all the facts in this case."

"What does the Magic Council need from me to ensure this is dealt with swiftly?" Talise spread her hands. "The role of Commander is soon to be available. Should I suggest your name? Or would a new budget for the Dark Magic Crime division be appropriate?"

"Bribery is also a crime," I said. "But keep talking. You're only making things worse for yourself. Add bribery to murder and you won't see your supporters ever again."

"Stop! Chance isn't dead," Pepin blurted out. "I can bring him here. He's close by. I'll kill him in front of you. Then you'll know this is over."

Talise sucked in a breath, obviously torn between offering the kill command and saving her skin.

Pepin's panicked gaze shot from Talise to me and back again. He opened and closed his mouth several times. "What would you have me do?"

"Get Chance," I ordered. "Olympus, go with him. Don't let Pepin out of your sight."

Pepin turned to Talise. "Is this your wish?"

Although her face was composed, the tiny red dots on her cheeks revealed her anger. "Do not kill the young man. Bring him here."

Pepin dashed away with Olympus, leaving me with the Grimlow family and Sirius, who seemed to be enjoying the show.

"You should work for me." Talise was giving me a thorough visual inspection.

"I have a job."

"When your name came up in this investigation, I looked into your background. I need talent on my team, and a witch who challenges my commands would be stimulating. I enjoy being kept on my toes."

"That'll happen when you go to jail."

She chuckled. "That is not an option. Join me. We could be powerful together. I have a desire to stretch my magical muscles again. It has been too long."

"I only work for myself. Things get messy when you involve other people." My gaze slid to her nervous grandchildren.

"You would be well-rewarded. Name your price."

"I'll pass. What do you plan to do about Chance?"

She tapped her fingers against her thigh, the silk rustling as she moved. "I do not enjoy controversy tainting my family. My idiot grandson—"

"Grandmother, I'm right here. You don't have to keep calling me an idiot. I know I made a mistake."

"Yet you don't learn from them. And you keep making the same mistake. It's fortunate there aren't a dozen more children trying to lay claim to the throne. There aren't, I trust?"

He hung his head. "No."

"Chance is your legitimate firstborn grandson," I said. "He has every right to his claim."

"And if he pursues it, I'll support him," Sirius said. "Anything to cut out the corruption festering on that throne."

Talise simply glared at him, then dismissed him with a wave.

"I want nothing to do with this family." Chance staggered through the door, assisted by Olympus, Pepin on their heels. "I wish I'd never found out. I want to forget it all."

Talise turned, her power flickering off her as her gaze ran over Chance several times. "You look like my older brother, although you must have your mother's eyes. No one would be surprised to learn you are born of this family."

Chance flashed a look my way. He looked rumpled around the edges, and there was a cut on his forehead, but otherwise, he seemed unharmed. "I may have a royal father, but that's where the connection ends. Lord Valdemar means nothing to me. Everything this family stands for means nothing to me."

"Don't be so quick to discount us," Talise said.

"You're offering to include Chance in your family?" I said. "Don't you fear the scandal?"

"We can't let him be a part of this family," Lady Arabella hissed. "He'll ruin everything. Think about your other grandchildren. You know them. You've been around them since they were babies. By letting this... this mistake in, it'll destroy everything. We could lose our royal seat."

Talise continued her inspection of Chance. It looked like she was deciding whether to eat him or squash him.

"I have a suggestion," I said. "It would mean no more murders, and you can keep what you covet so badly." At least, for the time being.

Talise shifted her attention to me. "I'm listening."

"I have the original birth and marriage certificates showing Chance's parentage and Lord Valdemar's marriage to Rose. I'll destroy these in front of everyone so long as Chance remains safe."

"That's not enough," Lady Arabella said. "While he's walking around, he could still spoil things. He'll get greedy and take what's ours."

"What are you suggesting we do?" I said. "Or do you want to cast the spell to kill Chance with all these witnesses watching?"

"Oh! I didn't mean that." Lady Arabella's cheeks flushed. "Can't he be locked up somewhere?"

"No! Why can't things go back to how they used to be?" Chance said. "None of this is my fault. I wish I'd never found out."

"That could be arranged," I said. "With Chance's agreement, I will wipe his memories. I'll remove all trace of him ever knowing about his father."

No one spoke as they considered this option.

I focused on Chance. "Only if you agree. Wiping memories isn't simple. There's a risk I could take memories you cherish. You could forget some of your time with Micky. I know how much he meant to you."

He looked around the group, his gaze stopping on his father for a few seconds. He turned to me and nodded. "Take them. I want nothing to do with these crazy royals. I love my simple life. I had a best friend, fun every evening, and I woke with a chance of excitement every day. I know I can't get Micky back, but I want to live for him. I want to have fun in his name. And I don't want to be stuck in this shell of obligation, always looking over my shoulder for my so-called family to strike me down."

"We're not stuck," Lady Arabella said. "We have everything we desire."

"Do you have happiness, freedom, and a marriage that brings you joy?" I said.

Lady Arabella spluttered out a few words before turning a dagger-like stare on her husband.

"Thought not. So, what does everyone think? If I destroy the evidence and wipe Chance's memory, will that be enough? Do I have your word you'll leave him alone and never bother him again?"

Talise stepped forward and held out her hand. "I agree. Everyone will follow my decree. Ensure there is no trace of this knowledge left, and Chance will be free to live his life. But he'll have no claim to our family. That will be gone forever."

"I... I'm not sure about this," Lord Valdemar said. "After all, he is my son."

Chance turned to him. "I'm not. You may have spent time with my mother, used her for your own pleasure, but you left her and had nothing to do with me. I don't want you in my life. You're not my father."

Lord Valdemar bowed his head. "I understand why you feel like that. If this is what you want, I won't prevent it."

"Let's get this over with." Lady Arabella clutched her husband's arm in a pincer-like grab. "Then we must talk about our marriage."

"Of course, my love," Lord Valdemar said. "Whatever you desire."

I caught Sirius's eye. He simply shrugged and headed to the door with his gang, passing Olympus as he did so.

I pulled out the birth and marriage certificates and handed them to Talise.

After she'd looked over them, she passed them back. "Proceed."

I tossed them in the air and blasted them to ash with a fireball.

"Chance, are you ready?" I said.

"Yes. Get these memories out of my head. Make me forget. When I wake, I want to be somewhere fun. Somewhere I can enjoy myself. Maybe a casino."

I smiled at him. "I have bigger plans than returning you to your trickster ways. You need a life with purpose. A way to give back. You may even earn money while you do it, and legally this time. Won't that be novel?"

"That doesn't sound so terrible."

"Trust me, you'll love it." I rested my hands on either side of his head, closed my eyes, and sifted through his memories, breaking anything connected to his birth father, the Grimlows, and the murders.

It took twenty minutes, and I was sweating and shaking by the time I'd removed the last memory. This kind of magic wasn't my specialty, and I felt drained and faint.

Chance slumped down, unconscious. Having a memory wipe was exhausting on both sides.

"It's done. When Chance wakes, he'll remember none of this," I said.

Talise stepped forward, her gaze on her firstborn grandchild. There was no fondness in her expression, simply cold acceptance. "This matter is closed. Storm Winter, your help is appreciated. I never expect to see you again. Grandchildren, we're leaving." She turned and swept out of the storage unit, Lady Arabella and Lord Valdemar following her.

Pepin had been mute this whole time, but a glance at his pale, sweaty face showed he knew exactly what was about to happen.

Olympus marched over and stood in front of him. "Pepin Flowerbottom, I'm arresting you for murdering Gaian Grimm, Edith Osman, Shaman Goody, and Micky Cox."

Pepin hung his head. "I did it for the greater good. I did it for the family, to make them happy. That's all I want to do, make people happy."

"Try making yourself happy first," I said. "It should lead to less murder."

Olympus patted me on the shoulder. "Good work, Storm. I'll take it from here. You take a break. You look like you need it."

I was happy for him to deal with the arrest and questioning, and was done with dealing with royal sycophants. All I wanted was a hot shower, a long sleep, and breakfast in bed.

Chapter 23

"We should go." Fire Fang danced around my legs. "We missed the grand opening yesterday."

I pulled on my jacket, searching around for my keys. "It's a candy store. What's the big deal?"

"They were giving away free candy. Let's go." He headbutted me in the thigh.

Fire Fang was happier than he had been in weeks, so I wasn't missing the opportunity to keep his cheery mood buoyant. "The wait will be worth it. I wanted a couple of days off without having to deal with people. Those royals were intense. And I haven't gotten over how easily Pepin tricked me. I must be losing my touch."

"You'd be more focused if you took better care of yourself, you crazy buttoned witch. That includes stopping at the candy store for free treats. Treat yourself. Look after yourself. And me."

"I'm trying, but I need to find my keys before we go anywhere." I didn't argue with Fire Fang. These last two cases had taken it out of me. I was trying to do it all on my own, and I wasn't giving myself enough downtime. My friends always nagged me about looking after my magical health, taking breaks when I needed, and recharging, so I was in top form. That hadn't mattered so much when I was young, but every witch goes through cycles, and I was on a downward pitch at the moment.

"Found them." Fire Fang dug my keys out from between the couch cushions and slung them at me.

I caught them. "The candy store is on our way to Luna's. We can stop there first, but then I want to see how Chance is doing."

Fire Fang growled his happiness, then raced off to dig Binky out from under the duvet. She'd spent most of the time there with me after I'd gotten back from the storage unit. On the way home, I'd dropped a sleeping Chance at Luna's and persuaded her to take him on as an assistant at her animal sanctuary. She'd been overwhelmed the last time I'd been there, and it would do Chance good to focus his energies on helping others rather than himself. I even offered to pay his wages for the first three months to sweeten the deal.

Once Binky had been prodded awake, we left the apartment and headed into the main shopping area of Witch Haven. Fire Fang bounded ahead, making a beeline for a crowd outside the candy store.

I hadn't even realized a new store was opening, but it seemed I was the only one who hadn't gotten word. There was a long line outside, and an excited buzz came from the waiting crowd. There were even a few shoves as people tried to get through the door and not wait their turn. The candy in there must be amazing.

I didn't do crowds unless I absolutely had to, so hung back.

Binky headbutted my calf and nodded at the store.

"You, too? You want the free candy?"

She bounced on her paws and chased after Fire Fang.

"Storm, I was coming to see you later." Olympus walked over from his office. "I thought you'd like an update on the case."

"So long as Pepin has confessed, that's all I care about."

"He has. He killed them all. The guy is still pleading the greater good angle, but he doesn't stand a chance of getting away with this."

"What about Rose? Was her death a tragedy, or did the Grimlow family have a hand in that, too?"

"We're looking into it. I think she died from a broken heart. She loved Lord Valdemar. He promised her everything and then abandoned her. Rose lost it all because she took a chance on love."

I shuddered. "Which is why I stay away from it. Too messy."

He chuckled. "Indigo was complaining you hadn't been on a date for ages. Not so long ago, she was asking if I had any suitable single friends."

"You told her no, I hope. Dating is off the table for me."

"I told her it would take a special guy to catch your attention and hold it."

"And you don't know any of them, right?"

"I promise I won't force you on any blind dates, no matter how insistent Indigo is."

"I appreciate that. Any news about the Grimlows?"

Olympus huffed out a breath. "I don't want them getting away with this, but their involvement must be handled sensitively. I've had an off-the-record conversation with Talise Grimlow and am yet to be convinced she's innocent. We've scheduled a committee, which she'll be forced to attend. We know her power can influence others, but we need evidence she knowingly influenced Pepin to commit those murders. If we can get that, she could face jail time."

"We know it won't come to that. Those families are untouchable. She'll get away with a slap on the wrist and told to be more careful. And of course, she'll smile and pretend to oblige."

"You don't think highly of the Magic Council's ability to hand out justice, do you?"

"You're the only decent Magic Council member I've ever met. The rest are like Pepin. They want to please the powers that be, rather than see wrongs righted."

"So cynical for someone so young."

I snorted out a laugh. "I'm not that young. And I definitely haven't been feeling full of youthful excitement lately."

"Indigo also mentioned how hard you've been pushing things. Taking time off wouldn't be a bad idea, especially now this mystery is solved."

I was going to say I'd sleep when I was dead, but that mantra hadn't been working out so great lately. "Have you visited the new candy store?"

"I've not had a chance. There's always a queue to get inside. Indigo's been with Luna and Odessa when it opened. She raved about it. She bought me a bag of candy but ate it before I got any. Must be good."

"They went without me?"

He shrugged. "Don't take it personally. You've been busy on this case. They'll ask you along the next time."

"Yeah, you're right." Still, I didn't like being left out. But I wasn't surprised. I had a habit of not showing up when I was supposed to and cancelling at the last minute. No wonder they were annoyed with me.

Fire Fang bounded over, his mouth full. Binky trotted beside him but wasn't eating anything.

"Did you get your free samples?" I said.

He nodded, his tail wagging.

"Then let's go see how Chance is doing."

"I appreciate you setting him up at the sanctuary," Olympus said. "So long as he keeps away from the casinos, he'll have a better life."

"I agree. Being around animals never did anyone harm." I said goodbye to Olympus, and we strolled to Luna's animal sanctuary.

When we arrived, Chance was coming out of a barn, pushing a wheelbarrow full of soiled straw.

He raised a hand. "Hey. Good to see you."

It had been tricky, but I'd kept a few memories in Chance's head, so he remembered me, although not my connection to the case. He thought I did something in an employment agency, which was how I got him this job. That worked for me.

"How are you getting on?" I said.

"I'm still pinching myself I got this job. I have no experience with animals, but it's a perfect fit. And the animals love me. Luna also brings me amazing treats from her uncle's bakery. I'm thrilled there's so much manual labor to do. Otherwise, I'd get a cake belly."

"I'm glad you're settling in."

"It feels like I've always been here. Although the last few weeks have been a blur." His smile faded. "I told you about Micky, didn't I?"

"You've mentioned him."

"I've been finalizing details for his funeral. He didn't have a family, so I decided to do it. It's so strange, I know he only died recently, but it seems such a long time ago. I miss the guy like crazy, but I've been feeling for a while it was time for a change. You can get too dependent on one person, can't you?"

"I guess. People come into your life at the right time and leave when they're no longer needed. It's good you can have a final goodbye with Micky."

"Yeah. He was great fun. But it's time for me to take on responsibility. Settle down." A protesting bleat came out of the barn. "Got to go. This lot need new straw and their food."

Fire Fang and Binky raced over to Luna as she headed my way.

She petted them both before stopping in front of me. "Hi. Are you here to adopt?"

"Good one. As you can see, I already have an odd hellhound and a stray cat who's no longer stray. I don't need any more misfits in my life."

Luna tilted her head, a puzzled expression on her face. "Then why are you here?"

"Hey! There's no need to give me a hard time. My last case was intense. Did you hear about it?"

"Sorry we're late."

I turned at the sound of Odessa's voice. She was hurrying toward us, with Indigo beside her.

"Some of the scarecrows were misbehaving. I had to give them a scolding and tell them to be on their best behavior. I don't know what's wrong with them. I think they're jealous because I've not spent much time with them." She nodded at me.

"I made another visit to the candy store first thing this morning," Luna said. "They had brandy apple snaps. I got as many as I could, but people were practically elbowing me out of the way. I'm going back later to see if they've been restocked. They melt in the mouth."

"We stopped on our way," Indigo said. "We heard there were peppermint cream brownies. We got three."

"Only three? I guess you didn't know I was dropping by," I said.

Indigo glanced at me. "Sure. Let's go inside."

They turned and headed toward Luna's house. I followed them to the door.

Indigo stopped and glared at me. "This isn't part of the sanctuary. You can't come in. The animals available for adoption are in the barn."

"This is the most unfunny joke you've ever pulled," I said.

Her glare intensified. "I'm not trying to be funny."

Ouch! They were making me work to get back in their good books. "I know I've not been the best friend to you all, but my last two cases distracted me. I'm here now."

"If you don't want to adopt an animal, you should probably leave," Luna said. She glanced at the others. "I get annoyed by time wasters coming here and thinking this is a petting zoo."

Odessa and Indigo hummed their agreement.

"What are you talking about?" I said. "Don't you want to hear about the case of the poisoned pumpkin pie? And I need to talk about Fire Fang. And Eden. I could really do with your advice."

My friends exchanged a puzzled look between them.

"We're not your support group," Indigo said. "Go talk to someone who cares."

Odessa pinched Indigo's arm. "That's not nice. You know Storm doesn't have any friends."

"I don't?"

They all shrugged.

"I know I've got some making up to do, but we'll figure it out. You always say I never ask for help, but I'm here now asking. And I don't know what to do about Fire Fang. He's—"

"I'm not taking your hellhound, if that's why you're here," Luna said. "This place is almost full, so I'm only accepting small animals. I'll take the cat if you want to get rid of her. She's cute, though. Are you sure you want to give her up?"

"No. That's not what I'm talking about. I need advice about Fire Fang's... condition."

"Go find someone else to bother. Come on, let's go inside." Indigo ushered the others in and made a show of shutting and locking the door behind her.

I stood on the porch, stunned by their behavior. What was going on? Had they finally realized what an awful friend I was and had given up on me?

I considered barging through the door and confronting them, but that was petty. Maybe they needed a few days off from me. I'd turned down their offers of help so many times, they thought I didn't need them. But not letting me in the house for brownies and gossip was ridiculous. And childish.

My fist hovered by the door, but I eventually lowered it. I'd leave them alone and come back in a few days. Everything would be back to normal by then and all would be forgiven.

I walked away from the house, whistling for Fire Fang and Binky.

Fire Fang raced over. He lowered his head and growled at me, his eyes glowing a startling red.

"Hey, quit that. It looks like you're stalking me. I'm not in the mood for being messed with."

The red glow in his eyes faded, and he shook his head. "That was weird. I don't feel so good."

"Probably because you ate too much candy. Where's Binky?"

He growled at me again, then burped. "No idea. Can we get more candy?"

"No, not if it's making you grouchy and gassy." I looked over my shoulder at the house, shrugging off the blanket of sadness that attempted to engulf me. I wasn't alone. I had Fire Fang and Binky. They were enough.

As I walked along, I looked at Fire Fang. Maybe I wouldn't have him for much longer once I told him the secret I'd been keeping.

He glanced up at me. "Something on your mind?"

I took a deep breath. His world was about to tip upside down. "There's something I've been meaning to tell you..."

You know what's coming? One epic, final book featuring Storm and Fire Fang!

The Case of the Cursed Candy is waiting for you.

There's a new store in Witch Haven, and what the owner is selling could be the death of you...

My life has always been complicated, but I've always been in control. Not anymore. I'm injured (by Fire Fang), friendless, and scared. For the first time in my life, I know pure terror. And it sucks.

And to add to the weirdness, a candy store has opened in Witch Haven. It's run by the sickly sweet Sherry Brown, and everyone is obsessed with her treats. Until someone chokes to death on her candy.

Galaan shouldn't have died. I was there to save him. But nothing I did worked. He turned up his toes and that was it. Or was it? Everyone thinks his death was an accident. I don't. And when I learn he left his old life and moved to Witch Haven, my witchy senses tingle.

When I discover he fought with an angry half-dragon, broke up with his girlfriend, and dated Sherry, the dead guy's life (and suspicious death) gets complicated.

With Fire Fang wanting to eat me as a snack, my friends ignoring me, and the Magic Council as handy as a chocolate teapot, I must deal with this mystery alone.

What I uncover will rock magical foundations, change my life forever (if I survive), and mean things in Witch Haven will never be the same again.